Starling

SARAH JANE BUTLER

Fairlight Books

First published by Fairlight Books 2022
This paperback edition first published by Fairlight Books 2023

Fairlight Books
Summertown Pavilion, 18–24 Middle Way, Oxford, OX2 7LG

A CIP catalogue record for this book is available from the
British Library

1 2 3 4 5 6 7 8 9 10

ISBN 978-1-914148-25-5

www.fairlightbooks.com

Printed and bound in Great Britain

Designed by James Lewis

For Mum, with my love

The sweetest delights are trampled on with a ferocious pleasure.

—William James

Garlic. This was anciently accounted the poor man's treacle, it being a remedy for all diseases and hurts (except those which itself breed).

—Nicholas Culpeper

Chapter One

Spring had come too early and frost had blackened the first buds. Under the soil the seeds and roots waited again, and Starling waited too. *Everything to its time*, Mar always said. Mar would leave when it was time to leave.

At least the van was warm inside. It smelled of woodsmoke, damp wool drying, onion soup.

Dawn was a way off and Mar was still asleep. Starling could hear her breathing, slow and steady below the pebble-dash rattle of the rain on the roof. It had rained ever since they'd arrived, a winter of rain, and the van wouldn't make it out of the wood even if Mar said it was time. The mud at the start of the track had been axle-deep when they drove in, the puddles glittering in the Luton's headlamps as they closed the gate behind them, twisting the blue nylon rope back over the post. They were miles from the nearest house, and safe for a while, she hoped.

'Fate smiles upon us,' Mar had said, and the bare dark trees had swallowed them up.

Starling slept on her left side, eyes part open, the mattress shaped to her hip, just below the narrow shelf that ran high along the van's side wall. She fitted into small spaces. Along her shelf lay a line of pale shells, a hagstone ready to hang, a jay's turquoise feather. Everything that mattered was in the small bag under her head.

She didn't need to look to see Mar. She would be lying on her back, eyes closed, breathing evenly as a midsummer's sea swell. Mar released her hair at night and it spread deep red across the pillow, hung in great hanks over the side, touching the floor.

Unlike Starling, nothing about Mar was small. She filled every space. Not that she was a giant – she stood a couple of fingers taller than most, and she carried no fat – but when she came into a room or stepped into a fire circle, people moved back. Only Starling fitted beside her.

*

Starling sensed a vibration out beyond the clearing. She opened her eyes wide in the faint light filtered by the curtains. Nothing. It was a nothing. She let out her breath slowly and sat up, pushed her hair out of her eyes and slid down to the floor. She let Mar sleep on.

It was probably a fox. She lifted the door so it wouldn't creak as she opened it and stepped out, sniffed. Yes, a fox. She pulled her boots on and squelched across into the wood to pee, remembered she'd need to dig a new pit soon.

Back in the van she lifted the kettle. No water. Mar had been up late the night before and must have made tea to keep herself warm. Starling had lain in bed listening to her rocking in her chair by the burner. At about midnight the rain had stopped briefly and she'd heard Mar open the door and stand in silence, listening to the night noises outside – an owl's cry, a badger's claws clattering over a log, a fox's scream. The whisper of a dark wood. Starling had turned over and slept.

She took the water container and headed out, long-tailed tits lifting out of the bare branches ahead of her like a crowd of excited children on a windy day. The high sky held a handful of light. This wind might blow in new weather, carry away the rain at last, but she didn't think so. She stamped through the wood, swinging the container, watching a patch of blue sky grow and vanish over the hill.

She chewed on a pinch of early blackthorn flowers, enjoying their bitter crispness, and started to hum. When she reached the field gate on the edge of the wood, she climbed over, and left the container tucked in by the fence. Here, where the wood reached into the field, a small sheltered patch of grass held the sun and the first nettles had pushed up through the damp soil a week ago. Now they were knee-high, leaves unfurled, startling green against the earth. Starling pulled a bag from her pocket and cut a cloudburst of nettle tops into it. Slim pickings, but she could smell the green in them, the spinachy tang they'd give the day's soup.

*

As she came back through the trees she saw fresh smoke coming from the chimney. Mar must be up; she must have found something to get the burner going.

A curl of white fell through the air. Starling caught it, and another, held them on her palm: two scorched fragments of printed paper falling like seeds, sowing letters on the wood's floor.

She went in. Mar was folding up her bedding, completely engaged with the task. *Every task matters equally.* Starling placed the kettle on the burner, bent and opened its door. Paper spilled out, not quite burned through, the print blackened by the heat. As the air reached the scorched edge of the book, the words turned to flame and twisted up through the smoke into the flue, forcing Starling to pull her hand away.

Mar stood by the table, hands flat in front of her, leaning forward and looking out of the window. She straightened, pulled her hair up and tied it.

Starling reached for the tea tin and shook it, the last few leaves skittering inside. Mar picked up her empty mug and went out to wait.

Mar's silences were volcanic. Since she last spoke, Starling had kept out of the van as much as she could, being useful, quiet and invisible, hoping the eruption would be quickly over when it came. Sometimes they were more smoke than fire. She never could tell. But this had been a long wait.

Hearing the creak of the metal chair outside as Mar sat, Starling turned to the bookshelf. It held all their books, battered from rereading and sharing and passing on. Sometimes they came back years later from a friend who'd say, *Hey, you should read this, it's awesome. Changes your mind, you know, makes you see things differently. Thought of you when I read it.* And Mar and Starling would take it back and put it on the shelf like an old friend in among the others. Starling liked to take them all down sometimes, put them into a new order: alphabetical, or by colour, or by category, or by the way they made her feel when she thought about them when she wasn't there. Mar didn't care what order they were in. She barely read these days. Starling tried to picture what was missing. They were only words, but Starling needed words.

Even when she wasn't brewing a silence, Mar spoke less and less these days. She measured out words carefully, as if she and Starling were running out of sounds, the way they were running out of tea. Starling wondered what Mar had been turning over and over last night in the darkening van, what was coming.

She poured water into the pot and went out to her.

If you sat silent long enough, you could hear the rain coming through the air two fields away, even before the blackbird warned you. Starling passed Mar her mug of tea and stood beside her looking at the brightening sky, clutching her warm mug.

Silence doesn't lie.

She knew better than to ask Mar why she had burned the book and sent the verses spiralling up the chimney to rain down on the earth. *We need no possessions. Truth lies within us.* She watched the steam rise from her mug. Mar sipped her tea and closed her eyes, the sun pale on her lids.

The wind lifted the treetops and a handful of drops fell flashing from the branches onto the wet leaves at Starling's feet. She drank her tea in quick gulps. Mar said nothing. Maybe she had used up all her words. She didn't need to say more, after all. Starling wondered if Mar's head was as full of words as hers was, chattering like the starlings she was named after. Mar spoke like a slow river, tried to teach her to flow with the day, to breathe, hear, see in rhythm with the natural world. Mar was moving away from human time.

Starling put her mug down, pulled out the kindling box from under the van and shook the twists of birch bark and tiny twig ends into one corner. Mar's cheek twitched. She didn't need to say anything. Starling knew it. *Start your day as you mean to live it, in peace and stillness.* She set off to gather kindling.

*

They were parked down a narrow track that would be grassy come high summer but right now was two runnels of thick mud. They were stranded. Their beautiful van hid in a clearing deep in the heart of an old English wood, smoke trickling out of the chimney. It could have been idyllic.

Mar had created paradise on the sides of her Luton. She was an artist, and her trademark was the kind of heaven that Henri Rousseau painted: luscious velvety and glossy leaves you could see the lifeblood running through, profusions of perfumed flowers, huge and singing with energy, but in Mar's version every plant was native to the woods and fields they passed through, and twice as glorious and a hundred times more scented and vibrant. There were columbines, daisies, woodruff, and the herbs of the earliest spring were there too – nettles, cleavers, dead-nettles, wild garlic, dandelion leaves, hawthorn leaves, all shining in the low sun. Ground ivy too, though Starling dreaded the day they were reduced to eating ground ivy. The day she put more than a sprig in a stew was a sure sign the winter had gone on too long. It had its place, though, curling round the handle on the van's rear door.

It was an advert for Mar's work, though that's not why she kept on painting it, filling in chip marks in a dog rose's petal, refreshing the brilliant white of a snowdrop. One day she had transformed the bonnet into a wild and generous vegetable patch, hiding stories and friends in the shadows. The van seemed to be part of her, and while others tried to conceal theirs, pretending they were workmen parked up for a quick brew, Mar saw no need. And it was true, for years wherever they went people stopped to look at the van, and asked who painted it, where were they going, how did they live, and sometimes they asked to look inside. Time was, Mar used to let them look – she'd say *Let them see that our van is more beautiful inside than any of their houses.*

That was long ago. Starling pushed the kindling under the van and sniffed the air. 'The garlic'll be flowering if we get more of this sun.'

Mar tilted her face to the weak spring light. The low sun chiselled out the lines of her jaw, cheekbones and brow. She was splendid, a warrior whose energy burned inside her.

People who didn't know them never guessed they were mother and daughter. Starling was used to their surprise when they found out. It wasn't just the way they looked: Starling was dark and smart and snap-twig skinny, and as restless as her namesake next to Mar, stiller and stronger than a mountain.

'I'll make another brew.' She reached for Mar's mug, watched a blackbird skip into the winter-bare bramble patch. A squirl of dead leaves lifted from the ground and fell again. She tried to concentrate on them. She tried to keep her feet still, and counted her breaths in and out, felt the energy of life breathe in, the toxins of her negative thoughts snag and fail to flow away. But the sun was shining. She gave up and tiptoed back to the van. Mar would be there for hours, pulling the energy of the land to her.

Starling had wood to cut.

*

Out on the edge of the woodland Starling placed her hand on the trunk of the fallen oak. Its bark was harsh and resistant even after months of rain and sun. Standing tall on the wood's edge, it had been first to feel the gales two autumns past when the wind had turned and driven in from the east. The storm had caught the oak's westerly roots by surprise, and one vast gust had filled its canopy of golden leaves and toppled it, ripping its roots from the earth as it fell. *When a wind comes from a strange direction, even the greatest trees can be caught.* Starling thanked it for the warmth it would give them. They had to keep the burner alight. Its smoke above the trees was a signal to anyone, but they had no choice. The winter had gone on too long. They needed to move on, draw the fresh air of the road through the van. Their breath alone set condensation running down the windows, and under the smell of Mar's herbs and the soup pot there was a mustiness, the signs of damp creeping into their mattresses and clothes. The air coming in through the windows was as moist as the air inside, so there was nothing for it, the burner stayed lit, and they'd have to leave soon before someone found them. Starling looked out across the fields through roots that splayed like dirty sunbeams against the grey sky.

They were doing no harm, but even if the sun came and dried them out, they would never be allowed to stay. They never were. The bailiffs would impound the van. Mar and Starling had no fuel, and there was no one left to give them a tow, no one to lend them a few quid to get a couple of gallons to see them on their way. No one to protect them against a rock through the window.

Beyond the roots, on the horizon, a row of trees ran high across the rim of the field, swaying in the wind. Rooks exploded into the air above them, circling, climbing and twisting above a single figure walking from left to right. Starling crouched and watched until the walker passed under the trees and out of sight, waiting for the rooks to drop. She measured in her mind the thick branch that lay by her knees. It should last a while, and oak that had lain a couple of years would give them good lasting heat.

She unzipped her coat and felt in the lining for her phone. She hadn't turned it on for weeks, saving its last charge. She thumbed the volume all the way down, though she knew it wouldn't ring. She had no credit, and it was months since she'd last used it so she'd been cut off. But Mar's hearing was like an owl's and you never knew. The screen brightened, and Starling peered at the last message she'd received, almost a year ago.

Hey Star, are u nr? Come see us. Gotta floor if u fed up with mud.

Where was Luc now? She'd no way of knowing if he was still at the address he'd texted her. She turned the phone off and pushed it back into its secret pocket. *These phones serve for surveillance and control of fools. They suck people in with promises of friendship that mean nothing. See these hands? These eyes? They are where truth lies.*

Luc had given Starling the phone not long before he left, an ancient Nokia good only for texts and a call if she had credit. She touched her pocket and picked up the bow saw.

Each trip out here she risked someone hearing the saw. At first its teeth struggled to settle into the gnarls of the bark, but soon the sawdust piled on the dark soil and she let her mind empty as she worked. That was the good thing about chores: the pull and push tugged the thoughts out of her head if she let them.

She used to long for quiet, a moment of silence with no shouts, dogs barking, kids crying, hammering, clanking of pans and starter motors. Now that she lived in silence she missed the racket of a full camp.

Starling sawed enough logs to last a week. They were her offering and she let the bark cut into the skin on her hands as she shouldered the first length, shifted her weight and started back towards the van. Rain hissed across the field towards her, and by the time she had carried all the logs to the pile, she was soaked.

*

Starling could hear the sound of Mar moving around inside the van, her feet shifting the boards of the floor, the clank of the cookpot lid. They were coming to the end of their winter supplies, but Mar could always make something to eat. Last week Starling had caught a pheasant and they'd make the stock last a while yet. The nettles would be good. Still, they were both thinner than they'd been a month ago. This was the hardest time. But they'd keep going.

It would be easy to walk away, get a job, a floor, a room, always have a meal that filled you on the table, and more in the cupboard where it came from. But such a life held no meaning – what was the point of living as if you were not part of the land? Of buying a sauce in a jar that tasted of chemicals? Of never smelling the cold jade of midnight in February or the feel of a pike nudging your leg in the river in June? You might as well not live. The real world was here. If Starling and Mar wanted to eat, they had to know where the first dandelions would come up in January, how to save seeds and nuts in autumn, how to make jam and salt meat for the lean months. They were survivors. More than survivors. *We are women who live needing nothing, needing no one. We are women who live in full connection with our mother earth. We will never betray her.*

They bartered sometimes, the old way. A pair of rabbits for a jar of honey. A bag of ink caps for a bottle of oil. *This is how the earth's people have always lived.*

And they made just enough cash to buy the few things only money could pay for. Fuel. Parts for the engine. Credit for the phone, in Starling's case. Starling took the small axe and split a boxful of logs for the burner. *Only the earth, sky, air and water will always be here. They do not need us. We will all be gone and we need nothing while we are here. We need no one.*

Except each other, of course. Mar and Starling always had each other.

Still, Starling kept some things secret from Mar: the phone was one. Her box was another. Small and smooth as a conker, she kept it safe in her pocket. Any time they arrived somewhere new, she hunted for something small and put it in the box. It could be a leaf, a sweet wrapper, a fragment of coloured glass, a wasp's wing. It had been all these things over the years. Berries and nuts too, a nub of crayon from the Skool Bus, a photo of a monkey off a leaflet, a strand of sheep's wool. When she arrived at a site she shook out the box and placed something new inside. It didn't matter what. She'd had it as long as she could remember and she didn't know where it came from, but she knew every grain of its wood as well as she knew her own knuckles. On its lid were carved three tiny birds flying in an endless circle and she could run her finger round and round them without anyone knowing. As long as she kept it safe, hidden even from Mar, they'd be safe too. It would always bring her home. Starling knew what Mar didn't: rituals matter when you're never sure what's coming next.

Standing in the rain before she went into the van, she thought about Luc's message and wished she could ring him, say hi for a second. He'd laugh, probably, and forget about her call by the time she'd stepped into the van, but she'd know he was there, somewhere. She tugged on the tarp and pulled it tight over the logs, and went inside.

Chapter Two

That night the rain returned strong and heavy from the west, beating against the door and windows, hammering on the roof. From the roar in the trees Starling knew the storm would stay all night. She rolled a cloth and laid it along the bottom of the door and put her boots by the burner to dry out.

Mar sat under the tilley, the burner warm by her elbow. Her cloak, green as moss, was spread over her lap and she began to go over it inch by inch, fingering the seams, holding the fabric up to the light, pulling out the pockets. The smell of high summer crept into the fug of the van, hay seeds and lavender nudging into the woodsmoke.

Starling didn't ask where they were going, why Mar was fixing her travelling cloak. You didn't ask Mar that kind of question. She would tell you when it was time, or she wouldn't.

Starling returned to the bench seat. It folded down from the wall, fitting neatly behind the table. Mar had her chair, and this was where Starling belonged. If she reached up she could touch the underside of her bed. A log settled inside the burner. On a hook beside her a candle lantern lit her face, leaving the rest of her in shadow.

The walls and ceiling of the van were lined with wood that had turned golden over the years. A dark smudge rose up the wall above the burner where the smoke billowed out when they opened its door. Brush-lines up the tall cupboard marked the years of Starling's life. Nineteen years since she was born in Mar's bed above the cab, barely four strides from the corner she sat in now. Mar had painted a line every year, and each line grew into a different plant: daisy, buttercup, dandelion, forget-me-not, pansy, marigold, balm, sorrel, mustard, cornflower, bramble, hawthorn, elder. At fourteen, Starling had stopped growing, so that year Mar painted dog rose, then bindweed, angelica, blackthorn and nettle emerging in a burst of leaves and flowers from all the years before. She had painted every cupboard door, every window frame, every shelf too, winding them with plants and animals so even inside they were always out in the wild, and the wild was always watching them.

On the table sat the remains of their meal. Two bowls. Two spoons. The crumbs from the flatbreads Mar made each night. The van was quiet, contained inside the rain. Starling kept still. In a moment she would clear the table, rinse the bowls, wipe the spoons, sweep the crumbs. For now, though, she held the silence like she used to hold the bubbles Mar blew for her when she was a child.

This was Mar's idea of heaven, a space under the trees with no one else for miles. It was a place you could breathe easy, she'd said, the day they pulled in. They'd had to stop, almost out of fuel, passing lay-bys they could have spent a night in, Starling willing Mar to pull in though they both hated a lay-by. Verges were a last resort, but they needed to find somewhere before the needle teetered over the red. And then Mar, who knew all the paths and lanes that tied places together, Mar had turned down an invisible track though a half-open gate, bumped over the ruts, and the fuel had run out as they rolled into the clearing.

Mar had seemed so happy that Starling had thought maybe they just needed a lay-up here, time away, time to let things calm.

When the rain didn't stop after two weeks – two weeks of keeping to the van, waiting for a break in the clouds – she'd offered to go and find fuel. She could get just enough money to get them out and they'd find a way to go on. They always did.

But Mar had said, 'No, Starling. No more.' And from that day she had journeyed closer to silence, her few words melting into the growing winter darkness.

One night, weeks ago, Mar had said to her, 'The only truth is the track we choose to follow. We must be led by the lines of our land, finding our stories as our feet carry us.' Starling had begun to ask her what she meant, but Mar had stood and walked out into the rain, closing the door behind her. She had returned when the owls fell quiet before the dawn and it was as if she had pulled a heavy hood over herself, hiding her thoughts from Starling.

As Mar's silence lasted, Starling felt as if she was watching her travel away through a long lens, as if Mar was climbing a far mountain, slowly pulling herself to the peak.

She stood and gathered the crumbs, licked them off her fingers. She took the bowls and spoons and slid them into the metal bowl warming on the burner. Mar looked up and pointed at the sewing box, and nodded when Starling reached it down from the top cupboard.

Starling pulled out her pad and pencils and settled in the corner, pushing her back hard against the wall, arms wrapped round her knees, watching Mar. She began to sketch. It was almost like it used to be. Maybe it could be, if Mar was mending her travelling cloak. Maybe she was ready to move at last.

*

It took Mar two nights to mend her cloak, stitch its seams, wax its cloth. Starling worked and waited for her to reveal their new journey, but when Mar had hung her cloak back in the tall cupboard, she sat in stillness watching the clearing through the open door, the rain falling ceaselessly, chain mail holding them in and keeping them safe.

She wondered what Mar was planning. Maybe she wasn't planning, but waiting to see what the days would bring. Waiting for the land to wake with spring and tell them where to go. There was an art to feeling what the land was saying, allowing yourself to sense the sap rising in the oaks, to hear the robins' song before they opened their beaks – always the first to welcome the new growth. There was a day every year when you felt the warmth from over the seas calling you out onto the road while the frosts still settled nightly on the thin winter grass.

This year, though, the maps stayed in their box under the driver's seat. They kept to themselves their stories of journeys past and journeys to come. With barely any fuel the van wouldn't make it out of the wood.

Then a morning came when Starling woke to quiet – she could hear the robin sing clearly from the holly, the rusty creak of birch branches rubbing against each other above the van. It had stopped raining. Leaving Mar sleeping, she tiptoed out of the van and sat on the step as she tied the knots on her boots, breathing out with the land and the sky, feeling the world expanding at last.

Every cell of her knew that spring was coming, that the mud would be drying and a new journey was ahead.

She wandered beyond the wood and into the fields, down to the stream, and came back to the van with a bagful of early-growing fat hen, nettles and garlic mustard, a clutch of yellow morels – a real treat – and a fistful of violets. She'd found a warren where she'd be able to set snares later so they'd have rabbit stew. All gifts for Mar. She'd make coffee, fry the morels for a late breakfast, and they would sit out in the clearing and Mar would be happy.

But when she got back, the van was empty.

Starling kept on with her chores, stoking the burner, digging the new pit, hanging bunches of garlic mustard and fat hen to dry. When the light began to fade and Mar didn't return, she began to wonder. She chopped an onion and added it to the pot, took Mar's place by the burner and stirred, added the greens, fossicked in the jars for a scrap of dried chilli, stirred again, tasted the pot and pulled it off the high heat, putting the lid on to keep it warm. She put the violet in the egg cup she had made for Mar the summer they made pots and set it on the table, then moved it to the window so it could see the last of the sun. Sitting beside the violet, she watched the sky above the trees turn pale, then orange, then darken. The morels began to lose their glow. The air grew still. The evening star rose.

Finally, Starling made herself open the tall cupboard, feeling her stomach clench like she'd eaten a bad mushroom. Mar had taken her cape and her bag.

Maybe she'd gone for a night's journey to feel the soil beneath her feet and hear the earth's messages in the quiet of midnight.

When the damp night air began to fill the van, Starling pulled the door closed, quietly, so she would hear any sound outside. A footstep. A low call from the far edge of the clearing to *Come see the barn owl, Starling.* But the clearing gave her only the rustle of a mouse in the leaf litter, then silence.

She sat on her bench. She got up and took a book from the shelf and tried to read but she was listening too hard for sounds that weren't there. She sat with her hands on the closed cover, pressing it as though the pages had the answers if only she could read them. The van was too still for reading. She had to hold it safe by staying still. Her candle went out and she sat until the burner grew cool and she felt the van settle into its own night. Only then did she climb into bed and lie with her eyes closed, feeling the feet of every beetle crossing every twig outside as if she were laid out on the earth beneath the dark sky, waiting.

Chapter Three

Starling stayed close to the van for days, tethered, in case Mar came back. She looped in and out of the clearing like a dog checking on its master. She looked for a message. Always before, Mar had said goodbye and left her with a note. When Starling was as small as a mouse, Mar would go away for days or weeks, and any time she left for more than one sunset, she would draw where she was going – a map or a sketch of a sandy beach or a festival in a forest, or maybe simply a path through trees towards the sun – and she'd write in her looping script that she'd be back and that she was carrying Starling in her heart so Starling would always be safe. And Starling would show the note to Em, and Em would hug her and smile. *Wonderful,* she would say. *We've been missing you when we wake in the morning.* And Starling would keep Mar's note under her pillow in Em's van until the day Mar returned, swinging her van back into the camp with a hoot on the horn that caught her like a fish on a hook, reeling her in from the stream, or the highest tree, or the furthest field. Mar had always said goodbye to her and she had always come back.

This time, though, Starling found nothing.

She looked under her pillow, on her shelf. She shook out the pages of the book she'd been reading and all the books she hadn't touched for ages. She pulled down the sun visor in the cab, where they left messages for anyone who knew them. The van was so tidy, though, she'd see anything that wasn't in its place.

She sat in Mar's rocking chair and looked out into the clearing, her guts flickering in fear and hope that her mother might stride back down the path and find her in her chair.

She couldn't let herself think that Mar had left.

Starling gave herself jobs to do. She washed down the van's paintwork. She carried back more water, though the water tank was almost full. She dug out the foot pump and topped up the tyres, ready to leave when Mar came back.

Maybe this was a kind of preparation for a journey. Mar needed to spend time away, and then they would be off.

Starling had been a nomad all her life. She was born on the road, delivered in the van, lifted into her mother's arms a squalling scrap of Mar's own flesh as the sun rose and cast her light into their bed, and Mar had carried her along the threads of the land from that first day, weaving a new way of being, side by side. *We are pioneers*, Mar taught her. *We are strong women, bound to the land and always free.*

Travelling had its own rhythm, its own song. Some journeys started slow, a few notes carrying them sweet out onto the road. Other journeys began with a shout and a clamour, but they all had their pattern. Life was in the travelling, in the music, in the joining of journeys one after the other to make something whole, but never finished.

Mar chose their life. Even digging a shit pit was part of the music, a grinding bass note that grounded the tune. Not that Starling loved it any more for that. No one loved digging shit pits. But Mar had always valued hard work. When she was younger than Starling was now she had turned her back on the lies and insincerity, on her dad's falseness and the sad hopelessness of her parents' stale lives. *I live honestly, taking nothing, owing nothing*, she said. Mar didn't want life to be easy, but she did want it to be true.

Above the burner Mar had painted, *This woman was born free, and never will be in chains.* Rousseau had no idea, Mar said.

Bloody privileged over-educated cock-obsessed man, is what she said. Not that Mar despised education. She'd taught Starling her Henri Rousseau from her Jean-Jacques and much more, priming her to catch fools out. They underestimated a kid from a van at their peril.

Freedom, though, was something not learned from books. There were people on the road who didn't understand that freedom wasn't the same as letting your rig rot, your shit poison the land, not the same as blagging off mate after mate and never giving back. They thought just not having a job meant you were free and sticking it to the Man. Mar and Starling's freedom took hard work. Water run. Wood run. Kettle on. Gather food. Light the burner. Tat down. Move on. Take your own route. Start again. People didn't understand that you had to make your own life for that life to mean anything. Anything else was fake.

While she waited for Mar to come back, Starling ate scraps of food between jobs, an oddment of flatbread, spirals of dried apple peel, but she wasn't hungry.

Where was Mar?

At midnight she lit a fire in the clearing that glimmered off the bare trees around the van and turned them to dancing cave figures, and in its light she demolished the log pile and restacked it, the clunk of log on log echoing off the dancers in an unsteady beat. She wished Mar had a phone. How would Starling know if she was well and safe? How would Mar know if Starling was?

She searched the van methodically, working out what Mar had taken with her. Her cloak, her travelling bag – those were easy. From the box under the chassis, the tarp had gone, and a groundsheet, the makings of a shelter. A bender was easy to hide, easy to build with a couple of long branches and a patch of level ground. Cold and uncomfortable too, but the closest a human got to sleeping on earth, to living on the move, to being animal.

What else? The small pan. Mar always had a knife in her bag, a fire steel, a mug. She'd taken a bowl and a spoon. Oats, Starling thought – they'd had plenty of oats, the winter saviour when all else ran out, and she thought Mar had taken a bagful. Flour for breads. Herbs, maybe, dried greens? She couldn't tell. The hazelnuts they'd gathered were gone, and the dried damsons.

Mar had taken what she needed for a lone journey across country. She was travelling light, her life on her back, the earth beneath her feet, moving slowly, step by step.

Starling should have seen it coming. Mar refining. Mar stripping back to her spirit, paring back the layers, revealing her live wood, ready to enter fully the wild world beyond the van.

Starling sank down onto the ground finally and the knowing of Mar's leaving bubbled up inside her like a kettle left on a slow flame that gradually, inescapably begins to boil, filling her whole body, roiling through her, out of her, reducing her to nothing more than the overwhelming fact that she was gone.

Mar had left her.

Starling held her hands up in front of her eyes. Did she still take up space in the world? Mar's going was so vast that it engulfed her, a black hole pulling everything in.

*

Starling became a hollowness that had no boundaries.

The thing that had been her body moved slowly around the clearing. It saw the robin skeeter from holly to birch. The first shoots appear on the bramble. They were like scratches on a window pane, not really there; they meant nothing.

The morels rotted on the chopping board. The burner went out.

The rain came back, drifting across the trees, tapping the roof of the van to rouse her, growing insistent, rough and wild when she lay on her bed, eyes open and seeing nothing.

*

Starling didn't know why she was so afraid. Mar had left before, when it was just the two of them. *I am making a small journey, Starling. You are in my heart.* Starling had been alone then too, no Em, no tribe, just the van. Starling was strong. Mar had told her so. They had left Em, the tribe, the camps and made themselves stronger. *We don't need them, Starling. Our strength is within us.* There had been times, the last year or two, when Mar had left without words, but she had always left something. A tiny sketch of a bird against the sun. A book half read on her chair. A note on the board of a date they had agreed to be somewhere.

This time, Mar had left nothing. What if she never came back?

Without Mar, how was Starling to be?

*

It was the fox that roused her in the end, stepping delicately into the van and sniffing the damp air. She watched him from her bed as he nosed the cushion on Mar's chair. He stood on his hind legs to investigate the rotting mushrooms, then trotted over to the table and looked up at her. It was as if he was saying, 'What are you doing up there? There's food to eat. Water to carry. Are you not an animal like us?' He turned and jumped neatly out of the door, leaving behind a foxy musk that said, 'I have been here. I claim this space, if you won't.'

She pushed back the cover and felt the way her hip bones jutted.

Mar trusted her enough to leave her like this. She knew Starling would understand what she was doing. *A true child makes no claims on her mother.*

Starling made a bowl of porridge and sat at the table, eating it slowly, feeling the warmth of each mouthful travelling down her throat and into her gut. Spoonful by spoonful, she gave herself permission to go on.

Water run. Shit pit. Kindling for the burner. Thin flames against its cold black interior, wavering and uncertain. She blew on them, lifted them to the burner's roof, added more kindling, and felt the heat. She filled the kettle and sat, exhausted, in Mar's chair to wait for it to boil.

Starling gathered food from the fields and hedges. She soaked a bowl of beans. She set a trap on the field edge and caught a rabbit overnight. Next morning she brought it back to the van, skinned and gutted it, and later that night she ate stew thick with nettle tops and beans and soft morsels of flesh, and she let tears run down her face as she ate because Mar wasn't here with her, but she ate a deep bowlful.

After dark, Starling sorted through the van. She pulled out the small square drawer below Mar's bed, its front painted with a sheaf of wheat. She knew its contents. She had played with them on wet afternoons and slow evenings all through her childhood. The curl of her own hair wrapped in tissue. *The Story of Mar and Starling* written in purple crayon in a tattered exercise book. Coins from far countries. Bits and pieces that Mar had kept over the years. But the tiny carved hand holding a shining black bird was gone. Starling had made it secretly as a birthday present for Mar, and placed it in her hands as the sun set over the Stones and the tribe's voices rose around them. Mar had taken it with her.

From the box beneath the bench, Starling pulled out all the mess of paper: a wiring diagram for the Luton's electrics, recipes for remedies, scraps scribbled with lyrics, tickets for gigs and festivals before Starling was born and through the years of her growing, sketches of plants and places. Addresses and phone numbers. Pencilled maps to find camps and fields and friends' mums who'd let them stay a night, and mates who'd keep their post. Sketches of people. Here was Starling, a tiny, dark-eyed baby. Em, laughing, flowers in her hair. Luc, Davey, Stevie and Gabe, just their faces, so clearly brothers. So many people they'd travelled with. Some she didn't know, from before her. Right at the bottom, folded in four, were worn-edged sheets of an old sketch pad, faces Mar had drawn over and over. A young man Starling had never met sat in the door of the van. She looked at his face, narrow and angular like hers, and stuffed all the pictures back, shoving them out of sight.

*

Mar had always been strong for both of them. When the moment was right, she'd always known when to go and she'd done it over and over. No one left Mar, even when they were walking away.

Em was Mar's best friend. She had wept as Mar told her they'd never speak again and Starling never knew why. She had heard the metal in Mar's voice and had picked up the shovel and gone to dig a new pit. When she came back, Em and Luc and the boys were driving out of the site, gone, never seen or mentioned again. Mar had so much certainty. She never needed to explain herself.

The only thing Starling was certain of was how to find food, fetch water, gather firewood, stoke the burner, keep the stock pot bubbling, keep herself fed and warm. She could do all of this. Here in the van, in the wood, she could turn the days over and over as the year circled.

The van sat in the clearing, holding all of Starling's life. All of life. What was beyond the clearing and the wood that held more? Perhaps she belonged here.

The birch trees around the clearing sent out their first pale catkins, and a filmy cloud of gnats spun in the morning sun above the bramble patch. But the year would turn round again and carry her into winter, into long months in the van by the burner, night after night, one bowl on the table, one mug on the drainer, her face reflected against the dark in the window.

No one knew where she was, except Mar, and where was Mar?

The van was home, it always had been. But alone in the van, Starling was too small. She tried to make herself fill it, banged the spoon on the pan, flung a log into the burner, sang as she pulled on her boots in the morning. But the noise she made had no echo.

She made up rituals. She would jump out of bed the moment the blackbird started to sing from the branch above the van. She sang 'Polly Put the Kettle On' as she waited for the water to boil. She polished her boots before she left the van. She led herself this way through the day and into the evening, until the night's measure of candle had burned and she blew it out, put her book back on the shelf and climbed into bed.

Was this how you built a life? Made a home? Starling could live truly with the land, take little, make no mark, be like the fox or the badger, padding gently over the soil seeking food and water. And one day she would die, her flesh gathered back to the soil in thanks for all it had given her. But the fox, the badger, the blackbird on the branch, none was alone. The thought of so much silence terrified her, yet so did the thought of leaving.

Was she free now? Free to make her own life and find her own way? The world beyond the van was dirty and corrupt. It rejected her, as she rejected it.

But Mar was out there, somewhere. Luc was too, and Em, and all of the scattered tribe.

*

In the end, it was the sounds of voices that told her to leave. People were coming into the woods with the spring. Before long they'd follow the track and find the van, and every day as Starling lit the burner, cut logs, crept the paths back to the clearing, she led people towards it. She was safe here only as long as no one found her. The moment the van was found, she'd be forced out, back onto the road.

The people's voices were soft, out on the edge of the wood. Like a scent they drifted into the clearing and pulled Starling to find them. She left her chores and her routines, and followed the felty voices until they clarified into threads. From behind trees she watched a mother and child singing a rhyme as they jumped through puddles, two women laughing a shared story as they puffed up the hill, an old couple murmuring beneath the catkins.

They reminded her that she'd become a single string, stretched and untuned with no one to hear.

When she returned to the van and the voices faded for another night, she knew she had to leave.

She pulled out the maps from their box under the driving seat and ran her fingers over their lines. They told her she could walk this curl of a contour, feel the wave of a hill rise under her feet, turn down that lane and find a tiny woodland by a stream. So many places called out to her that maybe they could be home. On paper, she owned the world. *The world is your home. You need no walls.* She traced field edges and farms, finding paths and tracks and towpaths and quick shortcuts through copses that would lead her almost all the way.

She would go to the Green Man and ask if Mar had been in. She would start there.

She folded the maps carefully and slotted them back into the box. She didn't need them. *A journey with a destination is no true journey. Follow the lines of the land. They will take you where you need to be.*

Mar had been right: she knew when it was time to go. Her feet would carry her where she needed to be.

Chapter Four

At first light a misty rain fell. Starling put out the burner with a bowl of water and sat on a log to drink her tea and watch the last smoke drift up through the trees. She washed up her mug and tucked it into her bag, tied her boots and stood up. It was time to go.

She hung the key in the empty hen coop beneath the van where Mar would find it.

Would she have driven the van, if she could have? She'd been tempted to try, to see how far she could get on the breath of fuel in the tank. But the van was Mar's. Starling couldn't imagine driving it without her. And anyway, she didn't have a licence.

Walking away from the van, she felt it hold her. She lengthened her stride and stepped out of the clearing without looking back. She knew this feeling of starting a journey, of looking forward, of letting go.

Starling had been leaving places all her life. Still, though, every time she arrived somewhere new she was like a sprig of mint in water – she couldn't help but put out hopeful roots. In this wood, they'd begun to reach deep and hold her fast. She wondered if she'd left part of herself in the soil. Were there traces of her all over the country? Nineteen years of rootlets broken off in woods and fields, yards and lay-bys? Maybe she belonged everywhere. Or nowhere. *All people are made to be nomads. The rhythm of walking is in*

*our bones, Starling. We sing, we speak, and our hearts beat in
time with our walking feet.*

In the clearing her universe had shrunk to the inside of the van, the
kicked-up patch of mud below the step, the skinny track to the pit, the
shape of the sky above the trees. She had to go and find the world again.

Some journeys were easier than others. Starling reached the
road and started walking, hood drawn over her face against the
chill, singing to herself to make a space the damp and cold couldn't
reach. Some stupid song of Mar's that kept winding its way into
her mind. She changed her tune and pulled her hood down to feel
the cold air on her head. She walked taller, striding out like she
knew where she was going.

Mar had taught her long ago to turn from the place she was
leaving and to keep on moving. *Tread lightly on the earth. Take
little and leave less. We are only here a while.* Yeah, but she had
always thought Mar would be there forever.

The air grew heavier as Starling walked along the verge. A
single drop fell loud on the tarmac, then another and another,
and in moments the rain was hissing all around her and running
through her hair and down her neck, filling her eyes. She pulled
her hood up again and the world retreated. The tarmac blackened
and shone; a car swished past and away.

She tried singing 'Blowin' in the Wind', a good trudging song,
but the open fields around her seemed to swallow her voice and
she faded into silence, the only sound the squelch of her boots on
the grassy verge, the rain on her hood, and the rooks cawing as
she passed. Starling and the rooks, wherever she went. She stopped
to watch them circling in the air above her, the only other living
things around. As she stood, the swirling mass of them fell together
onto a single oak tree like a fisherman's thrown net. They sat and
watched her, and she watched them back, but nothing changed so
she turned and went on.

She wanted there to be nothing in her mind. She had to keep moving, that was all. One foot in front of the other, the beat steady, not thinking, not looking, just walking. Not stopping because stopping let stuff in, stuff she didn't want to think about. People said walking was a kind of meditation. Bollocks. Walking was numbness.

She tramped on. She passed houses with lights on though it was midday, cars in their drives, figures moving across windows. Then she was alone on the road again.

The rain faded sometimes, as if some god was turning down the volume ever so gently. She'd lift her head and push her hair out of her eyes for a moment and then they'd turn the volume up again. Her boots tick-tocked beneath her like she'd been wound up and set to walk away.

The road entered a wood of pines and hollies that held the rain off in semi-darkness that was loud with wind. It was even colder in the shadow of the trees. Starling walked faster. She'd left the van alone in its wood, unprotected without her inside it. She should have stayed. It was her job to keep the van safe. But how to keep herself safe? How to stay sane alone in those four walls month after month?

There was that woman in Norwich who'd been walled up in a cell. Starling wondered how you stayed yourself, never seeing beyond your doorway. Maybe she felt safe there. Or maybe she was keeping everyone else safe. Julian. That was her name. *All shall be well.* Maybe. They'd had her book once. She'd anchored herself to the world. Her cell wasn't an escape. Appearances are deceptive. *All manner of thing shall be well.* All those years in one small room and yet, so free. Was it letting go of other people that gave you freedom in the end?

Other people always let you go, in the end. Get rid of them all. *Depend on yourself. Remember who you are. You need no one*. That's how she'd always been, or tried to be. She marched in rhythm with her words, an army of one, sending herself into battle.

*

Mid-afternoon, the light sank, drenched and exhausted. Starling kept walking, splashing through inky puddles, head low beneath her hood. She might as well. There was nowhere to stop here, nowhere she could hide out unseen for a night. Every foot of land was claimed and set behind a fence. Keep out.

The world of men is without mercy. Ask it nothing. Give it less. Stand alone and you will always be sure. She remembered Mar's hands turning the wheel of the van beside her as they pulled away from the site, leaving the tribe for the last time, reaching out for the dial of the radio. *Let's have some music, Starling.* She and Mar had been together against the world for so long. She had no one except Mar. That was her strength: she went out into the world with open eyes, expecting nothing from anyone. No one could trick her, deceive her or let her down.

A couple of cars went past, lighting her briefly in their headlights, casting her shadow along the muddy verge ahead of her, splashing gutter water up her legs.

She kept her head down. A small white van slowed beside her, matching her pace, its wheels turning inches from her feet. She pushed her fists deeper into her pockets and kept her eyes to the ground. There was no one else around, no gates or tracks she could escape onto, just her and the road and this van, and whoever was inside it. The window beside her hissed down and a man's voice spoke. 'Get in, I'll give you a lift.' Starling pulled her pack tighter onto her back. The van pulled ahead of her and swerved to a sharp stop in front of her, blocking her path, and the driver's door opened and she heard heavy feet pounding around the van towards her. Shit, shit,

shit. She ran, stumbling down into the soaking ditch and up and over the barbed wire fence beyond, and across the grass into the trees. A shout behind her, angry. Fucking pervert bastard. Why couldn't he leave her in peace? She kept running, clattering into trunks and dodging branches that grabbed her hair until she tripped over a root and fell. She held her breath. She heard rain and wind, nothing more.

She lay there, cold and wet. How far was the Green Man from here? Maybe a day, maybe two. Less if she kept on the straight roads like the one she'd just run from. More if she turned off and kept to the lanes. More, but safer. Even better if she moved cross-country where no one would see her, though the mud and ditches would be hell. She wished Luc was here.

Last time he'd texted, he'd been in Wincombe. But Luc never stayed anywhere long, and there wasn't much chance he'd still be there. Why would he be? He belonged on the road, like she did. But he used to keep her safe.

Starling scrabbled through the wood and out into heavy wet fields of ploughed clay that weighted her boots until she could hardly walk. Eventually she found a gate that led her onto a narrow lane. She walked cautiously, always aware of the nearest gate she could escape over. But no cars passed her. Around a bend, a row of cottages crouched by the roadside, their doors lit to welcome their people home. She could almost feel the warmth on her face as she trudged past, could smell dinners cooking inside. In old tales, a wanderer would knock at a cottage in the woods, ask for shelter for the night. She'd be welcomed in, warmed by the fire, offered the hay loft, or a space in the attic. Not here, though. That wasn't real life. No one ever welcomed Starling.

As the night lifted from the fields, she kept going, looking for a roof or a shelter of any kind. She'd left it too late and wished she had the tarp. She could have made a quick bender, sheltered in the dark hours and tatted down before daylight.

It was almost completely dark when she turned down a half-made track with potholes a stride wide and deep with rainwater that filled her boots.

The rain was relentless. She huddled in the lee of a hedge, holly and last year's beech leaves filtering the wind as poorly as a sieve. She chewed the last corner of a flatbread, and drips ran down her neck.

Starling needed to get dry. If she could light a fire she would be all right. She pulled herself up, shouldered her sodden bag. The puddles at her feet glinted black as bitumen, sucking the night sky into them. She splashed straight through them. She had to keep moving.

The hedgerow swallowed the small crunch of her footsteps, but on a small bend in the track, she heard an echo. She stamped, listened and turned to the sound. There was a wall. She felt her way along it to a gateway. She climbed over and moved into sudden dryness. Her knees met a bale of hay, scratchy and solid. Rain clattered on some kind of roof. She swung her bag down, and slid to the floor, leaning back into the itch of tight-packed grass. She could stop.

She stripped her soaking clothes off and hung them over the bale. She had nothing dry apart from the hay to make a fire with, and was too tired even to be ashamed of having kept on walking as darkness gathered. Mar would have scouted out a place to sleep hours before. Tomorrow, she would think ahead. She would be lucky. She huddled in her sleeping bag listening to the rain pouring off the roof.

Hours later, a small space opened in the sound of the rain and she was held in the stillness of the night. Finally, she slept.

*

In the morning she woke to find herself curled up in the back of a half-broken barn, the remnants of an old store of hay piled against the wall. The tang of mice and rats rose from the rotting grass and water poured in curtains from the unguttered roof, but she was warm and dry in her bag.

She had made it through her first day and night on the road. Maybe she could stay here for a day, make a fire and dry out her clothes.

A true survivor needs nothing. She makes her own way with no more than her eyes and her hands to guide her.

She pushed down her sleeping bag and stood to see what lay beyond the barn. The track she'd walked down last night dropped down the hill, a slick of ochre mud between ill-cut scanty hedges. Through the hedges, the near fields were ruled with faint lines of green: winter barley just getting going. No one would walk these fields in this mud. She turned a half-circle. Only a couple of hundred metres away, the curtained windows of a house peered over a hedge. She dropped down to the floor. How had she missed it? She had no chance of making a fire. She poured a palmful of oats into her mug and set it under the curtain of rain for a moment. She shivered, goose pimples all over, and looked at her cold wet clothes and boots. There was nothing for it. She dragged them on, filled her pockets with dry grass, stuffed her sleeping bag back in her pack and stepped out into the weather, spooning damp oats into her mouth as she walked back up the track.

*

Her second day on the road, Starling kept to small lanes, zigzagging around fields and through sleeves of woodland, following the ridges and furrows of the landscape. The ploughed fields were impassable with mud, but at least the lanes were quiet. Where the fast straight roads had numbed her mind, these lanes held it still, though she could always hear the hiss and roar of big roads somewhere out of sight. It was a land where people rushed but the earth still breathed slow.

The rain fell, pouring off fields across the road, filling small streams and ditches, uniting sky and earth and all the animals who moved through them.

Sheep looked up as she passed below high fields. Cows called from barns in valley bottoms. Dogs barked when she passed through farmyards. A post van tracked ahead of her, in and out of long drives to invisible houses. She met no one on foot bar one woman walking a pair of Labradors. She greeted Starling with a wry comment about the weather – 'but we're glad to be out in it, eh?' – assuming Starling too had chosen to walk in the rain. And maybe she had. She was a woman who made her own choices. She was unfettered, free to do what she wanted. For a moment she felt sure.

Mar was out here somewhere too, moving with purpose, treading new stories into the land, listening to its songs, healing its wounds. Or was she crouched shivering in a field corner, unable to light her fire, soaked to the skin even through her cloak in this ridiculous rain?

Mar was a survivor. That's what she lived by. Starling had to trust her.

Solitude is a blessing, Starling. Only alone can we find our true strength.

Mar's path wasn't Starling's now. Starling had to find her own purpose, her own way. The wind shifted and took a cold edge. She kept walking.

Was she wrong to return to the Green Man in search of Mar? It was the only place she might have left word, the last place they'd stopped before winter.

So she went on, along the small lanes, despite the endless rain, despite her hunger and despite the chill that rose from her boots and fingered its way down her collar and through her clothes.

But she was lucky. On the second night an old caravan in the corner of a field waited for her just as the sky's light began to leak away. She pulled its back window open and slid in. She'd passed its farmhouse almost half a mile back and the fields between were empty, gates open, thick with mud poached into shin-deep holes by cattle she could hear but not see. They were stuck in a barn now, no doubt. So for this night, she had four walls and a roof and no one knew she was here.

She tried the cooker, but there was no gas left in the bottle. In the cupboard above it, half a pack of macaroni spilled over the sticky formica shelf.

She pulled the hay from her pockets, added a handful of twigs she'd gathered and dried beneath her coat, and lit a fire she could reach from the caravan's step. Water from a cattle trough, a handful of nettle tops, the pasta, the flickering flames, and a responding flicker inside her said *yes, yes, I can do this*.

*

She dried her clothes on sticks propped above the fire, and the darkness danced outside the light of the flames. She felt the low murmur of old friends around her, passing mugs, laughing softly, leaning shoulder to shoulder in the warmth. How many years was it since she had shared a fire with anyone but Mar?

Before all of this, long before, Starling and Mar had travelled with the others – never the same people all the time, that's not how it went, but around the year they came together like migrating birds, always moving, staying a while, homing back, moving on. People were seasonal; some you saw in spring, some in summer, and the closest of them you spent winter with.

They used to tell stories round the fire at night, maybe two or three friends, sometimes fifteen or twenty: everyone on site would gather once they'd finished their chores and they'd pass round a joint and a brew and someone would pull out the thread of a story, and they'd all begin to weave it, passing the tale back and forth across the flames. In the darkness stories could change their shape as they crossed the shadows between the people. From when she was young, Starling knew that stories kept the darkness and fears away and bound the crew together for another night.

Now there were no voices in the wood. Over the years the others had given up – even Luc and Em. Only Starling and Mar had stayed true.

She'd learned to carry the memories of her friends silent inside her. She held them carefully, knowing how fragile a friendship can be. The last summer the whole tribe was together, they'd worked the festivals. They were a crew working across the country, meeting up for a week here, another week there, every festival the same routine, raising the tents and the stages, setting up the toilets, clearing up, filling, emptying, gathering at the end of the night round a fire for a brew and a spliff.

By the end of the summer it was just Starling and Luc. They'd no idea it would be the last time they'd work together, almost the last time they'd see each other.

The rules said no fires, but rules were for punters. Starling and Luc knew how to make so little smoke no one would see it against the night, out on the furthest field. Behind them the festival was subsiding into its own embers. They sat with their feet to the campfire, beers in hand, exhausted.

'Pass us a beer, Star.' Luc picked up his guitar. He never went anywhere without it. It was how he relaxed, how he unspooled the day, how he spoke most clearly. He braced it against his leg and ran his fingers across the strings, his elbow pushing her away. 'Sorry.' He tuned it and picked out an arpeggio, letting it rise into the darkening sky with the sparks from the fire.

He began to play, slow notes like waves on a shore, an old Neil Young tune they both knew from years of campfires all over the land, a song of earth destruction and human sadness. Starling closed her eyes and let Luc's voice wash over her, unwinding at last.

When the song finished, she lay with the fire hot on the soles of her feet, the sky fading above. Luc twisted round and looked back towards the main fields, only a few lights still guiding the punters back to their tents. He plucked another chord, and began to sing, a song about leaving, about being the wrong man for his woman. He'd never been Starling's man. He'd always been in her life, a big brother carrying her on his shoulders when she was tiny, the only person she ever allowed to tease her about being so small. They didn't need to speak. He sat quietly at the end of the song, looking into the embers.

She leaned against him. 'You all right?'

'Mmm. You?'

'Mmm, too.' She pushed herself to her feet, warm and tired. 'I'm going to bed.'

A month later, Luc had gone, and she hadn't seen him since. It had been more than five years.

Starling sat on the caravan step and watched the fire burn down. How long could you hold someone's memory before they turned to ash?

You need no one. No one needs you.

*

She left the caravan early, as the first blackbird called the dawn. Her boots and coat were almost dry but the sky was weighted with rain. She wanted to get some miles in before the storm rolled over the hills and caught up with her. Though she'd started the night

45

warm, she'd barely slept. No matter how still she lay, curled on the floor beneath the table, the caravan creaked and split as it shifted in the night. Everyone knew caravans weren't made for winter, with their flimsy walls and no insulation, and this one was on its last wheels. Starling pitied the farm worker that pitched up for the season and was expected to be grateful for its skimpy shelter.

She could go back to the van and its solid walls, the burner and her soft bed. But she didn't want to go back.

Step into the world and let it find you.

Starling imagined Mar's figure striding along a ridge, her cloak streaming behind her, never looking back at where she'd been, fixing her gaze on the way ahead.

If Starling went back to the van she would be alone. Here on the road, she was alone, but by keeping moving she pushed her loneliness ahead of her, just out of reach.

Chapter Five

Starling dropped down from the ridge to the main road when it was already dark. She didn't want to be seen. It was pouring again and she'd found a falling-down hut to sleep in, though it was barely dry. She had around another day's walk until the Green Man; maybe she could buy something hot to eat from a service station before she retreated up the hill to safety.

But a car stopped. It was low, sleek and powerful, hissing to a halt just ahead of her, its engine thrumming as it waited. Starling was soaked and filthy and this didn't feel right. The car's headlights sliced the gloom, the rain darting white through its sharp beams. She heard a door open, and a woman's voice call out.

'Do you want a lift?'

Starling was freezing. She wanted viscerally to be somewhere dry and warm. The temperature was dropping, and a night out in this weather wouldn't be fun, even in the leaky hut. But she wasn't daft. You didn't accept the crocodile's offer of a lift across the river, no matter how much you wanted to reach the other bank.

But the woman walked to the back of her car and opened the boot. 'It's OK. I don't bite.' Her voice was low and sanded rough by years of cigarettes. She sounded local. Not fancy. Not that that meant anything. Her car's black paint glittered in the light reflecting off the rain. 'I'm going to Wincombe if that helps. And I don't care if you're wet. It's not my car.'

Starling started to shiver, like her body knew she was going to refuse the lift and trudge on into the icy downpour. 'OK', she said, her voice coming out a whisper. She tried again, 'OK.' She cleared her throat. 'Thanks.' How many days was it since she'd spoken? Three, four? More like a week, or two.

Inside, the car smelled new. It had cream leather seats and acres of carpet for her mud-crusted boots. The woman was as glossy as her car, but her face was wrinkled and the hand she reached out to turn up the music was bony. She grinned at Starling, teeth alarmingly white against her lipstick. 'Still love that song,' she husked. Back before she sought silence, Mar had loved 'Born to be Wild' too, swinging Starling round the van as they yelled the chorus over and over. Starling felt a wave of loss surge through her so fast she almost couldn't control it, but she shoved the memory back into its cage. The only way she'd survive was remembering that she'd always been alone, even when Mar was by her side, holding her in her arms. That's what Mar taught her. *Alone, we are powerful. Nothing can hurt us because we depend on no one.* Starling had always thought Mar meant they were alone together, but now she knew.

She gripped her pack on her lap. She'd refused to put it into the boot. It and the bag round her neck held everything she had.

Starling smelled the rank musky odour of months in the wood rising off her coat as the car's heat seeped into it. She'd probably stink even worse once the warmth reached her body.

The woman's bangles rang as she changed gear and sped up. Starling knew the rule. She had to talk to the lift, give them something in return. 'Thanks for stopping,' she said. 'I didn't think anyone would pick me up.'

The woman fiddled with the dashboard. 'We're steaming up. Hang on while I work out which button it is.' She pressed a couple of switches. 'Can you see it?'

Starling peered at the tiny buttons. In the van they just opened the windows or wiped the screen. She chose one, and a blast of warm air skimmed the top of her head.

'That's better,' the woman said. 'I didn't fancy reading about them finding your body in a ditch.' She looked over at Starling. 'Where are you going?'

Starling hesitated. It wasn't this woman's business to know where she was going. But she had to say something, and what did it matter? 'The Green Man? On the Wincombe road?'

The woman nodded. 'Got friends there?'

Starling looked out of the side window. She didn't know. 'Maybe.' Her breath steamed up the glass and she rubbed it with her sleeve. The road swept by. It felt wrong, like someone was fast-forwarding a film, pressing it against her eyes as it screamed past on the reels, ripping her from where she should be, out where she could smell the rain and the mud, and strapping her into this imaginary world of polish and recycled air.

The woman spoke. 'You don't have to talk. I get it. I'm knackered too. I've been driving all day.'

Starling couldn't do it, couldn't make herself make conversation. She felt herself pulling her mind inside a shell, shutting down. She managed to tug her mouth into a kind of smile.

The woman carried on, like she didn't need Starling to say her bit. 'Nice car, though, isn't it? Company car, so I'm paying it forward. I used to have some friends like you – New Age Travellers, they called themselves. They were on the road with the Peace Convoy, you know? Though you probably weren't born then, were you?'

Starling shook her head. She didn't care about some random mates. The woman accelerated out of a bend, the engine roaring. 'Soon be there.'

The road kept streaming by, gleaming wet in the car's head-lamps, lights from houses flicking past, the people inside them playing families, sure they'd always have a home, dancing to the music like nothing would ever go wrong. Starling clenched her hands tighter round her pack, holding it against her and feeling her heart beating fast through the layers of soaking cloth.

The woman's voice broke into her silence. 'Are you OK?' She paused. 'You don't have to tell me what's going on, but if you want a bed and a safe place for the night, just say. You look like you might need it. I've got a spare room.'

It was too much to get her mind round, a room in a stranger's house, this woman downstairs in her kitchen. Starling knew the road and the rain. It was where she belonged. She shook her head. 'No,' she managed. 'Thanks.' Out of the side window the verge was a grey blur. She counted lamp posts as they thrummed past, letting the engine and the road beneath the wheels carry her on.

*

The Green Man's sign creaked above Starling's head as the car's rear lights vanished. She wanted to step onto the tarmac of the empty road, walk into the darkness and find a place to hide. But an icy wind fingered its way inside her damp clothes. She was freezing again already. She looked up. The light above the sign caught Mar's painting as it swung back and forth. It was one of her best. The Green Man's wild green beard and hair sprouted leaves, branches and flowers around a perfect likeness of Dave's face, smiling a welcome to his pub. He had been Mar's friend longer than anyone: they'd played in the sandpit together at primary school somewhere up north. Not that Mar reminisced, ever. Dave had mentioned it once, and Starling had tucked the image away before Mar changed the subject.

But it was Dave who'd set Mar's anger alight until it burned down their whole lives. His casual comments, pushing back at Mar, challenging her as he always did, had changed everything.

But maybe Mar had come back to put him right? Maybe she'd been here and left a word for her.

Starling stood in the darkness looking across the car park in to the pub, empty but still lit, just after hours. Dave would be in there, pottering about as if nothing had happened. Maybe she could just go in and pretend everything was normal. But she felt like she'd been sharpened too many times and turned twisty and unpredictable. She couldn't pretend any more. Last time they'd been here, she'd helped behind the bar while Mar worked. She wasn't that Starling now.

The light above the sign went out. Inside the pub a figure moved behind the bar, polishing the optics and wiping the beer taps. She knew what it would smell like in there, the tang of beer on Dave's cloth. She could hear the clank of the keys on his belt. He'd be locking up in five minutes.

When she knocked on the door he jumped like he was startled. He frowned and pressed a switch under the bar. A light came on above her head. 'Starling?' He strode to the door, unlocked it, and opened his arms to embrace her.

'You don't want to hug me.' She took a step back into the night. 'I'm filthy and wet. And I'm not stopping.' Her words rushed out: 'Have you seen Mar?'

He didn't answer her. 'Come in.' She shook her head, glaring at the floor to avoid his eyes. 'Come in,' he said again. 'I'll make you a coffee and something hot to eat.'

Maybe he had seen Mar. 'I'm not stopping,' she said again but she followed him in, pulling the door closed behind her. She had to ask. There wasn't anywhere else. The empty pub felt vast, too big for her. Too small too, after so many days in the woods and fields alone. She touched the wall by the door, its ancient beam, and felt its solidity beside her.

He poured coffee into the machine. 'I won't make you stay. Not if you don't want to. But you need coffee, and so do I. Lamb masala OK?'

She nodded.

'Be right back.'

Her stomach rumbled as the smell of coffee reached her. Last thing she'd eaten was... was what? Was it yesterday? The coffee machine burbled, the old station clock ticked on the wall, and a log settled on the fire. It was a stage set, she knew that, designed to make Dave's customers feel welcome, stay longer, spend more. Fakery. Well, she had no money, and she couldn't afford to stay even if she did. But she pulled a chair up to the fire and dropped her pack beside her. Dave hadn't answered her question.

She ate the masala on her lap, her boots steaming on the fire-dogs. Dave poured himself a coffee and sat opposite her, letting her eat, watching the fire. She'd forgotten how patient he was. But it was easy for him, wasn't it? His life was so cushy. Mar had been rigid with anger when they drove away. 'How dare he?' she'd roared, skidding the tyres out of the car park. Thirty years, almost, she'd been on the road. Stripping back her life. And he, he with his greedy puffed-up lifestyle and his bitchy wife... How dare he?

Mar had always mocked Dave's life, the different paths they'd taken since school, but last time it was different. She'd gone off on one, really let rip about his brand-new car, his holiday to Costa Rica, the prices he charged for a fish stew – 'No, a *cacciucco*,' she'd sneered, 'I forgot, calling it fish stew's not fancy enough for you any more.'

But Dave wasn't a pushover. 'How much fuel does the van burn, though, Mar?' he'd said last time, calm as anything. 'And where was your food grown? We buy ninety per cent of our ingredients from local growers.'

'Only so you can charge more,' Mar had flashed back.

'Only when it costs more,' he'd replied. 'We're not a charity. But we are part of our local economy.'

'Fucking capitalist system.'

'Maybe. But you're part of it too. Unless you don't want me to pay you?'

Starling and Mar had been at the Green Man for Mar to touch up the sign. They came every year though the sign rarely needed much attention, but they'd park up in the yard behind the pub and stay a couple of days or more.

Was Dave remembering that last time too? The words Mar had flung at him as they drove off? Starling pushed the memory away and flattened the last forkfuls of masala against the plate, suddenly unable to eat.

Dave didn't seem to notice. 'Where did you park the van? You can bring it round the back.'

He didn't like it out front any more, that was the truth, not since he'd gone upmarket, all gastropub and clean shoes. Starling put the plate down and looked at her boots. 'I haven't got the van.'

'Mar's gone on a trip?'

'I don't know where she is.'

'Oh.' His silence was waiting for her to say more. Starling said nothing. What was there to say?

He drew in a long breath. 'Look, I know it's not my place. But it's freezing out there and there's another storm on its way. Stay tonight, at least. Gill and the girls will be glad to see you.'

And there was the rub. Gill and the girls, Dave's blind spot.

'So Mar hasn't been in?' she asked, just to be sure.

He shook his head. 'I felt bad,' he said, 'last time. I hoped you were OK – she was so mad. I'd never seen her like that, like she'd boiled over. Were you OK?'

'Of course.' Starling couldn't tell him what it had been like, Mar at the wheel driving like a maniac, fuelled by righteous over-powering rage that had fermented over the months since into deep, angry silence.

Dave looked at her over his mug and she looked away. He didn't know her that well. He'd never been on the road with them. No one could know her who hadn't made a journey with her. But he'd seen her grow up beside Mar.

'Look, I got a bit wet today,' she said. 'Maybe I could stay one night? In the yard building, maybe? I'll keep out of the way.'

Dave blew out his cheeks. 'The yard building's in a state, Starling. I'm halfway through converting it. You don't want to stay there.'

She felt cold grip her at the thought of going back out into the night, but reached down to pick up her pack. She'd get going.

Dave put a hand on her arm to stop her. 'Starling. Mar's a survivor. She'll be OK. And she'd be telling you to accept a bed for the night. Offered in friendship to a survivor.'

What *would* Mar be telling her? Sometimes Starling didn't know any more.

*

The spare room was small with a single bed, a wooden armchair by the window and a rug on the wooden floor. It felt like someone had left and their stuff had been cleared away. Dave had closed the curtains and switched on a lamp by the bed. A circle of golden light. A door she could close. Could lock, even – there was a key in the door. No rain. A bed.

She was filthy. She couldn't lie in that bed, with its clean sheet, white duvet and pillows.

And there was nothing here she would put in her box. She hadn't arrived anywhere real – she might as well be on TV. She touched the tiny pot, safe in the bottom of her pocket, knowing it still held the van inside.

Dave had given her a towel and shown her a shower room along the corridor. But Gill and the girls would be asleep already and she really didn't want to wake them. She'd shower in the morning. She pushed back the curtains and opened the window, unrolled her sleeping bag and lay on the floor beside the bed. When she closed her eyes, she saw the road, slick and wet with rain, felt the rhythm of her boots on the muddy verge, the chill pressing into her flesh as she got wetter and wetter. She was here now, she told herself. *Be here, not out there. Be inside yourself. The door is locked and till morning no one can touch you. Sleep.*

*

She heard doors opening along the landing, girls' voices, Gill's, and opened her eyes. A grey morning light sifted through the gap in the curtains. She was upstairs at the Green Man, the woollen rug on the floor itching her face where she'd turned over in the night. She licked it, the fibres rough over her tongue. She thought of a sheep out on a wet hill, its wool knitted tight against the days of rain, moving across the grass like nothing mattered.

Dave had told her he'd be up and out early, off to the wholesaler and the growers, so no rush. He'd see her later, and the girls would show her where everything was. Breakfast in the kitchen. Saturday morning. Take it easy.

She took her time in the shower, washing her hair, soaping herself, rinsing slowly, resisting her urge to wash in the time it took one bucket of hot water to run through.

She could wait in the room until she heard Dave come back. She could borrow a tenner off him to get credit on her phone. She'd text Luc and see where he was. He surely couldn't be in Wincombe still? Could he have seen Mar? More likely Em had. Mar and Em. Had Em found Mar?

But sitting on the edge of the bed, wrapped in the towel, she looked out of the window at the road. An occasional car passed.

A bus. No one on foot. And above it all, a mass of black clouds heavy with rain was idling towards her. It wouldn't be long before she was soaked again. And she was starving. She looked at the clothes she'd rolled tight in the bottom of her pack and pulled on black leggings and a baggy T-shirt that looked clean enough. The room was so warm she didn't need more layers but she put her jumper on and pulled the sleeves down over her hands, her knitted coat of armour. She felt her boots, almost dry after a night by the radiator. She should go now and release the tension gripping her guts at the thought of family breakfast with Gill and the girls. She should head back out onto the road and leave all this behind. Mar was right. The Green Man was toxic. A poisonous place where Dave and Gill lived off an illusion that meant nothing in the real world that Mar and Starling lived in.

But that was the coward's way out. The fool's way. Missing a good breakfast and the chance to get her boots and coat properly dry, all because she despised a pair of spoiled girls and their mum.

She walked down the corridor and pushed open the door. The kitchen had become an expanse of gleaming white since she was last here: white tiled floor, white marble counters, shining tiled walls, glaring white downlights from a white ceiling. Even the girls were dressed in crisp white T-shirts. A single black vase in the centre of the table held a bunch of gleaming yellow daffodils. There was no sign of pots and pans, mugs or knives. Everything was hidden.

Gill looked up. She looked exactly the same, deeply tanned despite the winter, blonde hair cut sharp as a helmet. Her jaw twitched and she stood up from the table. 'Off you go, girls.'

Her daughters looked at each other and clattered their cereal spoons into their bowls, pushing their chairs back with a squeal. 'Hi, Starling,' the younger one said. She'd always been the friendlier one. Her sister walked out of the room, eyes on her phone, the younger one following. Starling wished they'd stayed.

'Hi, Gill,' Starling said.

Gill picked up the girls' bowls. 'Cereal?' She was being nice today, then.

'Yes, please. Whatever you have.' She would be polite. She moved towards the table and dropped her bag by the chair nearest the door.

'Wait!' Gill rushed over with a plastic bag that she smoothed out over the white leather seat of the chair. 'OK.'

'Nice kitchen,' Starling said.

Gill had her back to her, looking into an open cupboard of white crockery. They must have replaced everything when they redid the kitchen. Where were the girls' favourite mugs? The hand-made bowls Mar and Starling had given them?

'Thanks,' Gill said. She was trying hard too. 'Coffee?' she asked, and when Starling nodded, she poured them both a mug. She stood leaning against the counter as Starling ate, taking tiny sips of coffee so she wouldn't have to fill the silence. In the end, though, she gave in. 'So. No Mar?'

Starling had a mouthful. She shook her head.

'Dave said she left you.'

Starling's throat seized up. She made herself swallow.

Gill continued: 'She hasn't been here, you know.'

Starling looked at her. She had to ask. 'If she does come, will you give her my number?' She needed Mar to have it, even if it meant Mar knew about her phone.

Gill took another sip and eyed Starling calmly over the top of her mug. 'If Mar dares set foot in here ever again, I'm calling the police. I don't care what Dave says. I'm not letting her anywhere near my girls. She's dangerous.'

Starling was stunned. 'But—'

'Now eat up and get out. I don't want you here when Dave gets back.'

Starling gulped down the mouthful of cereal and stood quickly. Dave would think she was avoiding him, but she couldn't help that. It was crap, though. Starling had known Dave longer than Gill had, but loyalty counted for nothing in this kitchen. 'Don't worry, I'm out of here.' She picked up her bag and turned to leave, casually knocking over the mug of undrunk coffee. 'Oh dear,' she said, as the hot liquid poured onto the shining floor and ran along the gaps between the tiles. 'I'll get out of your way, Gill.'

She jogged down the corridor, Gill yelling after her. Her pack was ready by the bed. She grabbed it and picked up her boots, but before she could pull them on Gill was in the room. She seized Starling's wrist. 'How fucking dare you, you little bitch?'

Starling shoved her away. 'Get off me.'

Gill slapped her, hard. 'Get out of my home!'

Starling ran out of the room, boots in one hand and swinging her pack back onto her shoulder where it belonged. At the top of the stairs she upended Dave's emergency cash jar and swiped twenty quid. He owed Mar more, but that would do. She grabbed a handful of crisp packets from the box by the bar door, and she was on her way.

Chapter Six

Wincombe sat on the flatlands of the flood plain, its back to the river. The rain was falling steadily on its main street; it didn't want to be here either. Starling hadn't been to Wincombe before but she knew what it would be like. They were all over England, the kind of small towns where you turned off the A road for fuel and a pint of milk, took a five-minute stroll in each direction to see if there was anything more, and left. If you lived there, you knew everyone. Nothing happened. It was stranded, a prisoner.

People do not live in towns. They cling together, existing and no more, because they are afraid to live fully and freely as we do.

Mar's voice was always in her head. There was nothing Starling could do about it – Mar was pronouncing, prodding, reminding her of truth. As she walked into the outskirts of Wincombe, Starling could sing as loud as she liked to drown out Mar, but she was still there.

It was late by the time she found the wholefood shop. Its green paint was peeling. A blackboard outside tried harder: *Open, Homemade soup, Fresh bread, Organic vegetables, Come and say hello! The window held a couple of wooden crates of squashes and onions, artfully arranged like they'd fallen from a wagon. Capitalists love to mimic our necessity. Never trust the pretence of poverty.* There was a heap of gnarly-shaped bread rolls. Nothing for her. She couldn't afford anything in a shop like this.

No way would Luc be here, propping up this bollocks show of fake earthiness. He'd be long gone, quick on his feet and off to find a new woman. Starling hoped the woman he'd discarded was still here and knew where he was, and wasn't too pissed off to tell her. He was good at letting them down gently, playing the troubadour, the man who had to keep moving, following his soul's music. They loved him even after he'd left.

Starling peered in beyond the window. Wooden shelving ran down one side, stacked with bags of grains, beans and pulses, flour, nuts, bottles of oil with arty labels. Along the other wall a counter heaved with cheeses, breads and fruit, taunting her. She was starving. A young woman about Starling's age came into the shop from a door at the back and looked out at her. She smiled and began to wipe the counter.

'Excuse me.' A man in a suit stepped around Starling and pushed open the shop door. A smell of day-old soup with an underlay of spices curled out and she turned away. She wasn't going to waste her time or cash here.

There was a door beside the shop, painted in the same green but with a letterbox and a bell. She peered at the grubby hand-written sticker above the bell. *K&L*. L could be Luc. She pressed the bell, heard a gnat's buzz somewhere inside.

The man in the suit emerged from the shop clutching a brown paper bag, the girl close behind him, pale blue cropped hair and nose ring signalling that she rejected the mainstream she so clearly belonged to.

'Hi,' she said to Starling. 'Was that you ringing the bell?' Her skin was perfect and she had just the china-blue eyes Luc fell for. Starling was soaked again and her road clothes were filthy. She scowled.

'Nah.' She turned away, hands in pockets, shoulders tight against this girl.

Down the street, she sat on a bench, hunched against the rain. She had a handful of oats left, but had eaten nothing since the morning. She didn't want to crack open Dave's note unless she had to. She started to shiver. Even her jumper was wet. She closed her eyes and thought herself out into the fields, sheltering under a scanty hedge, listening to the rain on the earth. She tried to block out the town, and failed.

She opened her eyes to see a small white fluff of down float past, an angel come to earth as Em used to say, and caught the feather in her upturned palm, so light it was barely there.

Maybe she was meant to stop here, just for a while. Luc had spent time here, even if he was long gone. Maybe she too could pause and take stock. Where else did she have, after all? She needed time to make sense of what had happened.

She dug in her pocket for her box, opened it and tipped out the acorn that had been there since she and Mar had arrived in the wood. She carefully laid it on the spoonful of earth beside the bench and placed the feather inside. She closed the lid and ran her fingers over the three birds. She had to stop, even if only for a day or two. This would hold her safe.

But every fibre of her was strung tight as a violin, vibrating with every passer-by, every raised voice, every look. A couple of teenagers slouched past and slid their eyes over her hooded face. Their glance plucked a high keening note inside her. She didn't belong. She wasn't safe. Stupid. Stupid. Stupid. They were kids. She made herself breathe. In. Out. No one cared if she was here – that was the truth.

She wished Luc had been here. He'd have understood. *But he left you.*

How did he do it? How did he learn to be at ease wherever he stopped, even in a place like this where people like him and Starling were never welcome? She'd watched him over the years, his easy smile to a stranger, the way he knew the best question to ask them, how they smiled back, offered him a cigarette, a job, a bed for the night. What did he do, the first night he arrived here in Wincombe? Where did he stay?

The rain had stopped but the wind blew through her wet coat and a deep shiver ran up her spine. She could go in the shop and ask the girl with the perfect skin if she knew where Luc was. Starling imagined the warmth of the shop. The smell of the soup. But she stuffed her arms into her armpits and glared at the pavement. She didn't trust this girl, this K, whoever she was. *We know our tribe. We bear the mark of wisdom born of truth.* Yeah, and mud and hypothermia. But Mar was right. You always could tell. And outsiders were quick to turn on the tribe. You had to keep your distance. Did Luc still bear the mark?

The clouds broke and in the late light Starling's shadow stretched across the pavement from the bench. She watched it fall into the cracks in the wall of a flower shop. A woman's arms appeared in the window and pulled a green bucket of daffodils towards her and out of sight. Tulips, roses, pots of hyacinth and single stems of amaryllis vanished, leaving the window empty. All that remained were the words stencilled on the glass: *Blooming Marvellous – flowers for all occasions.* The woman stepped out, locked the door and walked away, pulling her hat over her ears. It was getting colder. The streetlamps came on, though there was still light in the sky, and streams of people began to flow around Starling, most not speaking, hands in pockets or holding phones, walking fast.

The crowd thinned. She had to find somewhere to sleep for the night. She'd passed a church on her way into town. Even if it was locked, the doorway would be dry. Imagine if it was open, though. The pavements glistened as it began to drizzle, and a solitary figure turned the corner on the edge of her vision.

She'd have recognised Luc anywhere. He walked up the road, loose-limbed, his stride the kind of swagger that wasn't a boast but the strength of a man who knew his own skin. She had forgotten the way he was still even when he was moving, the way his quiet was so different to Mar's silence. She pulled her hood off and her pack closer. He greeted a hunched woman with a brolly who paused, taking time to exchange a few words despite the rain. Then he looked up and saw Starling, and waved, a slow, open-handed wave she'd know anywhere from a lifetime of festivals and fields, a wave like a smile.

He lengthened his stride and was with her in moments, reaching for her hands and taking them in his. 'Starling. You're frozen. Jesus.' He looked down at her, a small frown pulling his wide blue eyes together. 'Oh, Star. How long have you been here?' He didn't wait for her to answer, but pulled her up and wrapped her in his arms, his chest warm through his coat against her face. She felt tiny and enclosed. It had been a long time since anyone had touched her.

She pushed him away. He hadn't changed, though he'd cropped his mess of straw hair and lost his dreads. His eyes smiled and she hoped there was a chance, despite everything, that he was pleased to see her. *Don't trust him.*

'Come on,' he said. 'It's bloody freezing out here.'

She almost said no, almost walked away. She could hear Mar telling her to get away. Now. Her path lay alone. But Mar wasn't here, and Luc was. So she followed him back up the street. He unlocked that side door beside the shop and led the way up the stairs. The bulb had gone and Starling tripped on the carpet in the dark. She rubbed gritty dirt from the carpet off her palms.

They passed a tiny bathroom on the landing, its door open to reveal a little cluster of almost empty shampoo bottles and scummy soap bars on the floor beside the toilet. Luc kept on up the stairs through the gloom, pushed open the door at the top and stepped into a room washed with orange light from the streetlamp outside.

It was tall-ceilinged, with a single bulb hanging down. The glow from outside lit a stack of crates on the far wall that spilled out bundled-up clothes, chargers, hats, a tambourine, a towel. An unmade double mattress filled a corner; a heap of cushions was tossed across the floor.

The girl from the shop stood by the window, a mug in her hand, looking out at the street as if she hadn't heard their steps on the stairs. She turned to them, one eyebrow raised, and Luc walked over and kissed her on the lips. 'Kit,' he said in his low voice, 'I'm late.' He put his arm round her shoulders, pulled her to him and turned to face Starling. 'Starling,' he said, 'this is Kit, my woman', but Kit shoved him in the ribs and snorted, 'I'm no one's woman. Hi, Starling,' and Starling almost liked her for a moment.

Luc dropped his bag on the bed. 'You should have come in, Star. Kit was in the shop, weren't you?' He switched on a small light clipped to the crates and the room fell into shape.

'I'm so sorry,' Kit said. She rattled about in the mess of stuff on top of the crates until she found a lighter, and lit a pair of candles stuffed in bottles. She picked up Luc's bag and hung it behind the door. Starling could see the rhythm in their movements, that these were the things they did each night when they came home. 'I didn't realise it was you. She did come, Luc, but...'

Luc reached out to Starling. 'Give us your coat, Star. You're soaked.' But Starling stood by the door, holding her pack.

'Look, I can go,' she said. This room smelled of other people's lives. She didn't belong here.

But Kit said no way and jumped, light-footed, over the mess of cushions and cans. She tugged Starling into the room with a hand on her sleeve. 'God, you are soaked. I'll hang it in the bathroom.'

'I'll do it,' Starling said, not ready to take her coat off yet, not sure she would stay. Luc's guitar was propped in a corner but nothing else looked like his. He still travelled as light as she did, then. Kit pulled a clutch of mugs out of the sink and peered at them in the dimness. She filled the kettle. 'Tea? Coffee?

Something herbal? I've got some camomile, I think?' She didn't bother waiting for an answer but ran round the room picking up cans and emptying them into a black sack that she threw back into a corner.

'Tea,' Starling said, and she sat on the floor by the door, exhausted. It was dark outside now. She couldn't face walking back out into the rain.

Kit was all flash and buzz like a butcher's blue light catching flies. She forgot about the tea, kept talking. 'Luc's working long days at the moment... and the shop's so busy... exciting, of course, but manic... and we've never had a chance to sort out the flat... so...'

'Kit,' Luc said, 'hey, slow down. Starling's been travelling for days.' He looked at Starling. 'Let's just have that brew. I'll wash the mugs.'

Starling's boots leaked slow puddles across the floor. She pulled a finger through the water, traced a waving line across the boards and watched it soak in. Luc placed a mug in front of her; she held it in her hands until they burned, and breathed in the hot steam. She closed her eyes, heard Kit take a pan and clatter it onto the little hob, Luc's low laugh, the sizzle of an onion, and she shut everything out.

*

The first night at Luc's, Starling was too wired to sleep. Even with the window open his room smelled of socks and joss sticks, and every couple of minutes a car's headlights flashed a path across the ceiling, cutting over the top of the sheet Kit had pinned up instead of a curtain. Luc and Kit were asleep on the far side of the room, their breathing soft, entwined and unfamiliar. Starling wondered if Mar was asleep, wherever she was. Probably. She could sleep through anything. *The sign of a spirit at peace with itself.*

She stretched an arm out of her sleeping bag and reached for her small bag, checking it was close. She'd carried it since she could walk, ready to grab any time. Lying on Luc's floor she had it beside her, just in case. She pulled the strap that Mar had lengthened for her as she grew taller. In the van, she'd kept it under her pillow; on the road it hung inside her coat and she'd slept with it under her head each night. No need to open it. She was always ready. They liked to come at night when you were asleep.

She used to love to look down from her bed at Mar pottering: painting leaves along the handle of the teapot, or roasting acorns for coffee, or pulling the rocker over to the door so she could watch the sun set, the van's walls glowing around her.

Mar was good at making things. She'd made Starling's bag from scraps of velvet and if Starling pulled back the cotton lining she could still see the luminous lime green, the dark crimson and the periwinkle blue it had once been. When she was little, she'd kept grass and feathers and biscuit wrappers in it, and Florence, her tiny cloth doll, and her own name pinned to the lining: *Starling Shepherd, daughter of Mar.*

Starling pulled Florence out and stroked her unblinking hand-stitched eyes, thin-threaded after nineteen years of travelling. Palm-sized, she'd been rubbing against Starling's sketchbooks and pencils and small stash of cash – when she had any – for so long that she was as soft as moss. That was all Starling had in the bag, apart from a couple of photos and a small bundle of clothes, a tin mug, lighter, torch, penknife, a folded piece of sketch paper. The essentials. Mar didn't believe in possessions and she didn't believe in home, either. *The world's your home. Don't get attached to any one place. Pick up your bag and go: that's what I did.* Starling pushed Florence back into her bag and slept.

Chapter Seven

In the morning, Luc and Kit clattered about, drank coffee and headed off to work, like nothing was weird, leaving Starling pretending to sleep. She peeled herself out of her sleeping bag and stood in her pants and T-shirt looking round her. She supposed the room was dry, at least. And no one knew she was here, so no one could chase her away, for now at any rate. But what was she here for?

In Luc and Kit's space Starling felt like a fly trapped in a room. She trod from window to wall to door. She washed the clothes she'd come in and hung them over the bath to dry: underclothes, leggings, layers of T-shirts, and her favourite jumper. It sagged with the weight of the water and she wrung it out again, tempted to put it back on. She didn't want to leave it here. But that was stupid so she went back up to the room and sniffed her spare set. More black leggings and T-shirts, her second-best jumper, striped with all the leftover wools in Mar's bag and with holes in its elbows because she'd worn it forever. They'd do.

She could hear Kit's voice below in the shop, chatting and laughing with customers.

She washed up. She straightened the cushions. She opened the window. It had stopped raining and the sun flared against the dirt on the glass. She looked under the sink to see if there was anything to clean it with. There wasn't even vinegar. In the end, she went out. She had nothing to do here. She needed a job. She needed money. She needed to get out.

*

Starling pulled the street door to the flat shut behind her, locking herself out. She slung her bag over her shoulder and set off to explore, mapping out the town by following the rise and fall of the land beneath the tarmac, just as she learned the fields and woods whenever she arrived somewhere new.

It was a small town. The streets were quiet. Neat signs beside plain doors between shops revealed the upstairs offices of accountants, solicitors, land agents, web designers and beauticians. If she looked up she could see lights on ceilings and hear phones ringing through windows. People were busy, but the town's life felt enclosed, and out of reach.

She could feel her feet pulling her back out along the river path towards the open country. *Out here, who's to tell you what to do?* But her clothes were hanging above Luc's bath, and she needed money.

Mar hated towns. They were built to make a few bastards rich and to perpetuate the distorted social structures that enslaved people. What kind of life was it where the only way to eat was to sell yourself? Stand in a shop selling shitty clothes to people who worked in shops selling shitty food to people who worked in offices writing pointless emails to people who worked in offices replying to pointless emails, all to earn just enough to buy a loaf of bread full of chemicals. No way. But here Starling was. And she couldn't go back to the van. She had to find her own way, work out where home was when you might be alone forever.

Mid-morning, a flurry of young women appeared pushing buggies, talking on their phones. They vanished into coffee shops with carefully distressed pine tables and mismatched china. At lunchtime, they emerged, warm and chattering, and gave up their seats to a wave of smartly dressed office workers.

Starling found a scrubby little park and waited for the youngest workers to appear, the ones with worn-down heels, cheap plastic bags and DIY haircuts, the ones who ate bags of chips from the takeaway or lunches brought from home. She picked one with a nose piercing and scarlet hair pulled up on top of her head.

'Hey.' Starling smiled at the girl. 'Love your hair.'

The girl looked up, grinning through a sausage roll. 'Thanks. I just did it. Thought it might be a bit bright, but hey.'

'Nah, it's great. Look, sorry, I'm new here and I'm looking for work. Do you know anywhere I could try?'

The girl thought a moment. 'There's not a lot going. They just laid a load of people off at the place I work.'

She called out to a lad who was passing: 'Hey, Nick.'

He sauntered over, shoving a floppy one-sided fringe out of his eyes.

'Hey, Flea.' He looked at Starling and nodded, pushed his fringe back off his face.

'She's looking for work,' said Flea.

Nick put his hands in his jeans pockets and shrugged his shoulders. Then he straightened up. 'How about Dinah's? She can never keep her staff. She's bound to need someone.' He looked at Starling and raised an eyebrow. 'Depends how desperate you are.'

They sent Starling down the far end of the high street beyond where it turned the corner. She kept walking as it widened out and the shops got scruffier. She passed a discount carpet store with a windowful of nylon rugs, a tattoo parlour with blacked-out windows. The shops turned practical and she walked past a tyre fitter, a pair of builders' merchants and a row of anonymous corrugated-steel buildings with no-nonsense signs: *A1 Electrical Factors, Dina-Dent,*

M&B Autoparts. She began to wonder if Nick had been having a laugh, but there, out of place as a flock of sheep on a bus, was a row of Victorian shops. Dinah's Diner occupied the last of them, its windows steamed up beneath a yellow-and-red plastic sign.

Starling stood on the opposite side of the road and tried to see in through the condensation. It looked busy, judging by the tables against the windows. A couple of guys in decorators' overalls came out, pulling packs of cigarettes out of their pockets as they walked away. They didn't look at her. The smell of chip fat and vinegar swept out after them. A minute later three older men emerged in dusty steel-capped boots and climbed into a van they'd shoved on the pavement round the corner. Starling hung on while the café emptied. A matching pair of office boys on late lunch sauntered in, but it was emptying fast.

When a skinny, sharp-cheeked woman of about fifty came out with a bucket in one hand and propped the door open with a chair, Starling struck out across the road.

'Hi.'

The woman ignored Starling and flung the contents of the bucket into the gutter. Starling jumped out of the way of the dirty water. 'Looks like you're busy.'

'You're a genius, then,' the woman snapped back. She was wearing tight bleached jeans and a salmon lacy T-shirt and she clattered back into the shop on heels Starling wouldn't have fancied spending five minutes on. She had to be Dinah. Starling followed her inside. There were nine formica tables, each with salt, pepper, sugar and vinegar. A matching formica bar ran along the right-hand side of the café. The office boys were sitting there, and looked up briefly to see who'd come in. Behind the counter – which held just a couple of pies and a saveloy now – the back wall was covered with an illuminated menu, with photos of every permutation of fried food, tea and fizzy drinks.

'Do you want something, then?' Dinah asked, hands on hips.

'I'd love a cup of tea,' Starling said, 'but I'm skint. Someone told me you might be in need of staff.'

Dinah looked at her, lips pursed. One of the boys at the bar coughed and nudged his mate.

'We don't normally get your type in here,' she said.

'That's fine,' Starling said. 'I saw how many people you had in over lunch. That's a lot to deal with single-handed. Shame.' And she turned to leave.

'You done this kind of thing before?' Dinah called out.

'Uh-huh. Bye.'

'Handle a fryer?'

'Yup.' How hard could it be? She could learn. She was almost out the door.

'I don't take no nonsense.'

'Nor me. That's why I'm off.'

'Jesus. Get back here, you dozy cow. You need money. I need a hand. You can start now.'

'Cash?'

'What do you take me for?'

'Thought so. What needs doing first, then?'

'You can clear the tables. Take that bloody jumper off, though.'

So Starling started working at Dinah's. Nick was right. She was all bark and all bite. God knew why the café was always so busy. Dinah was just as rude to the customers as she was to Starling. It was like they came to see a show. And her chips were good, and her tea was half the price of the fancy coffee shops up in the town centre.

That first day, Starling washed up, wiped the tables, mopped the floor, and served tea and chips to the afternoon stragglers. She wasn't allowed near the fryers – they were definitely Dinah's domain. The customers seemed pleased to see a new face, for the most part, though some pointedly placed their orders with Dinah even though Starling was standing there waiting and smiling. Still, she was used to that.

She finished about four thirty and Dinah gave her fifteen pounds out of the till. 'Get here at seven,' she said.

Starling looked at the three five-pound notes. She felt Mar behind her shoulder and took a breath. 'Right. Fifteen quid for half a day. I want forty for a full day, starting at seven. And a bag of fish and chips to take home.'

Home. That felt wrong in her mouth, like it was someone else's word that slipped in while she wasn't paying attention.

Dinah glared at her, but nodded. 'Thirty-five. Take what's left in the fryer,' she said. 'But don't get used to it.'

Starling had a feeling that Dinah might be decent under her armour. A tough woman made a lot more sense than a silly soft one like Kit or a bitch like Gill with her brittle veneer of niceness.

She headed back up towards the town, looking for somewhere to hang out until Luc got back. She didn't have the energy to deal with Kit. Maybe she'd thought Starling would be like Luc, the nice, clean face of life on the road. He scrubbed up well, did Luc. But Starling couldn't be bothered pleasing a fake like Kit.

She found a bench in the park and sat, on her own again and glad of it after the last twenty-four hours. She was starving. All afternoon Dinah had watched her like she was about to strip the joint so Starling hadn't even been able to grab a single chip, and apart from the handful she'd just stuffed down as she walked she hadn't eaten since the night before. She tore open the bag and the smell of vinegar and oil filled her nostrils. There was enough here to feed two of her, but she worked her way through the heap of chips, licking fat and salt off her fingers, hunching to keep warm in the darkening park.

*

One long hot summer, when Starling was all knees and scabs, still a child, Mar and Starling had lived in a wood near the coast. On a day when even the trees' shade was too hot they'd gone to the sea, and Starling paddled and wrote her name on the beach in pebbles while Mar collected a bagful of clam shells to paint and sell. When the sun began to set Mar threw a line of hooks into the sea, and as the water turned pearly grey and then orange, she pulled out a stream of shining mackerel wriggling with life until Mar cut them open and dropped them into the bucket at her feet. 'Dinner for you and me, and Em and the boys.' She smiled at Starling. 'Let's get chips for the way home.'

Starling hopped up and down beside Mar in the queue, snuffing up the fat and vinegar, twirling on the spot in her excitement. Chips were a treat for special days when it was just her and Mar, and the cash tin rattled. She grinned at the couple behind them in the queue, a grey-haired couple who looked like a pair of pasty-faced gargoyles, but the woman hissed at her husband, 'Just look at the state of her. Ants in her pants and needs a good smack. And a wash.' The woman raised her voice so everyone in the shop could hear, 'Some people just shouldn't be allowed to have children. It's a crying shame.' Starling froze and looked wide-eyed at Mar, knowing what would happen next.

The miracle, the absolute miracle, was that Mar simply winked at Starling and paid for their chips. 'Time to go, Starling. Nasty smell all of a sudden. Wouldn't want to catch something.' And she took Starling's hand and led her back along the promenade to the van.

'I didn't have ants, did I?' Starling had asked Mar, sitting beside her as they drove off.

Mar looked across at her, heaving the van round a bend as they left the town behind them. 'She meant you're a fidget. Jealous because she couldn't jump a kerbstone. Or have a beautiful child like you. And ants are our friends. I'll show you.'

Back in the wood, the ant heap was taller than Mar's knee, a pile of pine needles and tiny leaf fragments that rose like a small mountain just back from the path. 'Watch,' said Mar, 'and don't get too close. They spray acid if they're being attacked. It smells like salt and vinegar but it stings.'

They stood side by side on the path and Starling saw a line of wood ants emerge and head along a narrow, ant-sized trail into the trees. 'They're off foraging,' said Mar. 'What do you suppose they eat?'

'Ice cream. Chips!'

'No. What do they eat here in the woods? What's sweet?'

Starling didn't know.

'They milk aphids – little creatures up in the treetops that give out a sugary liquid. It's called honeydew, and ants love it. Look.' And there, up a tree, was a line of ants, one after the other, climbing out of sight into the canopy.

'So many!'

'There are thousands and thousands in this one colony, maybe half a million in a really big one. Wonderful creatures. We could all learn from them.' Mar turned to look at Starling. 'The way we live, here in the tribe, we're copying them in a way. We share our food. We look after each other's babies and children. We protect our homes together. And for choosing to live in harmony and cooperation, people like that woman despise us.'

Starling kept still. Mar was like an ant heap, when she talked like this. 'Don't poke, just watch.' A huge ant emerged.

'That's a queen,' said Mar. 'She's in charge. She makes the babies, and the others are there to look after her.'

'Is that fair?'

'She's the strongest and healthiest of all of them. If they look after her, she'll lay good eggs and make more workers. Isn't she a beauty?'

That was so long ago.

When Starling finished her chips, she flung the bag in a bin, and walked slowly up one side of the high street and back down the other, looking into every window. Coffee shop. Estate agent. Charity shop. Boots. Stationers. Shoe shop. Another coffee shop. Mar hadn't always been angry with the world – or at least she had, but there was far more joy than anger in her when Starling was very young. Days out together, learning about ants, paddling in streams, dancing all night in teepees, snuggling in Mar's bed on a cold night, driving through towns like this and watching the sad-faced townies eyeing the van in envy. It had been fun, growing up with Mar.

Starling kept walking up the street. Bakers. Italian deli. Fabric shop. Post office. Pet shop. Bookshop. Junk shop. Nothing she wanted. Nothing she could buy even if she did want it. She watched a young man in a cheap suit come out of the estate agents, lock the door and walk up the street, leaving rows of bright-lit pictures of homes behind him. The lights went off in the pet shop, the interior glowing blue from the fish tanks, and two women with a small dog came out laughing, locked the door and walked the other way, heels clacking on the pavement just out of time with each other. All the shops were closing for the night. Lights off, doors locked, shutters down. People going home. She propped herself up in the doorway beside the post office.

The street began to empty, but that wasn't what made Starling pull her coat tighter round her. Even when the streets were bustling, if you didn't belong, and worse, if you didn't have money, towns were the loneliest places she knew. Starling had never felt out of place in an empty field or in a wood, but here, she knew she didn't belong.

She looked across the street. A woman about Mar's age, but in suede ankle boots and a smart coat, was waiting in the door of the bookshop opposite. She looked at her watch, pulled out her phone, glanced at it, stuffed it back in her bag, looked across at Starling, looked quickly away.

'Fuck you,' Starling muttered under her breath. 'You have no fucking idea.' People were afraid of her and Mar. Maybe they should be. Maybe they could tell that if anyone was going to survive, it was Mar and Starling. Or maybe they hoped if anyone wouldn't, it was Mar and Starling. Sacrificial victims. Scapegoats. The sins of the towns piled on their backs. Banished.

They were wrong. People who lived in a place like Wincombe, they thought they were safe. But no one was safe. There had been too many on the road with them who'd been safe once and lost it all. They found out that nothing is certain. They learned to take life in their own hands before anyone took it from them.

Even when she was a small child, Starling had been ready. Any night she could be woken at three in the morning, police beating on the van door. Two minutes to grab your tat. Get out. Run. Don't bother asking for help. No one cares except your mates on the site, and where are they? Seized too, or running over the fields to safety.

Evictions, hatred, anger. One time they were evicted five times in a week. Once, when Starling was tiny, the bastards raided the site and took her, wouldn't let her be with Mar. They put Starling in a house with a woman and a man she didn't know, who fed and washed her, scrubbed her too hard, hugged her, while all Starling wanted was Mar and they wouldn't tell her anything. Next day, Mar came, angry, and the man was angry because Mar was angry and she was late because she'd walked because they'd taken the van, and she'd come to get Starling first. *What do you expect?* And she was still raging when she banged on the door and demanded they give her back Starling. Mar had always come.

Kit had no idea.

Starling had learned. *Be invisible. Watch and listen. Trust no one.*

If she disappeared now, who would notice? Even Luc wouldn't look for her. He'd think she'd gone on another journey.

*

The street was almost empty now and if Luc was as late again as he had been the night before, he'd be ages yet. Starling stepped out of the doorway and walked up the road.

She liked churches. She wasn't one for God, but no one ever asked. And every town had one. If she was lucky its door would be open. The spire of St Stephen's caught the pale curl of the new moon on its tip as she walked towards it, holding it steady for her and Mar.

Inside, St Stephen's had the same smell as all churches, an underlay of damp, polished wood, wax and cloth, dust. An electric candle flickered above the altar. Rows of dark pews. The world outside muffled. She put her bag down and sat. She rested her arms on the pew in front and laid her head on them.

They used to go to Norwich a couple of times a year. People said it had a pub for every day of the week, so there was plenty of work for Mar. Starling could see Mar's signs talking to each other across streets, calling out over rooftops, Edith Cavell and the Wild Man having a natter, the Mischief's naughty boy teasing Adam and Eve. She would wander while Mar worked. One time, at the end of a day of creeping in and out of market stalls and side streets and tracking the river, she'd pushed open the door to the cathedral.

There had been that same hush you find in the smallest country church and the hugest cathedral. The scrape of a chair on stone. Early evening light washing pillars like avenues of golden elms at twilight. It was late winter and the darkness fell fast as she stood and let the place wrap her. A man in long black robes came past, turned to her and said, 'Are you here for evensong?' And because she might have been, and she liked songs, she'd followed him. He gestured for her to sit in a row of carved wooden thrones, and left her gazing at the candles flickering on the thrones opposite and on the wall of gold that leaped up behind the altar. Men and boys walked in, in twos, in coloured robes, and filed into the stalls right in front of her and opposite. Starling could have touched the soft black hairs curling on the man's neck just below her, if she'd dared. She sat, hardly breathing, fearing she should not be there, that her presence might bring it all to ruin. A woman appeared, shuffled quickly in to take the seat beside Starling, dropped her shopping bag at her feet, and nodded at Starling before bending her head. And then liquid singing washed through and over Starling, and she didn't want it to stop but feared, too, that it had some power that she didn't understand, that it might somehow change her, and Mar would know, so when she left the cathedral, she tucked that song, that light, that stillness, deep inside. She told Mar she'd been looking for the river and had got lost.

It was past time for evensong at St Stephen's but Starling didn't mind the silence. The latch on the door clacked up and a gasp of traffic noise quickly faded as a middle-aged woman closed the door behind her. She didn't seem to see Starling but walked up the side aisle, put a coin in a box and lit a thin white candle. She stood for a moment looking at the painting of Mary on the wall behind the candle, and walked up to the front pew to kneel.

Starling walked over to the candles, dropped one in her bag and left as quietly as she could.

*

By the time Starling pressed the doorbell it was gone ten. Luc opened the door and walked up the stairs ahead of her. 'Where were you?' he said quietly over his shoulder.

Starling didn't see why she needed to tell him. 'Out,' she said, and followed him into the gloom of the stairwell. 'I got a job,' she added.

'Kit made you dinner. Thai green curry.'

Starling said nothing, kept walking up behind him. Kit couldn't bribe her to like her.

In the room, Kit was sitting on the bed, knees curled under her. She looked up quickly, a small frown on her forehead. 'Are you OK, Starling? It's so late...' She trailed off. Starling said nothing.

She had followed a fox out of the churchyard down an alley, the white tip of its brush guiding her through the dusk all the way to the river. She hadn't been ready to spend a cosy evening with Luc and his new girl, pretending to be just fine with their cuddles and smugness. She'd sat on the riverbank until the chill and damp reached right through to her bones.

Luc looked at Starling. He lit the gas and pulled the saucepan onto the heat. 'I was worried about you.' He raised an eyebrow to show he was joking, almost. A spicy burning filled the air.

Kit jumped up and took the pan from him. She turned the gas down and stirred the pan's contents. 'Luc said your favourite meal is Thai green curry – I'm not sure I've made the best, but you must be starving so I hope it'll do. I can do rice if you want? You look freezing, too. Luc, pass a plate?'

Starling crossed the room and pulled out her sleeping bag. 'Thanks,' she said. 'I ate already.' She pulled off her trousers and rolled them up for a pillow, lay the sleeping bag along the far wall and snaked in. She turned her face away from the lights of the room and closed her eyes. 'Night,' she muttered, and fell asleep.

Chapter Eight

A week in, Dinah's was OK, she supposed. Starling added thirty-five pounds to her stash each night and that was worth a lot of grief from Dinah about the way she washed up, served too slowly, wasted time talking to customers. She learned to work faster, to keep the customers happy without Dinah noticing. It wasn't much of a life, but it was something. Something and nothing.

She felt empty. She kept moving, and her limbs worked and her mouth made words, and she could eat and drink, but inside she was a vacuum.

Two weeks in, it wasn't easier but she had a kind of routine. She didn't want to be there, but she was until she worked out where else she could be. Or something. Sleep, work, return late, sleep, work. Some nights she was so tired she came straight back to the flat from Dinah's and sat watching Luc and Kit potter about like an old married couple, sharing stories from their days, passing each other pans and cups like they didn't need to speak. It wasn't that they were all over each other, it was that they didn't need to be.

They chatted to her too, asked how her day was, who'd been in. She gave them just enough, the gristle of her day that she could do without: Dinah's refusal to serve three lads who came in so drunk they knocked the stools over, how they'd pissed against the café window and Dinah'd smacked each of them round the head with the mop; the blown fuse that shut down the fryers ten minutes before the midday rush; the new burgers that gave out so much fat she spent half her time cleaning out the grill.

She didn't tell them about the smell of the nettles along the riverside as the early morning sun touched their fresh tips, or the way the guttering candles in St Stephen's made the columns along the nave look like trees in moonlight. These things were hers.

Luc and Kit gave her a key so she could let herself in when they weren't there. They went out to see friends, films, gigs. They asked her along, but she shook her head. It was their life, not hers. Coming up the stairs from the bathroom one night she overheard Luc telling Kit that she was probably finding it hard, she probably missed the road, must miss Mar.

She had no idea how she felt. She wasn't even sure she felt anything. Mostly, she felt numb, and that was OK. Numb meant she wasn't remembering the van, or Mar sitting in the lamplight mending her cloak, saying nothing; wasn't wondering what the hell she was doing there; what the hell she would do anywhere now that her home and her life had vanished into smoke like the words in the book. Even if she could catch her life, it would turn to ash in her hands.

*

Luc and Kit had a party. It was one of those parties that doesn't look like one at first, people arriving in ones and twos, bottles in their hands or packets in their pockets, like they just happened to be passing and saw a light on, and suddenly you realise the room is full. When the first few rang the bell Starling was sitting on the floor looking out at the lit windows of the shop opposite, its spring-coloured fabrics wrapped hopefully round headless dummies with their hands on their hips, like if they had mouths they'd be talking about the weather or the price of Brie. Starling wasn't talking. A day at Dinah's exhausted her with all its smiling and *Can I help yous*.

The party trapped Starling in her spot by the window. Luc was on the far side of the room, chatting and playing the odd note on his guitar, a subtle punctuation that let him pause and look away, smile across at her, but he was out of reach. Every time she flexed her legs ready to stand, to escape, maybe to get out of the flat altogether, Kit would bring someone else over. This time it was a couple wearing carefully crumpled Class War T-shirts. They remembered not to smile, being anarchists. 'Hey,' they said. 'How's it hangin'?' Their mouths drooped with the burdens of the world. It took a couple of fake anarchists to make her want to smile – what did they have to revolt against? She grimaced at them, showing her gappy teeth: 'Great, yeah,' and turned away.

'Who are you?' she wanted to say. Who were all these people with their dreads and their dirty toenails, their cans of cider and vodka and their Rizlas and cake? All keen to be seen with the girl who really was from the outside, who didn't have a door she could close to shut them all out. They all knew who Starling was. Kit must have painted quite some picture of her, and every grudge-filled rebel with a mummy and daddy back home had come to breathe her in.

Come the Crisis, we'll be the ones, Starling. They'll be looking to us to lead the way, to show them how to live when the world they live in closes its doors against them. But we'll be gone. We'll be safe because we never let go of the Old World. Never let it go, Starling.

Kit was full of energy, the perfect hostess in that I'm-not-trying-hard kind of way. She greeted arrivals with a wave from the other side of the room, dropped cans in laps, wrapped a skinny arm round a lonesome kid's shoulders, and then she'd pad back to

Luc's side like a lioness with her cub and lean against him, laying her scent, warning Starling off. Warning everyone off. But she did a good act, putting her hand on Starling's shoulder whenever she was near, leaning down and saying quietly, 'You OK, Starling? Thought you'd like to meet some people. Need a drink?'

Someone turned the music up and the kid with the zig-zag shave who'd smoked way too much picked up his guitar again and started some dirge about the long, long road he'd travelled. And what Starling wanted more than anything else was to snap his strings and go to sleep. But her sleeping bag was somewhere under a mound of legs and arms and coats, and no one was going home.

She sat and watched, pushing her tongue into that pea-sized gap where her tooth had been. She did it without thinking. She never smiled wide because of that gap. She hated the way it labelled her, but it was a badge of pride too – the mark of her tribe, the people who pull their own teeth, spitting the blood onto the ground, their mum packing cloves into the bloody hole she's just ripped the tooth from. It healed, just as Mar said it would, no need for a dentist, drugs or signatures. *Ever seen a fox at the dentist?* Ever since, the smooth gum had comforted Starling, the shape of her mouth so utterly familiar.

The party dragged on, and when Luc finally began to play a tune on his guitar it was too late. Sitting there could have been like the old days back round the fire, notes from a guitar, voices singing, but in Luc's flat there was something missing, like the difference between plantation and ancient forest – the trees in this wood were all the same age, the same type. There wasn't a lot that held them together either, as far as Starling could see. Any one of them could walk away and the others wouldn't care. If that lad in the corner hit his girl, no one would stop him. They were all so determined to be laid back, right-on, whatever, that they had let go the ties that held them together. Who told the stories that bound them? She saw little love in their lives. She could hear no music and felt no poetry in the rhythms of their days.

*

The days grew longer. It felt too warm for spring. Back in the clearing the mud would be drying, the track would be drivable. They'd be able to leave, Starling and Mar. Starling sometimes thought in the moments before waking that she and Mar were still back there in the van. She found herself dreaming a journey. They'd go to the sea, maybe, to see the light on the waves, breathe in the vastness, gather mussels for the pot.

Then she would wake and remember where she was. Starling made herself see the truth. She had nowhere to go but here, for now. She did not have Mar's courage for living alone in the wild. She was weak. She told herself to be here fully, to let go of her urgent, constant desire to flee. She had to release it, like a child with a balloon, and watch it fly away, leaving her weighted to the ground.

She stopped putting her tin mug back in her bag each night. She made herself place it on the drainer, almost touching Kit's and Luc's. Did they notice that she'd taken a tiny, massive step by leaving it in the flat even when she wasn't there? She pushed against Mar's voice: *You need nothing. But what you want, keep close.* But when Luc left every morning, she heard Mar reminding her that Kit could throw her out any time, and why wouldn't she? So Starling rolled up her sleeping bag daily and stuffed it back in her pack, ready to run.

She walked lines between the flat, the park and the river, Dinah's and St Stephen's, and made them feel familiar. She made a rhythm. She began to leave for Dinah's before Luc and Kit got up, and to stop at St Stephen's on her way back. She'd head out to the park or the river when the flat got too much. She missed the van.

She missed the water run. She even missed shitting in the woods: those moments of purpose and solitude.

It was strange living in a building: press a switch and there was light; flush and your shit washed away. No sense of the wild outside. She'd never before stepped outside in the morning onto a pavement, no grass, no mud. Never lain awake in the orange glow of street lamps outside the window, listening to their tinny insect buzz. She heard no night-time flicker of leaves in the trees, because the nearest tree was too far from the window and there was no real night. She'd never had a window she could sit in any evening and watch people walking up and down carrying bags of shopping like they had every right to be there. Never watched people holding hands, talking on their phones, balancing a takeaway pizza in one hand and a can of beer in the other. She began to think that maybe, just maybe, she could learn to be part of this kind of living.

But at the same time, like sandpaper on new paint, the other half of her – the realistic half – scuffed off these thoughts. She knew this wasn't her life. She saw it in people's faces, the way the sight of her walking towards them on the street made them look away, or scowl, or spit in the gutter. No matter how hard she tried here, they didn't want her. She could wonder about finding a room to rent, somewhere she could lock the door behind her and call her own. But they all knew she didn't fit.

The flat felt smaller than ever the van had. She hated its mess. She'd forgotten that Luc could be happy no matter where he was or the state it was in. She wanted to clear and tidy, to wash the cups and plates and pans that Kit and Luc left to pile up until they ran out, to bring order to the overflowing crates of stuff that they surely didn't need. But it was not her home.

She felt invisible. Luc said nothing and asked nothing, and part of her knew that he was respecting her, that he knew she'd tell him when she was ready. Kit was always there, though, and Starling didn't have the words. So she kept her silence, and Luc let her. Why should she tell him?

The tribe looks after its own. But only you can look after yourself.

Each night, Kit and Luc whispered to each other in bed, while Starling lay on the far side of the room trying not to hear. There was never a time when Starling could talk to Luc even if she'd wanted to.

*

The evenings grew lighter. Low sun stretched between the buildings and called people out of their stuffy houses into the warmth. Most of them gathered outside the pubs, packing the benches and tables, laughing louder as the sun began to set, paying no attention to the swifts arriving over the rooftops to find their summer nests. Starling watched the birds swirl in the pale evening sky, her heart lifting with them as they shrank to dots against the fading blue.

She left the flat and walked down to the river, but where she'd found peace before there were couples strolling, children running, dogs scuffling in the undergrowth. Where had they all been?

She walked upstream, away from the town, walking against the water's flow, and the land began to rise on either side of the river, slowly forming a valley that stretched out until it rose into hills of fields and small woods.

She passed below a farmhouse, its roof and walls made of tiles whose rusty colour matched the soil. A row of cottages lay further along, children's toys in the gardens, shiny cars outside. A woman bringing in washing nodded at her as she passed. Woodsmoke rose from a chimney.

It was so fucking idyllic. And all an illusion. None of them worked the land. They'd drive to town every day like everyone else, buy their food in the supermarket. Or in bloody Wincombe Wholefoods.

If she had a little cottage out here she could live off the land. Grow veg, hunt rabbits, catch fish. Storybook stuff. Child's dreams. On the money she earned from Dinah's she couldn't even rent a room in town. And anyway, how would having a little cottage make anything better? She still had nothing.

Her feet carried her up a faint track across a grassy field, through a hedge and onto a ridge. She could see for miles, hills layered in tones of grey against the evening sky, the river below her veiled in a cool white mist. She didn't need a cottage. The Old World was here, beneath her feet, laid out all around, summoning her.

Out here was where she belonged, if she belonged anywhere.

A car exhaust rattled somewhere over the hill. A memory came, sharp and mean, of a freezing winter night somewhere in Suffolk. Someone crying in a truck. A distant car's engine. She was fetching logs for the burner and keeping out of the way because Em and Mar were in that truck with Little Lou and his mum.

He'd died the next day. He was so tiny Em carried him in her outstretched arms, wrapped in his blue blanket, like an offering, Mar and his mum by her side. Who were they offering him to? The tribe straggled behind them, wrapped in every layer they had against the icy fog that filled the whole winter, the whole world, the Old World.

As the last light dimmed behind the hills Starling turned back towards town, where only Luc knew what real life was like.

Chapter Nine

Starling sat with her back to Luc and Kit, looking out of the window. Luc was on the bed, a cold mug of coffee at his feet. He was immersed in his guitar, noodling around the strings, up and down, gathering notes into fragments of melodies. She'd always loved to sink back into his music, letting the notes carry her like a leaf floating on a current, but this evening she couldn't let go – when he hovered on a familiar tune for a bar or two he snared her, yanking her back to old times so sharply that she felt the heat on her face from the fire, the crackle and spit of the flames, the murmur of all the voices she had lost.

Kit didn't notice. She was adding up invoices, checking stock, clattering away, busy busy. She always was. Starling had nothing to do. She was watching the jackdaws up on the rooftops behind the shops, squabbling over the chimney pots. They could fly anywhere, but here they were, gathering as they did every night before they vanished to their secret roost. She could find it, maybe. Follow their straight-as-an-arrow flight to whichever woodland was their night-time home.

Luc shifted behind her and slurped his cold coffee. 'Ugh. You nearly done, Kit?'

'Mmm. Soon.' She kept clattering, not listening.

'Fancy a pint, either of you?'

Starling turned back from the window and shook her head. She was knackered. And she was saving every penny she earned. What was the point of going to the pub? She'd gone once and sat in the corner watching Luc surrounded by people, laughing, talking, telling stories. No one saw her. No one knew her.

'Kit?' Luc asked again.

'What?'

'Pint?'

She heaved a deep sigh and stretched her neck. 'Love to, but I've got to get the stock order in. Can't put it off any longer. I'm almost out of puy lentils and I ran out of quinoa a week ago.'

Starling snorted. 'Quinoa? Who the hell buys that overpriced shit?'

Kit looked up from her invoices, startled. 'Loads of people do.'

'People with more money than sense.'

Kit shrugged. 'It's not my favourite, but if my customers want it, I'll stock it.'

Starling crossed her arms. 'They'd be better off with honest English food that's not shipped halfway round the world.'

'Maybe.' Kit didn't rise to the bait. 'But quinoa's a good earner – customers who buy it spend a bit when they come in.'

Luc stared at Starling. 'It's a shop, Starling. You have to sell what people want.' He put his guitar down. 'Right, I'm going to make more coffee if we're not going out. You two?'

Starling pulled herself up from the floor and grabbed her bag. 'Nah. I'm going out.'

*

She followed the line the jackdaws had taken, over the river and into the fields beyond, tracking the slow rise of the land away from the river. The crops were growing fast now, cattle beans, rape, wheat, here where the soil was good. She wondered how far the jackdaws had flown.

She heard them every evening chattering like old women in the trees above the streets until at an invisible sign they'd lift into the dissolving light in messy swirling flocks, and fly east, fading over the fields.

So Starling kept walking east, though the birds were silent and out of sight. Back at the van, she'd watched jackdaws gather each night in the copse on the far hill, hanging out with the rooks, sociable and garrulous even on the stormiest days. All they seemed to need was a cluster of tall trees with a view, a gulletful of insects and seeds, and a stolen egg or two.

Ahead of her a handful of black specks wheeled above a silhouette of trees. There they were.

By the time she reached the copse the jackdaws were settled, the odd fidgety chuckle the only sign they were there above her. She sat beneath an oak, her back to its trunk, and looked down the way she'd come. Wincombe was invisible, tucked below the folds of the land, though a faint glow of orange hung low above the furthest hill. Even here the street lights stained the night. Everything about the town was toxic.

Fucking quinoa.

Out here, at least, she had space and silence. No one knew where she was. She could think whatever she wanted.

Starling dreamed of the van, the birch trees' branches tapping above her head, the badger's claws clattering over the log on the far side of the clearing, the scent of the burner telling her she was home. She wished she was like Mar, contained entirely in herself.

One last jackdaw flew towards her, calling. It landed on a branch above her and fell silent, home for the night.

Why did Mar choose to leave in March? Why had she been so desperate to leave Starling that she walked into the worst weather, the hardest time to travel? Maybe Mar wanted that, to embrace the cold, the rain, the mud. She didn't love them, or hate them; she needed to open herself to them. A kind of baptism. Maybe she wanted to become the mud and the rain.

Mar would have had no illusions. She knew it would be hard. But maybe she couldn't live disconnected from the earth any longer. They were held apart from living, breathing nature by the walls of the van, the softness of their beds, their jars and packets of food. Maybe, in the weeks of silence and anger, Mar had been grieving, remaking herself, preparing to live with the earth.

Starling didn't really know.

She looked out at the valley below. A drift of smoke hung over a half-dug veg garden. A small child cried. Mar had taught her to despise these lives, but here on the hill, the sun below the horizon, with no home of her own, Starling was filled with longing.

She needed to learn again how to be with other people. It had been a long time. Living with Mar, she'd absorbed the value of silence, learned to move through their days with intention, with no need to speak. They understood each other. When Mar was angered by ignorance and destruction, Starling's role was clear. She amplified Mar's rage, sang it true for them both and let it fly free. Without Mar, who was she? Who was she speaking for? Speaking without Mar's anger sometimes felt like betraying everything she and Mar believed in.

She couldn't be Mar. She couldn't be the Starling she was with Mar or she'd be alone forever. She had to find her own song, her own way of being. But she'd keep her edges sharp, just in case.

*

Starling offered to cook a couple of nights a week. She put money in the kitty. After all, there was an art to visiting. On the road, you welcomed anyone who came along but it was easy to outstay that welcome. Everyone liked someone who paid their way, did their share of the chores, kept clean, fixed the rig, looked after the kids. They liked someone who brought new stories, a change of scenery, a laugh and a song.

It was fine, of course, if you wanted to be left alone. No one asked questions. They passed you a brew, checked you were OK and made you welcome. It was the way things worked. You took in anyone who came. They stayed until they were ready to leave.

So Starling went shopping. She topped up her phone and headed to the supermarket. The man in front of Starling in the checkout queue had piled his trolley with pizzas, tins of beans, a stack of plastic-wrapped sliced whites and a mega-pack of crisps. She turned away and fixed on the checkout shelf's pots of nuts and mints, tiny gobbets of temptation and waste. When it was her turn, she placed on the conveyor belt a handful of apples, three potatoes, three carrots, two onions and a chicken she'd stew and make soup from.

Starling handed the cashier the money.

'Loyalty card?'

She shook her head. 'Busy, isn't it?'

'Been like it all day. One sunny Saturday and everyone goes crazy. Mind you, I do love a barbie, bit of sun, a few bottles of vino, your mates round. You got plans?' She smiled at Starling.

'Nah.' Starling stuffed her shopping in her bag. 'Nothing special.'

On her way back to the flat, she bumped into Flea and Nick. She saw them about town often and they'd wave at her across the street, call out hi, even if they didn't stop. Today, they were both loaded down with shopping, glad to set it on the pavement.

Starling nodded at the bulging cash-and-carry bags: 'You feeding an army, you two?'

'It's all mine,' Flea answered. 'Nick's helping me carry it home. He gets dinner with us for being my pack mule once a month. Join us if you like?'

Starling was startled. 'Thanks.' She hadn't expected that. 'I can't, I'm cooking tonight. But thanks. Appreciate it.'

When she walked into the flat, Kit was there already. She was cradling Starling's mug in her hands. She raised it in greeting before lifting it to her lips and taking a sip. 'Good day?' she asked.

Starling didn't trust herself to answer. She dropped the shopping on the floor and went down to the bathroom. She locked herself in and gripped the sink as she glared at herself in the mirror. It was only a mug. An empty vessel of metal and enamel. That was all. Her mug. She took a long shower, and when she went upstairs to cook she took her mug and washed it thoroughly before stashing it back in her bag.

*

A few days later, Starling came into the café from the back and found Luc there, chatting to Dinah. She'd never seen him there before but they seemed like old friends. Dinah was even laughing.

'You get off,' Dinah said to her. 'I'll close up. You two are mates, then?'

Starling gestured at the spray and cloth in her hands, 'I was going to clean the tables down.'

'Nah. I'll do that. Now get out of here before I change my mind.'

Outside the café, Starling gaped at Luc. 'How did you do that? I've never ever seen her be that nice to anyone.'

Luc shrugged. 'I like her. She's straight down the line, is Dinah. And I fixed a puncture for her when I first got here. She was stuck by the roadside and no one stopped. She's given me extra chips ever since, and that's the route to my heart. Speaking of which,' – he dug in the pockets of his jacket – 'damn, where did I put it?'

'Inside pocket?'

He patted his chest and grinned. 'Close your eyes. Don't get too excited.'

She closed her eyes, and Luc took her right hand and placed something in it. She knew straight away what it was. Starling loved Mars bars and they were her and Luc's secret vice, kept from Em and Mar and their puritanical approach to ready-made sweets.

He knew her too well. She tore open the wrapper and offered it to Luc: 'Bite?'

He shook his head. 'Nah, all for you.'

'Where's your bike?'

'I've got a half day so I walked down. Let's go back along the river.'

They didn't need to talk. Starling bit into the chocolate and let it melt in her mouth.

'Thanks, Luc,' she said eventually, swallowing the last piece.

'It's nothing.'

'No, I mean thanks for letting me stay.'

'As long as you need, Star. You know that. I'm not going anywhere.'

That Luc, he's a drifter. But here he was, not drifting any more. Starling looked at him, loping along beside her, the sun on his face, at peace with his world. 'Is this what you dreamed of, Luc?'

'Yeah, I think so. Not sure I had a dream.'

'How did you end up here?'

'By accident. I fixed someone's truck, got a job at the garage, and it was OK.'

'Is OK enough?'

'Most of life's just OK, isn't it? And then I met Kit.'

Starling said nothing.

'Kit's amazing. She reminds me a bit of you, actually.'

'She's a townie.'

'So are most people. Doesn't make them bad people. They're finding their way, same as the rest of us. And Kit's special. She's gritty. And I fancy her.'

Starling kicked a stone along the path, making it bounce wildly into the undergrowth. She wasn't even going to think about Luc fancying Kit. 'I miss the woods.'

'Days like this, I could too.'

'Not always?'

Luc shook his head. 'Those winters,' he said. 'I hated the winters. All that bloody mud. And so frigging cold – I'll never miss shitting into frozen ground, ice forming round my balls.'

Starling laughed. He was right. Only Mar could embrace the viscera-freezing cold of a mid-winter shit. A gaggle of teenagers swaggered past them, music blaring. 'There's too many people here, though,' she said. 'It makes me feel edgy. And you know what, mud's good – you just don't know it till you miss it.'

She was serious about the mud. You knew where you were with it. Mud meant soil, and water, and plants, and animals – and all of that meant a place people could live without money or rules.

'I miss it too, sometimes, Star. But this is where life is, you know. We were out of it too long. We were hiding, out there on the road.'

Starling protested: 'You call this life? Slaving for someone else, turning up when they tell you to, being sacked the day the wind changes direction?'

'Yeah, I know. But be honest, Star. I know we're cramped in one room here, but we're safe. We were so used to it. I've seen you, sleeping with one eye open. It was months before I could sleep at night with both eyes shut. Christ, we had no idea that it wasn't normal the pigs would break our doors down any time they wanted.'

He was right. Even her small portion of floor in Luc and Kit's room felt safer than anywhere she'd ever stayed on the road. She wondered if the van was safe, alone in the wood.

Luc cleared his throat. 'You don't have to tell me. But where's Mar?'

He'd caught her unawares. She wasn't ready, so she shrugged off his question. 'On a journey.'

He nodded and left space for her to say more but Starling shoved her fists into her pockets and kept walking.

A trio of kids ran past with a football. She looked at Luc. 'Jesus, do you remember the graveyard?'

They used to get water from graveyards on the edges of villages and towns: there were taps and clean water and there was mostly somewhere to park the rigs for an hour or two.

Luc and Starling's job was to get the water while Em and Mar went off to get supplies from some corner shop. This was well before, when Mar still laughed and she and Em would walk arm in arm down a lane singing to the hedges, inseparable as two leaves on a stem.

Luc laughed. 'How old were we?'

'I think I was about six. Wasn't it the summer your dad came to stay?'

'Yeah, could be. I was nine or ten.'

'Those kids were scary.'

'So were you.'

The graveyard was well out beyond the last house of the village, round a bend and down a steep hill past the football pitch. Luc and Starling had pulled the water containers out from under the rigs, watched Em and Mar vanish up the hill, and dropped the containers beside the lych-gate. Someone had left a football on the pitch, only part-deflated, and they had the field to themselves.

They didn't hear the village kids coming until they were on the pitch, eight of them, all bigger than Luc and Starling and roaring across the grass straight at Starling because she had the ball, and she was a girl, and tiny. She dropped it and ran. Even Starling knew there were battles she couldn't win.

They almost made it back to the rigs before the village kids caught up with them, righteous outrage on their faces, yelling like the war heroes in their games. Luc took Starling's hand and held it tight. He stood as tall as he could and puffed out his chest. 'Hey,' he said, surprising them. 'Nice warm-up. We'll give you a ten-goal lead if you want.' And he grinned at them like he hadn't just fled across the field for his life. But they laughed at him and kept on coming.

All these years later, Starling remembered it clear as day. Luc looked down at her and gave her a friendly shove with his elbow. 'I'm never going to forget your face, or theirs, when the grit hit them in the eyes.'

'I'd never have dared if you hadn't been there.'

'But you squared up to them, all three foot of you or whatever you were – you barely came up to their chests, but you were so angry!'

'Well, they could have asked for their ball back nicely.'

'Would you have given it to them?'

She pulled a face. 'Maybe?'

'You were bloody awesome. Sounded just like Mar.'

'I still am!' She could see the kids turning tail and running back up across the pitch. But mostly what she remembered was Luc's hand wrapped round hers, telling her it would be OK, whatever happened next.

Chapter Ten

The flat had Luc, and it was safe, but it was unbearable. Each day Starling would push her pack into the corner and try to make a moat around it, a clean line of floor between it and Luc and Kit's mess. Each night she had to shove aside their shoes and half-drunk mugs. She'd come home and find Kit had strewn her damp towel half over her sleeping bag. Once, Starling had to pick a pair of Kit's pants out of her corner with her toe and fling them back at their mattress. Of course, it wasn't her corner. It wasn't her flat.

And though she loved Luc, Kit was always there. She was impossible to ignore, like an infected mosquito bite that Starling just had to scratch. The flat was too small for the three of them, no matter what Luc said.

She could leave. She could work at Dinah's until she had enough for a rig of her own. She only needed something small, something invisible that she could park up and no one would notice. A stealth rig. With a rig she could work at Dinah's, or she could work the festivals and save for the winter. In a rig she could sleep without Luc and Kit's whispering and Kit's interminable positivity. She could shut her door against the world.

But the seat beside her in her van would be empty and she had nowhere to head for if she left Wincombe. She'd be the same Starling, wherever she was. And even if she stayed, every night she'd sleep with one eye open, hearing every step outside. And there was no one who'd be glad to see her pull up at the end of a long journey and stagger out of the cab unfolding her cramped limbs. What was journeying for if you travelled alone? Mar knew. And Starling knew that her plan to buy a rig wasn't hers, it was the plan of some other woman she wished she was.

More than that, Dave had been right. She and Mar might have lived off-grid but they had polluted the world every time they put fuel in the van's tank and set off on another journey. She wondered now why they'd kept journeying. But she'd been moving so long it had felt like the only true way to live, rejecting ownership of a piece of the earth, flying free as a bird. Leaving whenever things got hard.

All these years, she'd been placing something in her tiny pot to hold her safe in the place she'd come to. Was it time to stay still? To be held tight by a small white feather in a wooden pot?

Maybe. Luc was here, but he was only tethered by Kit. He'd left Starling before and he'd do it again. He'd probably leave Kit. Starling had no one else. She had learned very young never to ask Mar about her grandparents or her dad. Mar had cut them out of her own story, bad wood that could only bring harm, and they had no place in Starling's life. Mar was keeping Starling safe, she said. No need to know about people who had nothing good in them. *We make our own family, choose who to trust.*

Starling trusted Mar, but still she wondered. The day she'd left the van she'd torn out Mar's sketch of the man who looked like her. It was folded and out of sight in her bag, but it was there, twitching at her like a curtain asking to be opened. No. She trusted Mar. If the man in the sketch mattered in Starling's life, Mar would have told her.

*

It was early and Starling lay listening to the tits in a tree down the street, in and out of the nest at first light. Though Luc had left the window open, the air in the flat was thick and heavy. She let herself out quietly, took the long way down to Dinah's, paying herself out like a line on a kite. A couple of early joggers passed her, plugged into their music. A bin lorry screeched out of sight.

From the high street the only sign of the river was a row of trees that grew along its banks and rose behind the rooftops, the leaves in their crowns catching the early sun and quivering in the breeze. The unpaved footpath towards the river sneaked left down the side of a dentist's surgery, still closed this early, and Starling's feet crunched loud on the gravel as she pushed through the gate. There in front of her the river flowed slick and shining. It was so unlikely, as if an invisible hand had just laid a brush of olive-green paint right through the town. A twig twirled past, spinning slowly on the gleaming water. The current gurgled through a tree root and onwards. She let out a long breath.

She walked until she found a fishing stage and sat, her feet dangling down into the water, letting the current pull them as if it wanted her to let go, drop in and join it. The sun warmed her face, telling her to stay here all day. But it was time to get down to Dinah's. She followed the cool, slow river behind the houses. A couple of kids were playing catch in a garden; a woman hung out white shirts in different sizes on a line, a family suspended in the wind. The houses turned into workshops and industrial units, and the gardens turned into yards of bright yellow ragwort, broken pallets and waiting vans. She turned away from the river and emerged out onto the road a few hundred metres above Dinah's.

A skinny figure with bright red hair turned onto the road ahead. Starling waved at Flea.

'Hey, Starling.'

'Hey, Flea. Can't stop.'

'Me neither. How's Dinah's?'

'Ah, she's not bad.'

Flea laughed and started to walk away. 'I've got to dash, I'm late, but Nick's got a gig tonight. Do you want to come?'

*

The White Hart was crammed by the time Starling got there. A tide of aftershave, bellowing voices and high-pitched laughter surged at her from the open door and she almost turned around and left. But the only alternative was another evening in the flat with Luc and Kit, or wandering the fields alone again, and it was the first time anyone had asked her along to something in Wincombe. She had to get out and start living. So she pushed in, *'scuse-me*-ing her way through the hot bodies towards the stage. No one was paying any attention to the pale goth singing 'Tainted Love' because she let her voice seep out like she was scared someone might listen, so Starling climbed onto the corner of the stage and looked out across the room. Flea was almost as small as Starling, but her hair was flaming by the bar, Nick beside her.

They couldn't talk, it was too loud for talking, but they grinned and yelled across their pints about the heat, and then Nick went off to set up, so Starling stuck with Flea, who had loads of mates who all said hi and grinned and waved their pints, and then they pushed together to the stage because they were Nick and the band's mates, and Nick strode to the front of the stage, and the bassist dug deep with three notes, pulling them in, and Nick's voice flew high, and everyone was dancing, filled with the beat and the song, and Starling felt something far down inside come surging out, and she knew she'd remembered something important, even if she didn't know what it was. She let it roll through her, song after song, sweat dripping as she danced, nothing in her mind but the music.

After, they stood outside in the cooling night and no one wanted to go home. Flea put her arm round Starling and laughed.

'You were on fire, Starling – never seen anyone dance like that! Love ya!' And Starling laughed back, and leaned in to Flea and said, 'You ain't seen nothing yet,' and they shimmied arm in arm, happy to be alive and dancing.

*

The next day at Dinah's a group of lads came in all full of swagger. She recognised them from the pub – they'd been outside after the gig, blocking the door like a bundle of dogs in the park. They were off a building site by the looks of them, dusty tracksuit bottoms, boots, tans that came from working outdoors whatever the weather.

'Ay ay, weren't you at the Hart last night?' a tall one said, the only one whose head wasn't shaven, when it was his turn to order.

His mate shoved him, shouted so all the others could hear too: 'She your type now, Mac?'

The rest of the group laughed, but Mac just said, 'Fuck off, course not. Just being friendly, aren't I? Cheeseburger and two chips, and tea, white, three sugars. What's your name, darling?'

And Starling told him, despite herself, because just maybe it was time to stop being so damned careful. When she took his order over, she gave him a smile she wouldn't have given a week before, and said, 'There you go, Mac,' and they all jeered again and she came back and said, 'Know what, it costs nothing to be polite. You get more chips too. And he's not my type either.'

That was it, no more. They came in every day that week because they were working on a site round the corner, and by the weekend they were eating out of the palm of her hand. And she never gave anyone extra chips. Dinah would have killed her. But she was beginning not to be a stranger in town.

*

Flea texted Starling: *Hey babe, fancy a drink after work on Tuesday?*
They went back to the White Hart and took their drinks outside to the
benches on the pavement. Flea pulled out tobacco and a paper, and
held the pack out to Starling. Starling shook her head. Flea laid a line of
tobacco along the paper, nudging it into place with fingers whose nails
were chewed down to the skin. Starling stuck her own hands under her
armpits. Hers were no better. 'Bad day? Good day?' she asked.

Flea shrugged, licked the paper and stuck it down. 'OK day.
They're all the same, mostly. Pays the bills.' She lit up and took
a deep breath, closing her eyes to make the most of the moment.

'What do you do?'

'I'm an assistant marketing executive. So-called. Mostly I
correct my boss's shit spelling, organise her so she doesn't turn
up to the wrong client every day, and do most of her work, if I'm
honest. Some days I dream of working at Dinah's like you.'

'Can't be that bad.'

'Well, at least Dinah doesn't call you darling and pretend you're
her foolish little daughter while she does piss all and shafts you.'

'No chance. More like, "Stupid bint, get over here now!" Mind
you, I think she might be mellowing. I actually think she smiled at
me yesterday.'

Flea slow-nodded in appreciation. 'You're made, then. She loves ya.'

'I'd love not to stink of chip fat, though.' Starling sniffed at her
sleeve and wrinkled her nose.

'Could be worse. My dad used to clean septic tanks. Mum
made him strip off out on the landing, but he stunk the flat out
until he'd showered.'

'Gross.'

'Yeah, but someone's got to do it.'

'What's he do now?'

'Not a lot. He had an accident and can't work. Collects Jayden
from school – that's my little brother. How about yours?'

Starling didn't want to talk about parents. 'My mum's away. Don't have a dad. I grew up on the road, with the tribe.' She took a deep swig of her beer.

'The tribe?' Flea echoed. She raised an eyebrow. 'I mean, it sounds a bit like one of those awful old BBC documentaries in Africa.' She intoned: 'Here the tribe carries out its strange, primitive rituals...' She saw Starling's face. 'I'm sorry. I didn't mean to be rude. I was just surprised.'

Starling had never thought about it. 'Well, yeah. We've always been the tribe, since before my mum was on the scene. Nothing wrong with that. We are a tribe. We look after each other. That's what it means.' She squashed the thought that maybe that wasn't true any more. 'So, you and Nick? He's an amazing singer.'

Flea coughed up her drink. 'Me and Nick? No way. I've known Nick since we were in nursery and I love him, but not like that.' She laughed. 'I'm not into boys.'

Starling paused a tiny beat and Flea shook her head. 'This isn't a date, mate. I'm on time out. I had a tricky break-up and need to get my head straight. Don't worry.' She grinned.

Starling grinned back. 'You're not my type either. Not sure I know who is. Boys, though, that's for sure.' Right on time, a lad ambled past, earbuds in, abs tight under his T-shirt.

'He's a sweetie,' Flea said, following Starling's look. 'But his girlfriend's a mean bitch. No idea why he's with her, but keep clear if you want to stay alive.'

A woman in hiking gear walked past on the other side of the street holding a bunch of roses, and Flea waved at her. The woman smiled and waved back. 'My old primary teacher,' Flea explained. 'Mrs Nash. Lovely. She used to let Jayden stay late and help her when Mum was ill and Dad couldn't pick him up.'

A young woman overtook Mrs Nash. 'And that's Nora. Year ahead of me. She actually dressed up like Hamlet for a whole term, went

around spouting "To be or not to be" like her life was one big tragedy.'
Nora strode up the street, eyes straight ahead, head-to-toe in black.
'Mind you,' Flea added, 'maybe her life was tragic. No one knew what
was going on for me when Mum was dying, so who knows?'

'Jesus. I'm sorry.'

'Don't be. It's not your fault. I don't really talk about it.'

A plump older man appeared round the corner. When he saw
Flea he waved and crossed the road to the bench where they sat,
his hairy knees poking out from maroon shorts above boating
shoes. 'Flea!' he boomed. 'How are you? Glorious day!'

'Hi, Rupert,' Flea replied. 'I'm good, thanks. It's a lovely
evening.' She smiled sweetly up at him, scarlet hair flaring. 'Are
you off on your travels again, you two?'

'We're off to Rhodes next month. Always a spare room, if you'd
be interested?'

When he'd gone, Flea said Rupert always asked if she'd like to
join them. Her mum used to clean their house and she'd take Flea
along in the holidays when she was tiny. He and his wife were
really nice people. The kind of people whose door she could knock
on in an emergency, even if they were incredibly posh and had two
houses. She'd go round there sometimes after her mum died, and
they'd ask about school, and lend her books, give her dinner. She
hadn't been for ages. Maybe she'd give them a ring.

Starling couldn't imagine it. 'It seems like you know everyone
here. Don't you feel trapped? Like everyone knows your business?'
A memory of raised voices across the camp at night, everyone
knowing Loz and Su were breaking up. Living in vans with
paper-thin walls, shitting and working together, you couldn't
help but know pretty much everything about each other's lives.

'Yeah, but they don't really. Like, me and Nick reckon Rupert was
really a spy. Perfect cover, living down here, nice as pie. And Mrs Nash
definitely had a secret. She'd vanish every weekend and Mondays she'd

sometimes turn up at school really early, looking like she'd slept in a ditch – I knew because I did Breakfast Club and saw the state of her hair before she'd showered. Maybe she was on secret manoeuvres.'

'Or had a lover out in the wild lands.'

'Or tracked wolves.'

'Or trained special services and teaching you was her deep cover.'

Flea had gone to school with half the town, she reckoned. 'Though me and my mates, we were swots and hid out in the library most lunchtimes.'

Starling raised an eyebrow, and Flea went on, 'You know how it is. Your face doesn't fit and all that. I liked books, and never went out. My mate wore a headscarf. They called us the odd squad if they were feeling nice.'

'I can't believe you're still here.'

'I had a place at uni, but Mum got ill so I stayed.'

'Bummer.'

'And now Jayden needs me so I can't go. And family matters more than a degree and a load of debt.' She paused and passed the crisps to Starling. 'How about you?'

'Me? I never fancied university. I didn't even go to school. Not my thing. So, do you know Kit? The wholefoods queen of virtue?'

'Yeah, she was in my year. She was all right.'

'You know I'm living with her and Luc?'

'Cosy?'

Starling blew out her cheeks. 'I'm going out of my mind. She's so bloody right-on. Little miss perfect.'

Flea shrugged. 'Maybe. I don't know her that well. But she used to stand up for Shamira against the racist twats at school so I'm all right with her.'

Starling stood, not ready to hear it. 'Another drink?'

'Better get back, to be honest. Dad's with Jayden and he'll be freaking if he doesn't get out soon.'

Chapter Eleven

When Starling got back, Kit and Luc had gone out. For once, she had the flat to herself. Jesus, how did anyone live like this? There were a couple of books, spines broken, abandoned on Kit's side of the mattress. They'd been there, untouched, for weeks, but Starling wouldn't pick them up. *No Logo? Yawn. The End of Poverty?* More bloody words and no action. Even Kit had given up on them.

There was nothing worth reading in the flat except the copy of *The Songlines* she'd brought with her, and she'd read it too many times already. The junk shop down the street had a box of books outside now it was sunny, but they were mostly romantic crap and crime novels. She couldn't afford the bookshop. Starling needed a library.

Next to churches, libraries were Starling's favourite places in any town. Even the smallest was warm and dry, and she could sit there reading all day if she wanted. Back in the van Starling had quite a collection of library books. She took only those she really wanted to read and hadn't managed to finish before they had to move on. She'd have borrowed them if she could, but libraries don't lend to people without addresses, and Starling had never been able to leave a story unfinished. So she'd tuck the book inside her coat and keep it safe, give it to another library somewhere further along the journey. Mar didn't care. She wasn't much of a one for stories. She liked facts and anger.

The library in Wincombe was round the side of the old council offices, through a grand doorway in Victorian red brick. It was open three days a week. Starling didn't get breaks at Dinah's, and definitely couldn't take time off at lunch, but on Tuesdays the library opened until seven o'clock. She just about had time.

*

It had one room with two high barred windows that allowed twin patches of light onto a scuffed grey carpet. There was a small table with a pair of upright wooden chairs. There was another table with a computer, a desk with a screen, and a librarian. The wooden shelves filled the rest of the room. They were polished by years of hands and filled with murder mysteries and romances, biographies of film stars and footballers, battered old books of local history, and a poetry section with just two books. But there was a whole A to Z of fiction.

The librarian had mousy shapeless hair and her lipstick was too bright, but her face had wrinkles in all the right places. She tapped briskly at her computer and looked at Starling. Of course Starling could join. Did she live or work in the town? Both, Starling said, feeling sick at the thought of telling someone where she lived. But she needn't have bothered because it turned out she needed an official letter with an address, and ID.

'But don't worry,' the librarian said, seeing Starling's expression. 'If you don't have that yet, you can join as a temporary member. It just means you can only take out three books at a time and you can't reserve them.' She smiled her scarlet lipstick at Starling. 'You can go and start picking your books if you like. I'll get your card ready.'

Starling danced across the floor to the shelves. She decided to start at *A* and read any book that looked interesting. She skipped anything obviously slushy – she'd read plenty of that in the van and it was like eating too many marshmallows. And she didn't need crime to add grit to her life. Starting top left, she pulled down a book by some woman with a pointy face and gleaming eyes. If she wrote like she looked it wouldn't be pappy. Next was *Pride and Prejudice*, an ancient hardback with a plain cover and tiny writing, the page edges soft with turning. She'd heard of it, but never had a chance to read it. Third, she put something pink and glittery straight back on the shelf and skipped all the identical books beside it until she reached some bald guy in glasses called Ballard. He looked pretty miserable and his books sounded weird. Perfect.

The librarian was busy with someone else so Starling walked round the room, breathing in the books. At the computer table in the corner, she stopped. There was a sheet of paper taped to the table: *Half an hour, 50p. Ask the librarian for the password and help.* She wiggled the mouse and the screen lit up, a flashing cursor lighting up a line of blanks waiting for the password. She dug in her pocket for 50p. Nothing. Next time she'd bring coins.

As she walked out of the library into the evening, she looked up, her eye caught by thousands of dark, fluttering specks above her: starlings twisting in miraculous unison, dancing over the rooftops, coming together into a tight ball and exploding out into whirling, constantly changing shapes before they finally flowed up and up into the fading sky. She didn't believe in omens, but it felt like a good one.

*

Flea went quiet. *Sorry*, she texted when Starling suggested another drink. *Jayden's ill again. Speak soon.*

Starling slept, ate and worked. She cooked a couple of times a week, pulling her weight: bean stews, pasta and veg, meals to fill a hole. She kept out of Kit's way, out of the flat.

Everyone around Starling was doing pretty much the same, as far as she could see, sleeping, eating, earning just enough to live on.

They scrabble for a handful of grubby notes in return for their souls. Most never see the midday sun, let alone the dawn. I saved you from that, Starling.

All these years she'd rolled on past other people's lives, looking in at their windows from the cab of the van. She'd always wondered why they did it, what kept them prisoner in their houses and their shitty jobs, why they didn't leave like Mar had. She watched Luc.

When she walked up the stairs to the flat after work, Luc and Kit would be talking and laughing. She was sure they fell silent for a breath when she opened the door, before they smiled and asked how her day had been.

Was he still there, the Luc she loved almost as much as she did Mar?

He wasn't a townie like Kit. Luc was born in a Welsh teepee, drums and bells ringing him into this world. Em had told it so often that Starling knew it as if she'd been there. And three years later he was the first to hold Starling after Mar and Em. Em had carried her down the steps of Mar's van, the tribe's newest member. She'd given Starling to Luc to hold. Welcome to the tribe, they'd all said, and he'd kissed her and asked if she was his sister.

These were their stories, told and retold, binding them together.

But now, he was never there – he was working late, out with his mates, arm in arm with Kit – so Starling told herself their stories as she worked and walked and sat in her pew at the back of St Stephen's. She began to knit together the holes inside her where the stories had unravelled through lack of telling. She told herself the one about the day they made eyepatches and ran away to be pirates, and Nico picked them up and took them all the way to the sea. About the time she fell in the shit pit and Luc fell in too to keep her company. About the summer day they almost drowned when their raft went over a weir, and Luc pulled her out because she couldn't swim. About him teaching her to swim in the pool on the moor by pretending to be an otter so that she laughed and didn't notice the bottom was out of reach. About the spring when a pair of starlings nested in Em's van's roof and Starling wouldn't let Em and Mar leave until she'd seen every chick fledge. How she loved Luc like a brother. How he and Starling were family, real family. Whatever that meant.

Families broke. She told herself the story of the day they left, him and Em and Phil and the others. How Mar had gone inside and slammed the door on the van, shouting 'Good riddance' after them, leaving Starling looking at the squares of pale dead grass where their rigs had been. She'd cried that day because she was afraid of being alone with Mar, because so much anger was scalding her from the inside out and she knew she could only survive if she became like Mar, and that she could only survive if she kept a tiny part of herself safe, alive with hope, like the oak leaf in her pot. She wished she could tell Luc now that she wasn't sure if she'd survived or not.

She took the folded paper from the bottom of her bag and opened it. She stared at the man who looked so much like her. Why had Mar drawn him and kept this picture?

Luc would know, but Starling didn't know how to ask him.

She knew the answer anyway. Fucking cheating lying bastard who'd abandoned her before she was born.

She stuffed the paper back in her bag. Everything was broken.

*

A postcard came from Em, like the old days. Em used to go on a journey most summers to find her quiet and visit old friends and family. If the boys stayed behind, she'd send cards from all over. A strange blurry photo of a village street, a gargoyle sticking its tongue out, a pair of hairy ponies high on a moor – whatever she found as she journeyed.

Luc read it quickly and waved the card at Kit and Starling. 'Mum sends us greetings for the solstice. Way too many courgettes coming. Glorious sun, we are blessed. Phil says hi. And do we fancy a trip down to Bramblehill?'

Kit was cooking. 'That would be cool, yeah. How about it?'

Luc passed the card to Starling. 'There's a message for you, too. Yeah, it'd be good. We could all go.'

Em's rounded script filled the card. At the end of her message she'd written, *Hi Starling my love, I send you my hugs across the miles*. Em, who Starling once thought might save her.

Starling turned the card over and her heart clenched. The picture was a drawing of a bramble thicket, a blackbird singing from its centre, in Mar's unmistakable style. Her hand shook as she gave it back to Luc. 'So Em knows I'm here, then?'

'Yeah, I told her when you first got here.'

She couldn't ask if Mar was there.

Kit took the card from Luc. 'I love this picture. It's so Em.'

Luc looked at Starling. 'Mar drew it ages ago.'

Starling managed to say, 'I didn't know she'd ever been to Bramblehill.'

'I don't think she has. It's an old one.' He paused. 'From before. Anyway, Mum got someone down there to print Mar's drawing up into cards. She's got masses. Have I got time for a shower?'

And that was it, no more mention of Mar, like she'd been rubbed out of everyone's lives. Only Starling was holding on to her and stopping her from melting away. And there was Em, with her stack of cards, sending Mar out into the world with a stamp and a few meaningless words.

*

Starling was tired to the bone. She sat by the window in the dark, breathing the street's heat. She smelled the day's melting tarmac. She closed her eyes and searched out the cool green scent of the river, but it was keeping itself to itself, flowing its own way out of town, through the fields and away from all of this. She was still wearing her clothes from work, saturated in the smell of chip fat and bleach.

Be your own woman, always. Know what is true. Feel your heart's knowledge and walk a path that you will always be proud to tell of.

The moon rose slowly above the rooftops.

She pictured the tribe round the camp fire, passing a bottle of cider, pulling potatoes from the embers and handing them round, pouring a brew for a latecomer telling his tale of a long journey leading him back to them.

Luc and Kit slept on as she left the flat. She closed the door silently, crossed the street into the alley and crouched, listening. Nothing. She ran on her toes, making no noise, getting the town behind her fast. A shape lifted out of the trees by the river's edge and she dropped to her knees as a barn owl swept over her, miraculous in its pale silence, a guardian angel. And then she was out of town, trousers rolled up and cold dew running down her bare legs from the long grasses by the path.

She'd been remembering Johnno, the way he'd appear at the fire and bring them back to the land with his stories. He had taught her to set a trap. His first rule was never to leave it unchecked, always to treat our fellow souls with love and respect. He could live off the land all through the year, fishing, trapping and hunting. You'd never hear him coming, the way he crept through a wood not cracking a twig, the way he'd sit for hours waiting for the deer to trot by, and lift his bow slowly, slowly, not changing the light or catching the eye of a young hind, and then there'd be a breath of wood parting air, a brief look of surprise in the hind's clouding eye, a thud as it hit the ground, the arrow quivering like an eyelash, and silence as Johnno crept forward to thank the hind for offering herself to him.

Johnno liked to be on the move. He had no rig but kept his life on his back, made a home for a day or a week or a season out of his canvas tarp and a frame made from whatever he found. He'd appear one day and bring Mar a rabbit or two, tied through their hocks, their soft ears loose. He'd hang them by the window, crack it open so their fur ruffled in the breeze, and while Starling stroked their stiffening sides Mar would tell him to sit a while, ladle him a bowl of soup, push a plate of leaves towards him, a berry cake if he was lucky. Starling had wondered sometimes if there was something between them, the way he'd push open the door of the van and just raise an eyebrow at Mar before stepping in, but looking back now she didn't think so. Johnno was like a talisman for Mar, the man who lived true, barely grazing the land he trod on, giving back as much as he took.

He taught Mar, taking her out for days and nights to live quietly as animals do, catching what they needed, sleeping in the height of the day under Mar's travelling cloak, moving through the land with purpose and freedom at night. Starling was tiny then, too young to travel with them, but when Mar came home she shone with earth energy and joy, and she told Starling tales of burrowing like badgers, sniffing the air for fungi, of swimming with pike and diving for mussels. Starling wanted more than anything to learn to live free with the earth, and finally when she was strong enough to carry her own pack for a day, Johnno had said she was ready.

He said Starling was a natural. She wished he was her dad. He understood the world and chose how to live in it, quietly and at peace, entering a room as subtly as one of his arrows, giving his love to the foxes, badgers, deer and trees he lived alongside, one with Gaia. Across one long summer Starling slept in the arms of an oak tree's roots, feeling the tiny feet of a mouse run over her face, hearing the worms burrowing beneath her. She learned to make fire with a flint and a curl of birch bark, to heat a stone in the embers and cook a sparrow's egg on its heat. And she learned to bend a sapling, strip its branches, tie a noose of guitar string and hang it over a frame, trigger set to release the strength of the sapling the moment a rabbit put its head through the noose to bite on the apple spiked just out of reach.

She thought maybe she understood why Mar had left. Why for Mar it wasn't a leaving, but a seeking.

At the edge of the wood Starling waited for the first light to rise, clear as a baby's eye.

She stood to one side, keeping her human scent from the rabbit's path as she laid the trap, placing branches carefully, carefully, to guide the rabbit through towards the bait. She gave words of hope and thanks for the land's generosity, and turned back to town.

Chapter Twelve

Next morning Starling woke slowly to an empty flat, air thick as a blanket, sunlight scalding the dust. She closed her eyes and drifted on a slow current of last night, swimming with the stillness of the midnight wood and the cool of the dewy grass. She'd go back later, check her snare and spend the day out in the fields.

The street outside was Sunday-morning empty, despite the sun on the pavement. Music tangled in the air, Marvin Gaye leaking from an upstairs window in a strange duet with Skepta from across the road, backed by the plink of bhangra from above the bookshop and thrashing metal from somewhere further along. Voices rose and fell from the flats.

She felt suspended in the web of sounds, safe in the warmth of the air in the flat.

A door banged.

Footsteps ran up the stairs. Starling's jaw tightened. She'd known it couldn't last.

The flat door swung open and Kit bounced in, dancing on her toes like she couldn't stop.

'Phew! Lovely morning!'

Starling lay still, hoping Kit would go away, bounce back down the stairs and take her too-bright enthusiasm somewhere else for once. She'd been for a run, and now she was going to do stretches, breathing, and a bloody breakdown of every mile she'd gone, the same theatrics every Sunday. As if Starling would be impressed. Who the hell went running when they didn't need to? Only people who spent their days cooped up like battery hens. Had she noticed anything real on her run? Like the light on the water of the river, or the damsons by the bridge, or the badger hairs caught in the barbed wire where they ran into the oak field? Nope. She'd batter on about people Starling didn't know or care about, stuffing the room with noise, showing off her so-pure lifestyle. Every single bloody week.

'Hey, Starling! Gorgeous day!' Stretch. Breathe. Performative sigh of happiness.

Starling turned to face the wall. She couldn't make it clearer that she wasn't in the mood. She tried to think herself back to the field edge. This early, it would still be in shade, damp with night air, the sun sliding across the field towards it.

'Star!'

Fuck off. Starling gritted her teeth, determined to say nothing out loud.

'I just wondered.'

Don't.

'I went on a demo yesterday.'

Starling had seen the placard, propped against the wall all week like a badge of virtue. *People Before Profits!!!* As if Kit would share her own money with anyone. She probably didn't even pay the mate she got to mind the shop. Starling opened her eyes. 'Yeah? Did you change the world?'

Kit looked delighted. 'Probably not, but you've got to do something. And if I got one person to think differently that's good enough for me. But actually it felt bigger than that. It was amazing, so many of us determined to fight the system! It was brilliant. And I was telling this guy, he was from a radio station, how fucking easy it is just to fall off the edge, have no money, no home, and I said—'

Starling sat up. 'You said what?'

Kit took a deep breath. 'I didn't tell him anything about you. Not even your name. I just said you had a story to tell. It's so bloody unfair that banker twats sit in their second homes sipping lattes and planning their investments while people like you have not much more than a bag and a tiny amount of cash that you slog your guts out for!'

'How fucking dare you!' Starling scrambled to her feet, flinging her sleeping bag against the wall. 'I don't need your bloody sympathy. You're no better than a wanking banker yourself, you and your cosy little shop and your quinoa. Don't you think I know how you got it? Mummy and Daddy set you up, it's so bloody obvious.' Starling stepped towards Kit. 'You stuck up little cow. How about putting people before your profits? How about selling food real people can actually afford? Has that occurred to your spoiled little mind? That someone like me can't even afford to walk in the door of your fancy little fakey shop. Let alone buy a bowl of soup on a freezing day. Why do you think I didn't come in, that first day? Your shop's for exactly the kind of people you pretend to hate! People like you!'

Kit stepped back, wide-eyed. 'Starling, I'm sorry—'

'Don't be. Don't waste your sympathy on me. I don't need it. Don't want it. You make me sick!' Starling was a white-hot rod in a fire, terrifying and powerful.

Kit shook her head as if to say 'No, no, no,' but no words came. She backed up against the door.

Starling faced her, arms crossed, jaw out, breathing hard, trying to hold her anger, to control it, to use it.

Kit was motionless, eyes wide in shock. A tear rolled down her cheek. Starling began to shake. She'd gone too far. But it had to be said.

She grabbed her bag and her boots. She had to get out. Before she could even cross the floor, Luc appeared in the doorway, carrying a bottle of milk. He strode straight over to Kit and enveloped her in his arms, held her tight. He looked over Kit's shoulder at

Starling. 'I heard every word of that. The whole street did. You're completely out of order, Starling. And wrong. So fucking wrong.' Luc never swore. 'You'd better go.'

What had she done?

'Come back when you've calmed down. Come back and say sorry.' He spoke fast, firing out his words. 'Don't be like Mar, Starling. You don't have to be her just because she's not here.' He paused, and she looked away. He lowered his voice. She could hear the effort it took him. 'We love you. But you can't do that. Go.' He turned away from her, and murmured in Kit's ear, holding her safe from Starling.

Starling closed the door behind her, quietly, and walked slowly down the stairs.

*

Outside, the sun jarred hot off the shopfronts. An old woman shoved a shopping trolley across the path in front of her and Starling paused to let her pass without noticing the smile of thanks the woman gave her. She remembered those nights on her way to Wincombe, lying half-awake in the barn waiting for the dogs to find her, or a farmer with a shotgun, or some fuckwit who'd followed her down the lane and knew no one would ever come to her rescue. She'd forced herself back out into the wild in one angry outburst. Starling had always thought she could fend for herself out in the wild. And she could. But there was no wild she could be safe in. There was no wild in this country. There were people everywhere and no one wanted her on their land, in their town or in their homes.

No one wanted her. Luc had told her to go. He thought she was tough, and she was. Nothing reached her. Nothing could hurt her. Pain sliced through her and left scars that healed stronger. Pain made her impervious, like Mar.

Her phone rang. Luc? She pulled it out of her pocket and felt relief and disappointment to see Flea's name on the screen. She almost didn't answer, but she needed to hear a voice that wasn't drenched in anger and loathing.

'Starling?'

'Hi, Flea.'

'Are you all right?'

'Yeah.' A beat. 'What's up?'

'Not a lot. Stuck here with Jayden still so I thought I'd say hi. You sure you're OK?'

'Yeah. I just lost it with Kit. Finally called her out for being so bloody right-on and playing the poor girl when she so obviously never had to work for it. Know your privilege, right?'

There was a pause at the other end. Flea's voice was quiet and resolute. 'That was shitty, Starling. Kit and me, we both got free school meals. We were in the same queue at lunchtimes, no school trips, second-hand uniform, teased for being poor. It was bloody awful. She's got no more money than you or me except what she's worked for.'

'No way.' Starling didn't believe it.

'You owe her a massive apology, mate. That shop, she worked there every day after school and every weekend, for years. The bank wouldn't have loaned her the money but the old owner backed her to take it over. Her friends helped. Painted it, built the counters. She's worked her socks off. Kudos to her. I couldn't do it.' Flea was silent a moment. 'I gotta go.'

Shit.

*

Every fibre of Starling told her to run away again.

Luc might fall for a pretty girl and believe her lies, but Flea? Starling had to believe Flea.

She kept hearing Luc's words – 'Don't be like Mar.' She'd always been like Mar, or tried to be. Mar never took bullshit. She had no room for fakers, hippy wannabes, poverty worshippers. Mar told it the way it was, every time.

Starling remembered Em's face the day Mar forced her to leave. Her grief and love, and her desolation at Mar's rejection.

Mar had left them all. Was Starling going to be the same, cut off and alone because she never had the courage to ask herself, just once, if maybe she'd got it wrong?

All the while, Starling kept walking, her head jangling, oblivious to everything as she walked out to the open country.

She didn't know what to do. Or how to do it. She had never learned to go back, open that door and step in to face the person she'd confronted. Mar never said sorry.

She pictured Kit weeping in Luc's arms. Kit was pathetic, wouldn't last a minute with Mar. But who would?

Starling allowed herself to feel it. She was afraid of Mar, of Mar's intransigence, her refusal to hear the other side. Her gut-boiling, terrifying rage at anyone who stepped up to her and called her out.

She couldn't be like Mar.

*

Gradually, she began to see the river flowing past her, steady and endless. She walked on upstream, sat by the water for a while, and walked again.

She took herself over the fields to the wood's edge and crouched down over her snare. A small rabbit, not yet full grown, lay soft and still, its neck snapped neatly by her noose. She touched its side and felt a faint warmth beneath the fur. 'I'm sorry,' she said as she gently released the wire and took the rabbit into her hands. 'Thank you.'

Would she have to eat it on her own, over a small fire in the shadow of some hedge? She let her feet carry her where they wanted. She sent her thoughts up into the sky, calling on the greater powers that held the world in their hands. She needed their help. Old lines, dug deep, led her to Mar and Mar's way. She had to find new ways.

She pictured Mar alone in the fields, trapping rabbits, seeking a safe place to hang her tarp, making a small fire in a dark wood, warming her hands on the flames, seeing no smiles across the embers. She left Mar there.

Starling gathered sweet cicely and sorrel, nettles and hop shoots. She followed a drifting scent up a hedge line and picked a bouquet of creamy elderflowers and set them flouncing from the top of her bag. She looked for chanterelles and found none, but in an open field of shaggy grass she picked a ring of fairy mushrooms.

Gradually her feet took her back towards the town, and finally she sent a text to Luc: *I'm sorry. I'll leave if that's best.* He didn't reply.

She found her way to St Stephen's and pushed open the door. She sat in her usual pew and let the silence of the church seep into her like ink into blotting paper. The woman who'd prayed on her last visit came again. She lit two candles before padding to her pew at the front. Starling watched her become quite still, as if held motionless by the stone columns and the candlelight.

Starling checked her phone. She put it back in her pocket. He wasn't going to reply.

She looked down at her hands on the pew in front. They felt as if tiny electric eels were slithering through her veins, telling her to jump up, to run, to do anything but sit and wait, but she forced herself to watch them into stillness. Mar was right sometimes. *Find the stillness inside you. It is always there, it is your strength, and it is where you will find the answers. Be quiet in your ways. Hold that silence. Find your power.*

There were still no messages on her phone.

The woman left, nodding at Starling as she passed. Starling stayed sitting there, the scent of the elderflowers leavening the still church air. She was afraid and allowed the fear to flow, seeing it and acknowledging it. It filled her until she could hardly breathe, and she told herself that her fear was a sign she was doing the right thing at last.

Her phone buzzed.

Come home.

*

Luc and Kit were sitting by the window, looking out, silhouetted against the evening sun. They didn't move. Starling pushed the door closed behind her and stepped into the room. They turned to face her but said nothing.

'I'm sorry,' she said.

She could hear her heart beating loud and fast. 'I don't know what to say. Except, sorry.' She hadn't planned what she would say in this moment. She had half hoped that Luc would help her out. If he threw her out she'd know what to do. She knew about anger. She knew how to leave. But he said nothing. He left her to fill the emptiness. She took a deep breath, feeling sick. 'Kit. I was wrong, and out of order.'

Luc pulled himself to his feet, and reached a hand down to Kit, who put a hand up to hold his.

'It's never going to happen again.' Starling looked at Luc and then Kit. 'You were right, Luc. I don't want to be like that. Like Mar.' She twisted to show them the bag on her back, the elder-flowers bobbing. 'I brought dinner.'

Kit stood. 'You know my mum and dad didn't—?'

'Flea told me. I got it all wrong. I don't know what else to say.' Starling swung her bag down to the floor and took the pale flowers from the top. 'I can make fritters from these.' Luc loved elderflower fritters. 'But if you have a jar, we can put them in water first.' She held them out to Kit. 'Smell them?'

Kit looked at Luc and then back at Starling. 'Thanks,' she said, and made a small almost-smile. She reached out to take the flowers, and breathed in their scent. 'I'll get a jar from the recycling.'

Luc watched Kit go out of the room. He looked sombre. He shoved his hands in his pockets. 'Do you want a hand cooking?'

'No, thanks. I'm offering you the meal. It's the only way I can think of to say sorry. You and Kit just go and chill while I cook.'

He muttered, 'I never thought you'd be like that, like I was one of your enemies.' He was looking at the floor, couldn't face Starling.

'No! I could never hate you, Luc. I don't know what I was feeling. It was all wrong. That's all I know. It was all wrong.'

*

They ate quietly, pretending they were taking time to savour the flavours. What could they talk about? Silence spread as they chewed. Starling tried to talk. Of the heat of the day. Of the fish she had seen in the river. Rudd, maybe? She thought she'd seen a flash of red. Kit tried too. She spoke of her worries about Keith, the old man who ran the bookshop. He needed help. Of the girls in the flat opposite and their secret dog they smuggled out in a bag every morning. Of safe things that skated over the surface. The rabbit was tender, being so young, and Starling had made flatbreads, and they all wiped their plates clean. Across the street, children sang in high voices, their parents joining them to make a harmony of unfamiliar songs. The night air grew still. They went to bed.

*

In her sleeping bag in the corner that night, Starling lay listening to Luc and Kit murmur, turn over and sleep, their breathing the undertow beneath the chop of her thoughts. She vaguely heard Kit scrabble up and down to the bathroom in the night, but it was just another noise in the background. She finally slept, and woke as the first voices passed on the street below in the earliest morning light.

She could go to work early, before they woke. But Luc beat her to it. Starling lay facing the wall, listening to the clank of his belt buckle as he pulled on his jeans, the pop of the jam jar, the kettle bubbling. She heard him go down the stairs and out, leaving her and Kit.

She was shocked at the depth of Luc's anger. He was so like Em. Ridiculously gentle, stupidly hopeful. Always forgiving. Em gave Starling the biggest, warmest embraces. She'd nursed Starling through broken bones and high fevers. Starling had always known she'd be OK when Em was there. She'd felt that way with Luc too, before this.

She opened one eye and looked across the room. Kit was still in bed, snoring gently, though she was usually up and down in the shop before Luc rose. Starling called across in a low voice, 'Kit?'

Kit didn't open her eyes. 'It's still early. Luc went in for six thirty.' She sat up, pulling the duvet round her, even though the room was warm. 'Thank you for the meal,' she said. She looked away, fixing her gaze on the sky outside. 'You know, it was awful, what you said. It's not even because it wasn't true – it's because I hadn't realised till then just how much you despise me. It was frightening, and horrible. I don't know why, either.'

'I don't despise you.'

'It felt like it.' Kit turned from the window. 'The thing is, you hurt Luc even more than you hurt me.'

'I didn't mean to.' Starling wanted to pull her sleeping bag back over her face, but she sat up to face Kit. She owed her that.

'He loves you. He's been trying to help you, but he just doesn't know how.' Kit shrugged, like she didn't know either. 'He says you've been hurt, that something happened, but you won't let him in.'

'I don't need help.'

'We all need help sometimes. I do. Luc does. You do. Look, Luc hasn't told me much about you and your mum, but I know you've had some shit go down. It's none of my business. I'm not going to tell you my shit either. But—'

'You're right there. It's no one's business.' Starling could feel herself going rigid.

'No. It isn't. But it's obvious. The state you were in when you got here – you were like a statue, completely closed off. Luc was really worried. Maybe you needed to blow off steam, let it all out. I don't know. I'm not a psychologist. I just sell soup. And quinoa.'

Starling smiled. 'I'm never mentioning quinoa again. You're right, I can't talk about it.' She took a breath. 'Thanks.'

'We're here for you. Both of us.' Kit looked at her phone. 'I'd better get to work.'

'Me too.' Starling got up. 'I'll see you later.'

Chapter Thirteen

Starling felt like she'd been through a prize fight, all the bruises on the inside, swelling and stiffening her up. She got herself through a shower, dressed and made a mug of tea, drinking it slowly as she watched the street come to life outside, people striding to work, kids in school uniform running ahead of their parents and being called back, dog walkers and joggers. She couldn't face Dinah's but she needed to get out.

She bumped into Mac, literally, as she rounded the corner, head down, trying to tell herself she should go to Dinah's before it was too late.

'Starling, babe!' He was in loose tracky shorts and a tight vest T-shirt and flip-flops. 'What you up to? Got a day off?'

Starling was caught by surprise and didn't have an answer ready.

'I know I'm gorgeous, but I don't strike girls dumb. You off to Dinah's? Bit late, aren't you?'

'Yeah. No.'

'What?'

'I'm not working. Today, I mean.' She decided on the spot.

'Fancy a day out, then? With the lads? We're going fishing. Just off to pick up beers and pies.'

Starling hesitated.

'Up to you. If you want to come, now's your chance. It'll be a laugh.'

A laugh. She needed a laugh. 'All right. But I haven't got any fishing gear.'

'You can charm them onto my line.' He laughed. 'Come on. Day's getting on without us.'

*

The day was about the beers and the laughs more than the fishing in the end, but the lads caught a couple of perch, took selfies trying to make them look bigger than they were, threw them back, and cracked open another beer. They weren't fishing to eat, and Starling felt her load lift enough that she could almost breathe easy as she lay on the grass watching the clouds fly past high above, smelling the silty green river roll slowly past. She threw jokes back at the lads just enough to be friendly, not so much as to be at the centre of anything.

Flea texted. *You OK? Everything OK?*

Yup. Day out with Mac. You know him?

Be careful.

?

Don't be alone with him.

Starling wasn't daft. And anyway, how would Flea know? Mac wasn't her type.

He was quieter than Starling expected, sitting beside her, legs outstretched, wriggling his toes in the sun. 'Good to be out of those boots for a day,' he said. 'Dinah give you a day off?'

Starling laughed. 'I took one. You? Day off?'

They'd finished a job early – a block of flats on the edge of town. Nice enough, he said, but he wouldn't want to live there. 'Nah. I want a garden when I get a place of my own. Somewhere I can chill out after work, dig a few potatoes, maybe, drink a beer with my missus.'

He saw her surprise. 'I ain't got one yet. Just thinking ahead!'

One of the others called over. 'You watch yourself, Starling. He's a right charmer, he is. Wouldn't trust my granny with him!'

Mac lobbed his empty can at him. 'Fuck off, mate!' Then he turned to Starling and said, 'He's right. Don't trust me,' and winked at her as he pushed himself up in one move. 'Who's up for a kick about?'

*

They walked back into town as the midges began to gather round their heads and the swifts swooped wild spirals above them.

'My favourite birds, those.' Mac pointed upwards. 'My nanna used to say they lived in the river in the winter, and if I watched long enough I'd see them fly right out of the water in the spring. Silly old bat,' he said fondly.

'You always lived here, then?' Starling asked.

'Born on Orchard Street. Moved one street along when I was five. Haven't moved since. But I've got plans. Bought my own van this year. Next year I'm going out on my own. Plenty of work round here for a builder who know who's who.'

'And you do?'

'I keep my ear to the ground. This time next year, I'll be laughing. This time two years, I'll have my own place. Got it all planned out.'

'Do you live with your mum and dad, then?'

He shrugged. 'No choice at the moment.'

She wondered how it would feel to live in the same house for so long.

Mac interrupted her thoughts. 'It's rubbish. I need space to myself. Somewhere to bring a girl back to, you know. Where are you living, then?'

Starling hesitated. They reached the alley, the others way ahead of them by now. Mac was so close all of a sudden that she could feel his breath on her neck. 'Oh, just with some mates.' She sped up. 'Got a space on a floor till I'm sorted.' And she stepped into the alley.

'Come here.' Mac's hand appeared on her arm. She kept walking through the alley, the flat only a short way ahead now. 'Come on,' he said, 'just a quick one.' She walked faster but Mac grabbed her arm and spun her round. He yanked her so fast to him that she couldn't step back.

'No.' She pushed against him. 'No.'

'Come on, babe.' He clenched her tight, leaned down, his eyes fixed on hers, and shoved her against the wall.

'Get off!' She tried to knee him, quick and dirty, but he was twice the size of her, and he just laughed. Shit. Shit. She hadn't meant this.

'Starling?' A girl's voice. 'Starling?' Louder. It was Kit, coming down the alley towards them. 'Are you OK, Starling?'

Starling shoved Mac again, and this time he pulled away.

'Fuck you,' he said. 'Fucking tease.' He shouldered past Kit and vanished.

Starling was shaking. 'How did you know?' she asked Kit.

'Flea rang. We all know about him.' She tentatively reached out a hand. 'Are you OK?'

*

It wasn't the first time. She should have known. How stupid could she be? But it could have been – it had been – a fun day out, until Mac, bloody Mac, pinned her against the wall, grinding the bricks into her skull, his mouth shoving into hers, his hands grabbing her.

Back in the flat, her whole body shook like it had been sparked into life and didn't know what to do with the coursing waves of anger, fury and fear. She hated to admit to the fear, though she could barely hold the mug Luc passed her. 'You know it wasn't your fault, don't you?' he said, as if he could read her mind, and he put his arm round her shoulder and held her until she stopped shivering.

'Of course. Fucking arsehole.' But she knew what Mar would have said. Mar would have killed him. And then she'd have walked away from Starling, disappointed that she still didn't know the depths of arseholery that all men sank to. *Never trust a man. Dicks, the lot of them.*

Next morning Luc offered to take her down to Dinah's on his bike. But she refused to live like that. She clenched her fists in her pockets. She'd be fine. Every time she was knocked down she would come back stronger. She refused to be beaten. She'd use the anger as fuel.

She was late to the café and Dinah was already serving a bunch of office boys, slamming their chips on their plates, chewing her gum like a football manager. Starling hung back at the door – she'd missed a day, after all – but Dinah leaned out from behind the counter and yelled, 'What are you doing there? You want to work, you get back here.' Then she turned to the office boys and glared at them. 'Don't know what you're looking at. You want those chips?' They just handed over their cash and grinned and the people in the queue grinned too. No one expected anything else at Dinah's.

So Starling pushed through to the front of the queue. ''Scuse me,' she said to the people waiting to order. 'Coming through. Be right with you when I've got my apron.'

'Jesus, just get serving, you silly git,' snapped Dinah, but Starling went out the back and fetched her apron, washed her hands, and walked in with a smile on her face. 'Next, please!'

With Starling there, Dinah went out the front for a quick fag in the sun and when she came back in she sent Starling into the back. 'Get buttering those bacon rolls. The builders'll be here soon.'

Starling buttered the rolls and ran the dishwasher. She wiped the tables with a clean cloth and spray. She was glad to be busy. She was unloading a box of drinks into the fridge by the front door when Mac came in, greeting her breezily like nothing had happened. 'Hey, Starlin' darlin'.'

She turned her back so she couldn't see him. She hoped he couldn't see her shake, and pretended to sort the cans, clattering them loudly in the box to drown him out. But he came up close and said quietly, so no one else could hear: 'I'm sorry, Starling. Didn't mean to hurt you. I wouldn't do that.' Louder, he said, 'One coffee, white one sugar. Please.'

Dinah called out, 'Starling, get back here. I'll deal with him.'

Starling walked back towards Dinah and put the half-emptied box on the counter, willing her hands to behave. She would not rush. But she couldn't look at Mac. She lifted the flap and walked through to stand beside Dinah, glad to have the counter between her and Mac.

Dinah was pouring a coffee. 'There's a load of rolls need bringing in out the back, Starling. Get a move on.'

A couple of minutes later, Dinah stuck her head round the door to the store room. 'Don't you worry. He won't be coming back.'

Starling looked up, startled.

'I know his type. And I could see the state you were in when he walked in. He's not welcome.' She winked. 'Right, get back in here. There's people waiting. I ain't gone soft. Hurry up.'

The thing about Dinah was that Starling knew where she was with her. And she knew she could always walk out if she wanted to. Dinah knew that too, and Starling didn't reckon she cared, though maybe she did.

'I need to get back today, six-ish,' she told Dinah.

'Bloody picky you are.'

'I'll stay later tomorrow. Just got to get back today.'

'You hanging around in Wincombe, then?' Dinah asked. It was the first time she'd ever asked Starling anything.

'I'm not sure.'

'I thought not,' she said. 'Shame.'

'I might,' Starling said. 'It depends.'

'Sometimes you've got to stick at it.'

Starling had done nineteen years of bloody sticking, but she wasn't going to tell Dinah that. 'Yeah, but is this the thing I should stick at? That's the question. Mopping your floor is great, but you know...'

Dinah laughed a great gust that turned into a hacking cough that went on and on.

'You all right?' Starling asked, off-hand, like she didn't care. Dinah didn't invite concern. They were alike in that.

'Of course I am.' Pretty much what Starling had said to Kit last night. Starling went back to her mopping and began to wipe down the tables. Dinah took a swig of tea and stood up. 'That's enough. I'll do the rest. Git off now.'

Starling ran for her bag. She had an hour left for the library and coins in her pocket.

*

Mar Shepherd, she typed into the search bar. She wondered about *Margaret* but no one ever called her that. Only police and bailiffs. So, *Mar Shepherd*. Mar thought she was invisible, but no one could hide unless they knew how, and Mar disdained all digital technology. She had no idea how it worked. If she'd created a stir somewhere since leaving the van, she'd be here. Starling half hoped Mar was travelling the country, joining protests against fracking and new roads, bringing her beautiful anger to their banners, painting forests over developers' headquarters, entwining endangered plants and birds around the yellow angles of the JCBs lined up to ravage the land for a stupid bypass.

But Mar was keeping quiet, for now.

She hadn't always, though. Here she was, in a piece about a site Starling had loved. Mar was explaining to the reporter how they knew the locals and had work lined up; how they had every right to be there but the council was throwing them off, all because of a few people who didn't like the look of them. Starling had been about ten then. She remembered that time, how they'd lost a place they'd stayed every winter for years with most of their friends. House-dwellers driving past hooting in the middle of the night to send them mad. Throwing bottles. Nico and Nic moving to Spain. Others following. She remembered the day they left, glad to get away from the hatred, no idea where they were going, Em and the boys behind them. She wondered if that was when everything began to go wrong, when Mar began to stoke the anger and the pain inside her, no matter who else it burned.

Another story, from further back. Mar standing in the van doorway, the photographer loving the frame of the painted van around her pale face and wild hair. He'd persuaded her to let it down, a modern pre-Raphaelite, though Mar was no one's muse. *The art of the wild*, the headline said, and Mar had given good copy, handing the writer stories of lost nature and true community and living with the land. It was easy to forget that was how she had been, once.

The next story was Mar in full flow, a link to a crackly audio off some old hippy radio site. Who the hell dug this stuff out and posted it? She was talking to some guy, some earnest bloke with a posh accent, though he must have been on the road too, from the sounds of it. Plenty of them around back in the day. They'd all gone to ground now, built eco-villages in Wales with proper plans and permission from the council and fancy materials that no one like Mar and Starling could afford. But here he was, back-and-forthing with Mar about the Levellers. Mar's voice, the same as ever, strong and low, powerful as a river in full flow. It sounded like they were friends. She listened to the guy, his facts and dates and expertise, then Mar dived into the reality, the truth of inequality, the need for heart and love and revolution. Starling stopped listening to the words, and let Mar's voice run on, until a cough from across the room reminded her that this was a library. She hit pause.

Levellers, she typed into the search bar. She read the first article that came up. They sounded like her kind of people. Angry, determined to make the world fairer, shut out by the people with power. Even the people they used to fight alongside turned against them. Whoever wrote this seemed to think the Levellers were defeated. The pragmatists won, settled for something less. The Levellers lost. Except, Starling thought, their ideas flew out and settled in everyone's minds, they caused a flutter in the branches so every time people wondered about freedom and equality, the Levellers' thoughts were still perched there, refusing to let people carry on the old way. Mar was a Leveller, Starling realised. Starling was supposed to be. Never giving up. Always showing people who've taken the easy path that there's a better way.

She looked at the date of the audio. A year before she was born. The speakers: Mar Shepherd and Tom Bridges.

The librarian came over. She stood to one side so it wouldn't look too obvious that she was wondering what Starling was looking at. 'I'm afraid we're closing in two minutes,' she said. 'You can print the page if you like. It's 20p a sheet.'

Starling picked up the books she'd taken out. 'Nah, you're all right. I'll remember it.

*

The next day, for the first time, Dinah actually let Starling use the fryers. She even sat down and watched for a few minutes before she couldn't stand it and shoved her aside again, rattling the baskets like a dog with fleas. That got a raised eyebrow from one of the regulars.

'Blimey,' he said. 'She must like you.'

'I'm not getting any ideas. What'll you have?'

It was good to be working. And at the end of the day, Luc appeared. 'Walk back with you?' They took the long way round, heading down towards the river, taking it slow in the evening heat.

'I'll get out of your hair as soon as I can,' Starling said. They hadn't really spoken beyond the necessary since she blew up at Kit, since Mac.

'You don't need to. You're fine here.'

'Nah. You and Kit don't need me in your space. I get that.'

'Don't be daft. That's not how it works. You've got a place with us as long as you want.'

Starling's throat felt tight. She hunched her fists in her pockets and walked faster. 'I messed up. I'm too much like Mar.' She blinked. She was not going to cry.

Luc caught up. 'We all mess up sometimes. And I wouldn't be asking Mar to sleep on my floor, you know?'

Starling mumbled, head down, 'I'm sorry. I feel upside down. I don't know which way's up any more.'

Luc reached an arm round her shoulder and gave her a squeeze. 'I know. It's fine. And I'm just really glad you're OK. That bastard Mac—'

'I don't want to go there.' Starling drew in a deep breath. 'Look. Mar vanished one day while I was out. I can't talk about it. It's like there's this big black hole...'

Luc didn't speak and she was glad he knew that right now she couldn't cope with sympathy or anger about what Mar had done. He walked by her side, elbows almost touching, keeping her company, and it was what she needed.

They came to the river, low against the banks now after weeks without rain, half hidden behind thick curtains of reeds, balsam, bramble and nettles.

Starling snuffed up the earthy green scent of the river and the delicate sweetness of the balsam. It smelled so good. She looked at Luc: 'Swim?'

The water was a cool silk glove, welcoming them in. Starling let her legs dangle into the colder depths, the river's bed somewhere below her feet. A fish bubbled out of the water ahead after a fly. Martins scooped the air over their heads. Luc ducked down under the surface and came up, blowing like a whale, and she dived down, eyes closed until her fingers met soft silt. She rose gasping through the golden water for the surface. 'Race you!' she called to Luc, and they swam side by side, his lazy strokes easily matching her wilder splashing until they reached a willow fallen across the river and hung on its branches catching their breath, the current flowing slowly around them, holding them in its summer calm.

'I learned a thing in Spain,' Luc said idly. 'In Spanish, the word for starling is *estornino*, and it means a kind of mackerel too. Weird, eh? I used to think of you swimming underwater like a mackerel.'

'You were in Spain? When?'

'After. After you and Mar went off and Em and the boys went to Bramblehill. I spent a couple of years there, down in the Alpujarras.'

'Nice.'

'It was. Good friends. Easy living. No hassle.'

'Why did you come back?'

'I missed Em and everyone. I loved the sun and made good money busking. But it wasn't home. I missed you, too.'

Starling watched a leaf turn on the surface, and without thinking or looking at Luc beside her, she asked, 'Luc, you know my dad? I mean, do you know anything about him?'

Luc looked away. The leaf escaped the current and idled on around a bend.

Starling felt a knot in her stomach. 'You do, don't you? There's a guy in a drawing. It's Mar's drawing. He's with Mar and Em and Phil. And I think… I think he looks like me.'

Luc still didn't meet her eye. He began to swim back towards their clothes.

'Do you know him?' She swam, trying to catch up with him.

'You need to ask Mar,' he said when she swam up beside him.

But Starling knew what Mar said about her dad. Case closed. Don't ask again. And that's if the man in the picture was her dad. Mar said he was a fucking part-timer who only liked the scene while the sun shone for one summer and went straight back home to his nice warm bed when the rain came. Who abandoned Starling when she was born because he didn't fucking care. Mar had stood tall and loved Starling, and brought her up alone.

'I'm not asking Mar,' she said. 'And I might not ever get the chance to.'

Luc was ahead of her once more. 'I don't know much about what happened. And anyway, I can't say.'

'Can't?'

'Look, it's not for me to tell. Go and see Em. Come with us, and talk to her.'

Chapter Fourteen

Dinah's daughter was sharp-jawed and angry like her mother, but she thought she could hide it in shiny words and little feminine gestures, at least in front of Dinah.

'Oh, let me do that, Starling, you must need a break.' 'I made you some tea, Starling, it's thirsty work. I should know – I grew up on it.' 'Mum, you can relax now. I'm here.'

Dinah had never mentioned her daughter, but when Tabitha walked into the café she melted. Starling was disconcerted. She'd thought she knew where she was with Dinah.

She didn't reckon Dinah knew Tabitha was coming. Starling was clearing tables, Dinah behind the counter. It was lunchtime so they were pretty busy, knives scraping and clattering, the radio blaring out some dance track, a couple of guys yelling into their phones, but when Tabitha walked in there was a moment of stillness when everyone looked up and wondered what on earth this glistening, expensive woman was doing at Dinah's. Dinah was the only one who didn't look up – it was like a policy with her never to acknowledge a customer until they were right in front of her placing an order, and even then she gave nothing away, often only nodding in response, and usually ignoring any greeting altogether.

So she didn't notice Tabitha until she walked right up to the counter, skipping the queue entirely, and said, in a smoothed-out voice that revealed nothing, 'Mum,' and reached out a slender, tanned hand to Dinah's own scalded and scarred one. And Dinah looked up, and smiled, and everyone in the café smiled too – like they'd been waiting for a hundred-year geyser to blow and they'd been the lucky ones to be right there at the moment it happened.

Only lucky for a moment, though.

Dinah looked over Tabitha's shoulder at Starling. 'What you looking at? Those tables won't clear themselves. Get a move on.'

She let Tabitha in through the counter flap, slamming it back down behind her, and turned to the next customer. 'What?' she said.

'Two teas, a burger and chips and a hot dog,' said the sweet guy who always slipped Starling a fifty-pence tip when she brought his food to his table. 'Please,' he said, though no one ever said please to Dinah because she'd know they were mocking her. Dinah just kept on serving, like nothing had happened. Starling carried the dirty plates back through, expecting to find Tabitha out the back, but she must have gone upstairs, leaving a shimmering space waiting for her to rematerialise. Starling started to stack the dishwasher, and Tabitha appeared right behind her, making her jump.

'I'm Tabitha,' she said. 'Who are you? Mum's next little slave?'

Starling wiped her hands on the cloth, 'I'm Starling,' she said evenly. 'I just work here. Cup of tea?'

Tabitha turned away. 'White, no sugar,' she said, sitting at the back room table, facing away from Starling.

In slivers of quiet between the rattles and clanks of the dishwasher and the noise of the café, Starling picked up fragments as Tabitha rang round her friends. 'Bastard…' 'Course I did. He won't leave her.' 'God. Back at Mum's. No. No way. Don't come here.'

Starling kept her head down and kept working. She needed this job.

*

The next morning, though, Dinah sent Starling home. 'I don't need you now Tabitha's here,' she said.

Tabitha stood behind Dinah, a smirk on her face. She mouthed 'Sorry' at Starling, and arched a sardonic eyebrow. She picked up a cloth and dabbed at a table.

'You have to look after your own,' Dinah said quietly. Starling wasn't sure if she thought she was looking after Tabitha, or Tabitha her. But Starling threw the apron she'd been about to tie round her waist back in the drawer and left. *You were a fool to think you could trust her. Of course she'd throw you out the first chance she got.*

*

It was still early and Kit was sitting outside on the shop step when Starling got back from Dinah's.

Starling dumped her bag on the pavement beside Kit. 'I've been fired.'

'No way.'

'Yup.'

'But Dinah can't run it without you. And she'll never get anyone else.'

'Surplus to requirements now darling Tabitha's back. That's what Dinah said. Without the "darling", of course.' Starling didn't want to talk about yet another person dumping her. She leaned against the door frame and watched the street. The woman and her husband from the flat opposite came out, three small children bouncing around them chattering in a language Starling didn't recognise. The mum waved at Kit, and walked over.

'*Slaw*, Miriam!' Kit greeted her.

'*Slaw*, Kit, hello!' Miriam replied, beaming. 'It's a lovely day.'

'Isn't it? Where are you off to?'

The smallest child ran towards Miriam, and she gathered him in her arms as she told Kit they were going to the park to play football before school. The child hid in Miriam's shawl, but when Kit called out, '*Slaw*, Azad!' he peeped out and whispered, 'Hello, Kit,' reaching out a small hand to Kit, who took it solemnly and shook it. 'Good morning, Mr Azad,' she said, prompting him to laugh delightedly. He and Kit plainly had a routine.

The family walked off down the street, hand in hand. 'They're such a good family,' Kit said. 'Miriam always stops to chat when she comes to the shop.'

'Wincombe's a funny place to end up,' Starling said.

'Mmm. I don't know how they come to be here. They're Kurdish. It's a few years now.' She paused. 'Um, say no if you hate this idea.' She fiddled with her laces. 'I could do with a hand in the shop, if you're up for it. Proper wage,' she added quickly.

Starling looked at her. Was she joking? She didn't seem to be. 'Are you sure?'

Kit nodded. 'I'd been wondering if you'd be interested, before...' She hesitated. 'I don't want you to feel I'm...'

'You're what?'

'Well, I know you think I'm a hipster, pretentious and all that. And you're right that I've never lived off the land – I buy my stock from the organic wholesaler and the veg market. But it would be amazing to sell food we've gathered and made ourselves. I just don't know where to start.'

Starling didn't know what to say. Working at Dinah's, she wasn't even pretending to live off the land – the chips came in sacks, the sausages were toxic orange, the rolls arrived weekly in vacuum-packed plastic. And she was OK with that. She knew where she was with Dinah's. It was weirdly honest. And she'd known it was temporary – she could walk away at any time. This, though – this felt intentional, like if she did it, she'd be saying yes to something. What would she feel if Mar walked past? Mar would hate it.

She looked at Kit. 'Do you know how to make bread?'

'I'm shit at baking.'

'I'll show you. And there's masses of food out there, if you know where to look.' She considered. 'I'll go foraging. I can go now.' She knew exactly what food to make. 'I'll give you a list for the stock we'll need for bread and pies. Can you get it for tomorrow?'

Kit nodded, grinning. 'I've probably got enough to get started tonight, if you're up for it?'

'I'm up for it. Bloody Dinah can keep her fucking job.'

*

Starling took the river path out of town, the quickest route away from the houses towards the fields and hedges where the foraging might be worth it. Here near the town the dog walkers came, kicking the shit into the bushes, letting their dogs piss on the pathside plants, so Starling kept going.

It never took long to leave people behind. Town dwellers' nomadic instinct must have been crushed somehow, though Mar believed it was deep in every human. *Humans have always kept moving, Starling. It's our natural state to wander, stay a while, learn the land, share its harvest, move on.*

There was a footbridge over the river – a cow bridge, really, from the broken state of the farm track that led to it – where the town people turned back. The river path beyond it was overgrown with nettles, thistles, cleavers and grass, the soil beneath damp with dew where no sun had reached it yet.

She pushed through the growth, letting herself see what was there. That was the trick to foraging. Allowing the harvest to reveal itself by not looking for anything in particular, being open to whatever her eyes caught upon.

Just beyond the bridge, a damson tree sprang from a hedge end where the river curled round, the perfect place to fish amongst the weeds and shade on the slow side. She guessed a fisherman had sat there twenty years before and threw the damson stones from his lunch over his shoulder into the hedge. She thanked him, and picked a good couple of pounds of ripe purple fruit.

It was too early for blackberries, she thought, but right down on the river's edge they'd ripened faster in the reflected sunlight off the water. She pulled off her boots and stepped into the shallow mud of the bank, feeling it soft and cool between her toes, its silty greenness filling her nose, and gathered a fistful of first fruit. She ate one, pressing its tiny globules between her tongue and the top of her mouth to feel them burst their dark sweetness. She pushed the pips in and out of the gap in her teeth, her own personal eddy, her reminder of Mar, as she climbed back up the bank and walked on, barefoot, her boots in her hand.

Out here, getting further and further from the town, she was safe from Mac. She was safe from messing up. She knew what she was doing.

It was a funny time, July, for foraging. There were so many berries: elder, rowan, blackberries, early crab apples, raspberries if she was really lucky. But the greens were getting tough in the dryness and heat. Still, in every patch of green she found new shoots of nettle and sorrel.

By the time she walked back into town, she had a full bag of food that was fresher than any supermarket's so-called fresh aisle. Later, she'd get back out and set her snare.

*

Starling and Kit laid her gatherings across the table in the shop's tiny kitchen, heaps of purple blackberries, damsons and elderberries, squeaky green sorrel, explosions of nettle tops and caraway. Pale blue borage flowers to float in water and flavour it like cucumber, and the young leaves for salads with burnet and dead-nettles. Dandelion and fat hen, bittercress. A few late pignuts she'd dug from a bank by the edge of the wood.

'Wow.' Kit stood back, hands on hips. 'They're all so beautiful. It almost seems a shame to eat them. Just look at the colour of these. Are they plums?'

'Damsons from down by the river. They're a kind of plum.'

Kit reached out to take one.

Starling stopped her. 'Don't eat it raw. They're bitter till you've cooked them. We can make pies. Jam, too, so we'll have them through the winter. There's masses down there, easy pickings.'

She sent Kit upstairs to make dinner while she got started on the bread. She would teach Kit to bake, but not tonight.

In the store room, she found flour, seeds, salt and yeast and carried them through to the kitchen.

She made a dome of flour on the wooden table and drew a spiral from the centre with her finger, the warm flour soft and giving against her skin. She remade the dome and made a well in the centre. The yeast was coming to life in its jug of water, warmed to match her hand's heat, its earthy smell rising. She'd done this so many times and it was good to be pouring, kneading, pushing herself into the living dough, evening out their energies until they were both calm and ready.

She placed the dough in a bowl to work slowly in the fridge overnight and stepped into the yard behind the shop. In the half-darkness she explored the gritty broken concrete with a toe, looking up at the square of sky between the roofs.

'Starling?' Luc's voice drifted down to her from upstairs. He must have come in while she was making the dough. She went upstairs to eat.

She and Kit decided to bake the pies first thing so they could send the smell of fresh-made food into the street the moment they opened up. Starling could keep baking as Kit stood behind the counter. It felt chaotic – would she have time to make it all so nothing went to waste, so everything was ready for people's lunch breaks? Maybe she'd gathered too much, or not enough. She'd no idea. They could only try, and they'd learn as they went. Starling was glad she'd be out the back, leaving Kit to smile and charm the customers into eating their new offerings.

*

She woke at dawn to take the dough out of the fridge. She waited with a coffee as it warmed, then knocked the dough back and set it in the tins, listening to the early birds gathering their food just as she had. Luc and Kit were still asleep when she crept into her sleeping bag to wait for it to prove, and she lay watching the tits and finches flitting across the sky, listening to the others' breath across the room. It was the first time in months that she had felt her mind slow, at ease with a day of gathering food, making bread, living to live again.

An hour later, she tiptoed down the stairs again and placed the bread in the oven to bake. The sunlight was angling across the floor when she brought one of the finished loaves up to the flat to cool. It was fully day when Luc shook her awake and handed her a mug of tea and a slice of still-warm bread and jam.

'This is so good,' he said. 'I've missed fresh-baked bread in the morning. Thank you, Star.'

*

They had an hour before the shop opened, so Starling and Kit got to work, side by side at the kitchen table. They got the quiches in the oven first. Kit chopped onions, shook out the nettles and sorrel and started the soup. 'I thought I'd add some lentils to thicken it? What do you think?'

Starling nodded. 'Or sell it with a slice of bread for a bit more?'

'Good one. What next?'

'You could make a salad with these leaves, and the pignuts. I'll get on with the fruit pies. And some berry flapjacks. They won't take long and they're good with a coffee.'

'This is going to be so amazing. Thank you, Starling.' Kit began washing leaves. 'Will you show me how to make bread later?'

'I'll go out and get some fresh supplies first. Maybe more leaves and less fruit, but let's see how it goes. If there's time I'll show you. It's not hard, though really we want to get a sourdough going – wild yeast, and way more flavour.'

'I thought it was really difficult?'

'Nah. Not really. Just takes a bit of time to get started. Like all the best things.'

The bread she'd made wasn't a patch on what she could make if she was patient and allowed yeasts in the air to find the flour, bringing their ancient strength and flavours. Good food took time, like everything else. She heard Em's voice: *Let it grow, let it breathe, and you'll grow and breathe with it.*

Though Mar could make a good pot of soup and rustle up a meal from empty jars, it was Em who'd really taught her to cook, who'd had the patience to put her hands on Starling's and slow her down, to sing to the bread to make it rise and fill itself with their songs. Em believed that food made with love and care was at the heart of a community. She always shared what she had, set out tables in the sun for everyone to sit down together, and if all they had was soup, it was all they needed to be one people under the sky.

*

Moments before the shop was due to open, Starling knelt before Kit's pavement sign, opened the box of chalks and wrote in hand-high letters: *Hungry? Come and eat. Food is love! Fresh goodness from the fields, cooked today.* The smell of baking filled the shop: bread, quiches packed with hedge greens and mushrooms, lentil bakes, fruit tarts and pies, berry flapjacks, overlaid with the scent of nettle soup. She chewed on a handful of nuts and contemplated the sign. She drew a tangle of leaves and flowers around the edge of the board, nettles nestling behind blackberries, field mushrooms holding the corner, burnet, sorrel, borage, fat hen, a whole hedgerow of food. For a moment, she was carried back to the van and its wilderness in paints.

No. It was time to move on. She put the chalks away and headed back into the kitchen.

Chapter Fifteen

Kit opened the shop as Starling carried the last of the food through from the kitchen. Starling moved around arranging the pies and quiches on a bed of the greens she'd picked the day before, piling up the flapjacks with berries around the rim of the dish, stacking bowls next to the soup tureen. She had spent whole summers with Em and the others in tents and vans serving food in fields across the country. No one could ever resist those berry flapjacks; they were her secret weapon, guaranteed to fill her purse when times were hard.

They propped the shop door open so the smell of the soup, bread and pies would waft out. Starling looked at the sign. *Food is love.*

Don't be stupid. Food is life.

OK. Food was life, and love.

She and Kit stood back and admired the counter, piled high with food from the land.

'Just look at that,' Kit said. 'You're a star, Starling.' They grinned at each other. It did look good. It looked hopeful.

*

Kit had sold all the soup by midday, and the last slice of the second quiche half an hour later. Starling joined her behind the counter for the lunchtime rush, handing slices of bread, berry pies and salad bowls over to women in suits, men in shorts and sandals, girls in summer dresses. Miriam from over the road came in and bought a bag each of lentils and chickpeas and a single damson pie. 'I am glad you are open,' she said as she counted out the notes and coins. 'My cupboard is bare. Like the song I learn with the children. I am Old Mother Hubbard!'

One small damson pie between five wasn't going to go very far. Starling thought about the woman who'd bought a whole quiche from Kit almost as soon as they'd opened. She'd probably throw it away before it was half eaten. Starling added a second pie to Miriam's bag. 'No, it's for you. Free,' she said, when Miriam looked worried. 'For your children,' she added with a smile.

By mid-afternoon they had nothing fresh left to sell, so Starling left Kit to it in the shop. She had to get out and forage.

*

When Starling returned from the fields, Kit was checking stock in the shop, singing to herself as she moved from shelf to shelf.

'Those quiches, Starling – people loved them! And the flapjacks too – I managed to grab one before they all went, and they are gorgeous. Can you make more for tomorrow?'

Starling showed her the contents of her bag, berries heaped on top to save them from being crushed. 'I'll show you where the berries are, and how to make the flapjacks. I'm just going to shower, and then we can get started.'

That evening, they worked together again in the kitchen, prepping what they could to save time in the morning. They made more quiches and a mountain of flapjacks and when they'd finished they carried three plates of leftovers upstairs.

Luc wasn't home yet. 'He texted,' Kit said and read out, 'Back in half an hour.' So she and Starling collapsed onto the floor, and smiled at each other. 'Can we keep this up?' Kit wondered.

'Sure we can. And if we get a bit organised it won't be such a rush in the morning. I don't need to do so much foraging every day once we get going.'

'Did you use to forage like that when you lived in the van?'

Starling's throat went tight. Fuck it. She had to get over this. She realised she was biting into the quick of her fingernail and pulled it away.

'I'm sorry.' Kit looked worried. 'I didn't mean to pry.'

Starling shook her head. 'It's OK. Mostly.' She looked at her mangled nail. 'I mean, mostly I foraged, but not for everything. That's hardcore.' She pictured Mar, filling her pockets with berries, getting thinner by the day. Could she do it without Starling? 'We used shops too, and winter was tough. We'd dry leaves in summer to keep us going...'

'Can we do that here?'

'Of course. We need to get started, though – it'll be too late soon.'

'How come? There's loads of green stuff out there, isn't there? Just look at what you gathered!'

'The year's turning, though. We're past the solstice already.' Em's postcard swam into her mind. 'Winter's on its way.'

*

Kit and Starling got into a rhythm. Every evening, between them they'd make soup from the nettles and other greens, an ovenful of large quiches, followed by shelves of tiny damson pies and berry-laden flapjacks. They'd make salads in the morning while the bread baked. Starling foraged in the afternoons. And when Kit opened the shop, Starling would make a final batch of everything to keep the counter piled high until after lunch, adding lentil bakes and bean stews if she had time, sending the smells of the fields and the kitchen into the street to pull the shoppers in.

Starling would take a turn on the till sometimes. She handed out extra portions to people like Miriam and Flea – she trusted her instincts to spot the ones who needed good food and could afford it least. Kit saw her, and did the same. 'It feels right,' she said, 'since half our ingredients are for free. And we sold out again today.'

Sold out. Starling caught herself hoping Mar would never come to Wincombe. They'd travelled in opposite ways, and if Mar saw Starling selling food that the earth had given her with open hands, Starling knew they would never speak again.

But people needed food, and Starling and Kit were selling food that brought them the earth's love and goodness. They weren't peddling toxic chemical-filled crap. They had to sell it for money because – as Starling began to realise – Kit's costs were high. Rent. Rates. Power for lights and the till and the oven. Gas for the hob. And all the ingredients that Starling couldn't gather, at least not in the quantities they needed – flour, eggs, cheese. Always a trade-off, too. Buy cheap cheese, so they could sell cheap quiches that everyone could afford? Or buy the best organic and price most people out? It wasn't easy.

Starling's days changed shape. She went to the fields not to escape but with meaning in every step. In quiet moments back at the flat, she began to sketch again, her fingers remembering the feel of her pencils. She drew people passing in the street below, berries hanging on bushes, the bridge over the river that marked the edge of town. She filled her sketch pad, and with her first pay packet she bought a new one.

On the first blank page, she drew Luc. He was sitting on the mattress gazing out of the window, his guitar on his lap. Starling let her pencil find its own way, and Luc's feet emerged onto the page. She told him to keep still so she could catch the shadows while the sun was low and golden. 'Tell me about the boys,' she said, to hold him while she drew.

Davey, Stevie and Gabe were all younger than Luc. They'd always be his little brothers, no matter how grown up they thought they were. For a short while after he'd been at Bramblehill, they'd lived together, Luc trying to get them to school, to persuade them to wash though the bath was full of motorbike parts, trying to feed them in a kitchen that swarmed with mates and piles of muddy boots.

'I'm not even going to ask if anyone ever washed the boys' clothes. Where were you?' Starling asked.

'My dad's house. He was away.' He smiled, remembering. 'You know me, it was a bit chaotic, but it was cool being with the boys.' Gabe was still young, though, and his dad got a cottage with his new job, so they all moved there, except Luc, who ended up in Wincombe. He still dropped in every few weeks to see if they were all right.

'What are they up to?'

Gabe was about to finish school, though he really wanted to be out with Stevie, who was training to be a gamekeeper.

Luc and his brothers had different dads, but they shared Em's pale blue eyes and Luc's loping gait. Nothing would ever separate them.

Luc said scrawny little Davey was taller than him now.

'Seriously?'

'Yup, and twice as wide. All muscle. He made me this.' He shifted onto one hip and rooted in his pocket, pulled out a hank of iron knotted round itself. He weighed it in the palm of his hand. 'He's apprenticed to a blacksmith. He says he's given up his wild ways. Spends all day working and all night sketching designs to make. You should show him your drawings.'

Starling took the keyring and felt its heft in the palm of her hand, solid, holding itself in a firm twist. When she was younger, she used to pretend she belonged in Luc's shambling, messy family. They looked out for each other, and gave each other slack at the same time. None of them minded if another did their own thing for a day, or a week, or a summer. They always had a home at Em's or their various dads'. They had a bond that stretched as fine as a winter sky but never snapped. Her bond with Mar felt so tight it would break if she thought about it.

Starling looked up and out of the window. 'I used to want to be your sister.'

Luc looked up, his mouth curling, ready to smile.

'No,' she added quickly, 'not just yours – I wanted to be in your whole family so no one would notice me and I'd just be part of it like you were. It just seemed so much easier.'

'Well, you are part of our family, you know that. Come with me next time. The boys'll be glad to see you, they always are.'

'They'll have forgotten me.'

'And there's the difference,' he said. 'We don't have it easier, we just don't make it complicated. Come with me.' He blew out a long breath. 'Jesus, I'm knackered.'

He went quiet and Starling kept sketching. His feet were strong, high-arched, always ready to jump even in their stillness. Her pencil loved the sweeping lines of the tendons that ran up from his toes to the faint crease where his foot curved up into his leg. She looked at Luc's face to see what he was thinking. He was leaning back, looking out of the window again, humming a tune under his breath. Where was he? Here, or out in the fields where they belonged?

*

Next day, down in the shop kitchen, she sliced onions, setting them to fry, adding a potato and a kettleful of boiling water. She shook the tiny black beetles off the nettles and plunged them into the pan, the smell of living plants filling the air and pulling her back to an old place she knew well. She made a pot of coffee and sat in the back doorway, looking out at the yard. Behind her the soup cooked and the last pies baked. Voices sifted in from the shop. Kit's laugh. In the yard the sun moved slowly across the broken concrete, the piles of crates and empty olive oil cans. There was a row of pots, the soil in them parched, holding faded herbs – mint, chives, oregano by the look of it. Even the rosemary looked desperate. She fetched a jug of water and it poured straight through the soil and out of the bottom. Later, she'd find buckets for them and give them a good soaking.

Starling wondered where she belonged now. Could she be woven into this place of streets and bricks and orange light, and people who let their plants die of thirst?

In her pocket, she felt her small pot, its carved birds entwined on its lid, holding the angel feather inside. Maybe she should trust it. Trust Luc, and Kit and Flea. Maybe.

Later that evening she opened the backyard door and let in the evening light, gold-plating the floor and counter. Bread. She needed more flour and yeast. Seeds, too. She made a list for Kit. She could hear her clanking about in the shop with the bucket and mop, pottering and talking to herself. She'd be ages yet, tidying and cleaning after the day's rush. Starling tipped a mound of flour onto the surface and began to mix and knead. This was how she got through things and waited until she knew. Familiar routines. Finding food. Baking. Keeping a clean rig. She needed to keep busy, to fill the silences and the jagged gaps where her old life – where Mar – should be.

Mar could sit for hours. She never needed other people to define her. She was herself, complete, and Starling had always wanted to be the same. Here in the town, though, she needed other people. Not needed. But on her own, she was like a loose hem, threatening to unravel.

She placed the dough in the bowl to rise and wiped the sweat off her brow. It was hot in the kitchen. She stepped into the yard and stretched out her arms to feel the space, the cooler air held there by the walls' shadows.

What was she missing? It wasn't just Mar. The road? The van? Perhaps she missed a myth, an almost-truth. Remember winter, she told herself. A rig in mid-winter was grim and muddy. Luc was right about that, and it wasn't just the mud, it was being stuck inside the rig day after day, staggering out to do only the essentials, clambering back into the warmth as fast as they could, into the thick and over-breathed air, and the same old stories, the same books, the same faces. Friends were what made a mid-winter rig bearable. They brought new tales, old tales with new twists, news from the outside, and took old news with them when they left.

The gaps between those evenings of friendship – well, they were tough. And by the end, no one ever came to Mar's rig. Mar would open the door to no one, friend or not, so they shared no tales except their own. Mar and Starling had trodden the paths of those tales over and over, year after year, worn their tracks deep and inescapable. They gave no relief. They penned them in.

They were strong, though, Starling and Mar. That was the story they told themselves. They painted it on the stove, chanted it in their heads when their hands turned blue and their ribs began to show. Their rig was sound; they had supplies to last until spring, just about; they had timber or knew where to find it. They were lucky. They were skilful. They were survivors.

They had to be, because they knew the truth of winter.

Starling remembered finding Johnno frozen in his bender, his face sucked empty like an old balloon from months of coughing. That was in the days before, when they were together, Mar and Starling and all the others, twenty rigs or more on one site for three, four winter months. Starling had gone to see his dog. She'd wanted a real dog of her own but Mar wouldn't let her so she was going to draw Johnno's.

They'd buried Johnno in the copse on the hilltop, all of them gathered round the grave as Phil and Mar and Marky and Nudge lowered him in. Em had led the ceremony, calling on the winds and the earth and the sky and all the people there, and then they had walked down the hill to the site and crowded into Em's rig to keep the long night at bay with brews and every story they knew about Johnno's life, good and bad and best forgotten. They huddled round the burner, candles ablaze because they looked after their own. Starling was young, but even then she knew how to say farewell to a friend, and that friends mattered more than almost anything. It seemed like she'd forgotten.

Starling shook herself out and told herself to keep busy. 'Kit?' she called. 'Fancy a brew?'

Chapter Sixteen

Kit asked if Starling could mind the shop the following Saturday so she could go to her little sister's birthday. She'd prep and cook with Starling before she went, she said. She misread Starling's expression of surprise and jumped back in, 'Or maybe we should just shut the shop?'

'No, no. I'll be fine.' Kit trusted her to run the shop. Damn right, but still. *Yes.*

Starling and Kit worked late on the Friday night and piled the counter high before Kit left to catch her bus next morning. Watching her vanish down the street, Starling felt a surge of energy as she took her place behind the counter. The shop was busy from the moment she opened, and though she'd helped out behind the till before, it was the first time she'd spent a day selling the food she'd gathered and cooked, handing parcels of pies and flapjacks, salads and rolls across the counter to customer after customer. Many knew she'd gathered the ingredients – she found that Kit had been enthusing about her knowledge and skills – and they wanted to know where she found the plants, and how she knew what was safe to eat. By late lunchtime the shop was almost bare.

Luc came in with a mug of tea for her. 'Blimey. Looks like a horde of locusts went through.' It was Em's old wail after the kids had raided her cupboards again.

Starling sat on a stool and cradled her tea. After a moment she jumped up and pushed the last couple of rolls to the front of the counter, and stirred the soup to check it was still warm.

'Sit down, you mad fly,' Luc said. 'You're buzzing.'

'I'd better stay open for a bit in case people want dry stuff, lentils and all that. But I think I'll close in an hour. Do you reckon Kit would be OK with that?' Starling's legs jiggled with the need to get back to work.

'Definitely. I'll help you clear up if you want.' He held his phone up and took a photo. 'Smile!' A few seconds later his phone buzzed and he showed Starling Kit's reply, a string of smiling emojis and a photo of her grinning face surrounded with party balloons. 'I think she's happy.'

Later, they sat by the open window upstairs, feet up, cool beers in their hands. The day's heat rose, tarmac-scented, off the road below. A jangle of fairground music wafted over the rooftops. They both looked up.

Luc looked at Starling. 'Fancy it?'

*

The high street was crowded with couples and families, gaggles of teenagers and bunches of lads. Not much happened in Wincombe, so everyone went to the fair. A bunch of Dinah's regulars passed them; one called out, 'All right, Starling?' and the others raised their hands in greeting. 'All right?' she echoed. People she'd served earlier waved across the street. She thought she saw Flea's red hair bobbing along ahead. She'd catch her later. The entrance to the fairground was packed, and Starling, still fizzing from the day, led Luc in, elbowing into the crowds. It might be a small fair, but it was bright and noisy and everyone was glad to get out of their houses and step together into its illusions.

The fair was on the edge of town on rough ground that was used as a car park the rest of the year. It was the kind of place Em and Mar might have stopped, down at the far end where the lights from the town faded into the trees, before the Criminal Justice Act turned them into outlaws just for parking up.

The fair had grown up from the gravel and mud, become almost a village in its own right, a strange one of bright lights, sugar, vertigo and shadows where mischief could happen. The fair people were outsiders, like Starling but a whole other tribe. They kept themselves to themselves, looked after their own. And they knew that people would always need distraction, an alternative to their reality.

Luc smashed a hammer on a bell and won ten pounds. He shot targets and won a huge pink teddy. He said he'd give it to Kit to make up for her missing the fair.

'Really? Pink? Nylon?'

'Maybe not,' and he gave it back. Starling and Luc walked through the rides and stalls and it was good, it was just like it had been before he left her.

Starling's energy poured out of her, like filth down a plughole. He could leave her again. Any day he might walk away a second time, no warning, no goodbye.

The flashing lights, ringing bells and tingling music swirled round her, out of touch, plunging her in darkness.

No. She would not go there. She dragged herself back. Chip fat, elbows, whirlpools of light and music. Luc by her side. The Starships swooping bright against the darkening sky. The Big Wheel.

She grabbed Luc and pulled him over to the wheel. 'Come on, one last ride.'

It was slowing to a halt. A pair of lads tottered out of the chairs and tried to swagger off on shaking legs. The couple behind them kept on kissing even as they climbed down and walked away. The bloke on the gate held out his hand for Luc and Starling's money, wordless, keen to get them loaded and set the wheel moving.

The wheel began to speed up as they lifted to the highest point. They swung a moment, and then they dropped and the booths below rushed into focus, the gaggles of kids in micro skirts, leering youths yawing like sharks through the crowds, couples arm in arm. Luc and Starling flashed past the bloke on the box, and up again towards the treetops, screams and music and rushing air in their ears.

They whirled round, side by side, and when the wheel slowed again they were left dangling halfway up, facing out and away from the fair, as if they were perched on a branch of a tree. The noise fell away from below them.

'Are you OK, Star?'

'Yep.' She looked at her feet, dangling in space. 'No. Not really.'

'What happened?'

'I don't know. When Mar left...' Luc was silent. Starling swallowed. 'When Mar left, she didn't say anything. She just went one day when I was out gathering food. I'd no idea. I came back and she was gone.' She'd held it in so long, she couldn't contain her loss any more. 'Mar left me.' She couldn't look at Luc. She glared out into the darkness, away from the fairground lights. 'Mar. Left. Me. Everyone leaves me. You left me. Even you, and you said you never would.'

Luc began to speak, but Starling kept going: 'Shut up, Luc. You've no right to say anything. You've no fucking right.'

'But—'

'No, you left. Mar was right. She told me never to trust you. She told me you would leave, and I didn't believe her.' Starling drew in a jagged breath. 'Do you know what that was like? What the last few years have been like, alone with Mar?'

'No. I don't. But you're wrong.' Luc pulled her shoulder so she had to face him. 'I didn't want to leave. None of us did.'

'So why did you go? You abandoned me.'

The wheel started moving again. It crawled round to let people in below them.

Luc looked Starling straight in the eyes. 'I'm here. I'm going nowhere. And I've got your back. I'm not leaving.' Luc wasn't going to let it go. 'You know Mar made us leave, don't you? You've seen her do it. Anyone who loves her, she tramples on them. Em loved her. She hurt Em so badly. And Tom, your dad... you... she just throws us away. Why does she do it?'

The Starships swung past, tangling her thoughts in their cables and lights. But she suddenly understood Mar's need to break things. To break people. The strange joy she had in sacrificing what she loved. It was a kind of terrible energy that drove her on.

Luc kept talking, though she willed him to stop. 'Em wanted Mar to tell you about your dad. That's what they argued about. It's why Mar forced us to leave.'

Starling didn't want to hear it. 'He left us,' she spat out. 'He never even bothered to stick around to see me born. That's the kind of bastard he is.'

'He didn't leave you, Starling. Mar lied.'

Mar never lied. That was one truth Starling could always hold on to.

Luc continued: 'Mar kept you secret from him. She told your dad to get lost the moment she realised she was pregnant. She booted him out before he could see. He never knew about you.'

'No way would she do that.'

Luc didn't answer at first. He looked steadily at her, not letting her go. 'I'm sorry, Star. It's true.'

Starling's voice rose as the wheel began to turn again, bringing them back down. 'Mar's never lied to me!' She had to believe that.

'I know I should have told you. But I couldn't. And he's a good guy, your dad.'

'You fucking met him?' She had no idea what to believe any more. 'And you never told me? You bastard!' Luc flinched.

And then they were down, and the bloke on the gate clanked the bar on their seat open and Starling sprang forward, down to the ground and away. She didn't look to see if Luc was behind her. Didn't speak again until they were back at the flat's door.

He had betrayed her. Mar never lied. He knew about her dad and kept it secret. Mar never lied. Did she? Had Luc really met him? Had anyone told her the truth?

Luc put his hand on her arm. 'Star. Let's go and see Em. She's better at this than I am.'

'Fuck off.' Her hands were shaking. She couldn't get the key in the lock.

'Oh, grow up, Star. Look at me. I'm here. I care about you. But I'm not up for being called all the names under the sun because you still believe everything Mar says.'

'I don't.' The stupid key wouldn't turn.

He reached for the key and turned it in the lock. 'Hug?' he said as he opened the door.

'Go and hug Kit.'

She ran up and stuffed her things in her bag. Mug, sleeping bag, clothes. Books, sketchbook. Luc stood in the doorway and watched. 'Don't go,' he said. 'Please.' She ignored him. Pushed past him to get out of the flat. In the shop kitchen, she grabbed supplies and rammed them into the corners of her bag. Rice, lentils, beans. Her head was jangling with leaving, staying, the van, Mar. She needed to get sorted, to calm her head down, to work it all out.

She slammed the door shut behind her and walked automatically away without seeing the streets and people around her.

She'd told Luc about Mar leaving because she'd thought, despite it all, that he'd always look out for her, but he'd barely listened. Worse, he'd lied. He'd lied about Mar, and lied about her bastard father. Luc was a fool, always believing what Em said – Em the softie who wanted to believe every sob story, take in the stray, save the world, but couldn't see that the world wasn't like that, that she couldn't cure it with love. *Love makes you weak. Love is a luxury survivors can't afford. Trust, that's different.*

Mar loved her. She trusted Mar, wherever she was. She had to, or what was left?

At least it wasn't raining. Starling walked back out to the main road, and stuck out her thumb.

Chapter Seventeen

Three lifts through the night and she was almost there. Three threadbare conversations with drivers while her mind slipped on the stepping stones of Mar and Luc and her dad and Em. She couldn't think straight while she sat strapped in, rushed powerless along roads she couldn't smell or feel beneath the soles of her feet. She needed to walk. So she told her last lift to let her out and marched the final miles, beating a battle rhythm that almost filled her mind, pushing what had happened and what was ahead to the edges, jagged and lurking. She concentrated on the road as the sun rose. Dusty verge, pale dry grasses rustling, eggshell sky. Her nostrils filled with fumes and pollen. Her boots on the gravel, crunching. Two buzzards circled overhead. She paused to watch as they flew higher and higher, dancers on a silken web spinning almost out of sight. When she could barely see them any more, the silver threads of their cries twisted down to her. She walked on.

*

It was still early morning when she arrived at the end of the track. The grass was long now, and wreathed through the bars of the gate, which someone had pushed shut. A pale path looped around it into the wood, barely trodden. Was Mar there? Was the van safe? Starling's boots kicked up dust in the ruts the van had made when they drove it in. She told herself she was home. There would be woodsmoke ahead hanging in the heavy summer trees; its dark bittersweetness would tell her that Mar was there and the burner was lit and there was a pan of soup simmering. That everything was as it always had been.

Mar might offer Starling a mug of coffee, or she might not. She might turn to the door when she heard Starling's foot on the step, see her, and turn away. She might square her back against Starling. If she did that, Starling would have to go. She had seen it before, watched people she loved pushed away by Mar's wall of silence.

Maybe it was as it should be. Maybe it was natural. Mar had trained her to survive and to fend for herself.

She kept walking towards the clearing. The van was out of sight, hidden by the trees and undergrowth that had greened up since she was last there. They'd pitched it wisely. Had Mar heard the birds' alarm calls at Starling's approach? At the edge of the clearing she crouched out of sight and let the wood settle around her, absorbing its sounds back into the earth. A blackbird cackled noisy into the brambles behind her. A wood spider sprinted over a fallen leaf at her foot. A flicker in the corner of her eye told her a breeze had twisted a leaf down from the treetops. There was no woodsmoke.

She pulled herself to her feet and crept towards the van. She went slowly, placing her steps like a hunter on soft leaf litter, eyes on a rabbit. She drew closer to the van. The door was shut, but it was still early. Maybe Mar was asleep. Starling crept back to the trees to wait, lowered herself to the ground, her back to a tree, hidden from the clearing by the undergrowth. Gradually the woods around her calmed. She closed her eyes and pictured Mar inside, breathing slow and sure as the morning light crept in through the top window.

*

The blackbird in the bramble behind her clappered out of its cover. Starling looked up and held her breath. Someone was coming up the track. They didn't seem to be worried about being heard, and were walking fast. She risked a quick look.

A small terrier trotted into the clearing, followed by a stout woman out of breath. The dog sniffed about the steps of the van, lost interest, lifted its leg against the front wheel and vanished underneath, out of sight.

'Come here, Tobes. Come away!' The woman stood, hands on hips, calling the dog. 'Tobes!' She bent down to look under the van. 'Rats, Tobes?' She put a hand on the van and lowered herself to her knees. 'Tobes! Come away!' She struggled back to her feet and started to walk away, calling the dog. Then she stomped back, took a phone from her pocket, and took a photo. 'Outrageous,' she puffed. 'Tobes, now!' she yelped and the dog ran out. 'Come on, time to go home.'

Starling watched her go. Mar wasn't in the van or she'd have sent the stupid woman packing. Starling pulled herself to her feet and crossed the clearing, stripping hope away with each step. The wood pile was untouched. The water container was chained to the steps where she'd left it. She knelt and pulled out her key from the hen coop.

Inside, the van was musty and damp. Moist air always found a way in under the door or down the flue, and once in, it stayed. Starling opened the windows and let the warm summer scents of the wood flow in. A fly circled the van and flew out. She looked for signs that Mar had been back. Her mug out of place on the shelf, her blanket rumpled, a note for Starling on the chalkboard. But Starling had known from the moment she arrived in the clearing that Mar wasn't there, hadn't been there, wasn't coming back.

Was the van Starling's now to make her own? She stood and let herself feel its emptiness. It felt full of Mar, yet stripped of her –

she was here in every carved detail, every painted leaf, in the coffee stain on the floor by her chair, in the hook by her bed where she hung her bag, and yet all of these things told Starling that she had gone, and that the van was not the same place without her.

She wanted to tiptoe out again, as if she'd walked into a private museum and heard voices coming along a distant corridor. But she needed time alone. She needed to pause for long enough for her mind to stop boiling over. She didn't want to think. She wanted not to think, or talk, or hear anything new.

So she did as she always did, and started the daily chores, knowing what had to be done to keep the day afloat. She untethered the water container and set off through the wood, her old path hidden by a season's grass and brambles that tore at her legs. Cows gathered at the fence. They followed her at a hot-breath's distance all the way to the trough and stood round her while she filled the container. She patted the cow nearest her, its black face sweet-muck-scented in the mid-morning sun. She wished it could talk and tell her what to do.

Mar hadn't come back.

There were nettles above the ditch, a few late elderflowers along the hedgeline, rabbit droppings on the shallow ridge above the fence. There might be second-batch eggs in nests if she was lucky. Sorrel, dock, fat hen, cow parsley. She could milk a cow, surely? She could stay here.

But back at the van, about to light the burner, she thought about the woman with the terrier. She'd be back. Starling sat on her heels, lighter in hand. The woman had a photo of the van. She wasn't going to keep it to herself. The burner would send smoke up into the sky and bring them running.

Starling gave herself a day. A day was enough.

Maybe the woman didn't care, and Starling was safe. Safe, but alone. No one to share a brew with. Spin a tale with. Bake bread and flapjacks, crack open a beer with. She had begun to believe in Luc again. And in the promise of the shop with Kit. And in a friendship, maybe, with Flea.

Mar might come back. Given time and a little space, they could find a new way to be together, more like friends, two people who'd chosen to live this way. Maybe.

The van was made for two. Two berths, two chairs at the table. Two mugs, two knives, two forks, two spoons. Mar made the van before she knew Starling, before she made her. Starling was part of Mar. They were two pioneers remaking the world.

But Mar's strength came from what she had taught Starling all her life. *We are all alone in this world. We pass by others, touch for a moment, and then we're gone.* She pictured Mar alone in her van the day she left, Starling out in the wood, Mar measuring herself against her belief, and leaving, walking down the track, a single shadow under the sky.

Mar was a fundamentalist at heart. She had a heart, Starling knew that, but she steeled it against softness, against the warmth of others, because she'd learned that none of it mattered. That it never lasted, that it was based on lies. That no one would ever, could ever put another first, save them before they saved themself. Other people always had to leave you, betray you in the end. Except Starling; Starling would never have left Mar.

When the storm comes, no one will help us. Everyone has to save themself. And the storm is coming. The world is failing.

Luc had surely lied when he said Mar turned them away. They could have stayed. Em was a strong woman, as strong as Mar.

Mar had kept herself and Starling safe. She'd moved them further and further from other people and their compromises and the danger they brought. Alone together in the van they could hide out, avoid the bailiffs and the police, live true. Mar had pushed away outsiders like Dave and Gill. She no longer needed Em and Luc and all the others who'd been with them. It was like Mar was paring herself down to her essence, layer by painful layer, and the day they pulled off the track last winter, she knew exactly what she was doing.

Maybe she always had. The sketch of the young man who looked so much like Starling burned like an ember in the bottom of Starling's bag.

Luc knew him. He had kept her dad secret from her. Em had too. So had Mar.

Starling sat at the table. The violet she'd placed there to welcome Mar home had drooped over the rim of the egg cup and turned almost black. She felt its velvet petals, paper-dry now.

She was so tired.

She lay on Mar's bed, pulled the cover over, and slept in the warmth and smell of her.

When she woke, the sun was low above the treetops, slipping down towards dusk. She lay and listened to the wood settling for the evening, the pigeons clumsy in the branches, bees humming, a squirrel clawing up a trunk. She was hungry.

She took a bucket and a long knife and walked back to the damp dip in the land at the wood's edge where the ramson flowers had been forming in the early spring. She dug down for the bulbs, their sweet garlic scent filling the air as she cut them out of the soil. She cut handfuls of nettle tops and dropped them onto the bulbs, with a heap of hairy comfrey leaves for protein.

She lit the burner. Found a dreg of oil in the jar, breathed in the caress of garlic rising from the blackened pot, dropped in lentils and herbs, poured water on, watched it come to a boil. She had missed this self-containment. If someone saw smoke now, well, so they did, and she'd be ready, but she kept stirring, feeding the burner, listening for footsteps. No one came. Maybe no one ever would. She chopped and added the leaves, and watched them soften and swirl as she stirred.

She ate sitting on the step, her feet in the last rays of sun. The birds called across the clearing, claiming their territories as the light fell, before falling silent themselves as she went in and lit the candles.

She sat in Mar's rocker, not wanting to close the door until the dew began to dampen the air, watching the very last of the twilight warm the treetops and fade to dark. Only then did she come inside and shut the door.

The candles guttered as she moved around the van. She was awake now and could not settle. The van felt too quiet, though Mar had been silent so often. Starling put the kettle on, rummaged for tea, listened to the water judder and boil. Here was her mug, carried from van to town and back. She clasped it tight to hold her hands still, the hot tea scorching her skin through the metal. Was this all she had to hold on to? A tin mug and a bag of scraps?

The candlelight caught the gold threads in Jenny's dark mane, hanging from the back of the cupboard. Mar had made the hobbyhorse and given her to Starling on her sixth birthday, and even the horse-drawn children had wanted to ride her, jumping the fences they made from sticks and cans, stroking her wool mane, whispering into her soft leather ears. Mar had made many more, for Luc's younger brothers, for their friends, and then an entire procession to sell, every horse different, each buying them supplies for the winter to follow.

She'd made stools too, like the one in the corner beneath Starling's bed. When Starling was old enough she'd joined Mar, painting birds around the seats or a tree at their centre. Starling's own stool danced with starlings in their speckled spring plumage, picked out with Mar's finest brush, flying against a clear blue sky.

The van had always been her home.

She pulled out the box beneath Mar's bed and laid out its contents again, the stories of her whole life, and Mar's life before her. Here were the festival tickets, photos of Mar and Em and all the kids grinning by the van, swimming in the river, holding hands around the Major Oak. Here were flyers: *Bread not bombs, The dawn of a new era*. A rights card. A hand-drawn map of the ancient sites, the true threads of the land and the old ways between Avebury, Cantlin Stone, Chalice Well, the Tor and the Grail, linking the Iron Age fort at Cissbury Ring, the forest at Clun, Old Sarum, the stones at Rollright, the horses at Uffington and Westbury, Stonehenge, Salisbury, Clearbury. She'd trodden those ways all her life. Beneath the map, Starling's first sketchbook, kept by Mar all these years. All the words and pictures they'd ever wanted to keep, instructions, addresses, letters from friends, poems, songs. Mar's own sketches, right at the bottom. Starling pulled them out again and sat looking at the heap of paper and card, old scraps, torn pages from sketchbooks. Once, Mar had drawn all the time on whatever came to hand, compulsively putting down the people and the life around her.

Mar's sketches weren't in any kind of order. Starling spread them out on the table. She made a little heap of plants, another of animals, Mar's notes for the painting of the van, the stools, the boxes and signs she'd sold across the land. She spread out the places they'd lived, passed through, run from, and then the people – Em, Luc, Phil, the brothers, Johnno, Ears, Nat, Horse, so many, and all caught by Mar in a few quick lines – and Starling herself, a tiny baby, eyes scrunched shut, and then again, in Em's arms, growing all the time, sharp-edged, wild-haired, and always on the move. But never in the same picture as the man who looked so like Starling, here in a fistful of quick lines laughing beside Em, and here, in shadow in the van's doorway, and here, in profile, still for a single moment, his urge to move jumping off the paper. At last Starling pulled the sketch she'd been carrying from the bottom of her bag. Here he was, talking, brew in hand, Phil and Em beside him, Mar there too, her feet leading from the page to touch his. He was maybe Starling's age now when Mar drew him then. Younger than Mar. He was there for one summer of sketches, and then he was gone.

Starling turned the sketches over, but there were no names. Who needed names for the people they loved?

She put everything back in the box except that last sketch of Em, Phil and Mar and the man with her hair, her nose, and the fidgeting energy that she felt in her own bones. She folded it and put it back in her bag. She went round the whole van. Found the Rescue Remedy. The cassette they used to play on hot sunny days on the road, and on wet days to remind themselves of the sun to come. The seeds she'd saved ready for spring. She put them in her bag, blew out the candles and climbed into bed, boots ready on the floor below her.

She didn't sleep, she was sure, but she woke at first light to men's voices and a dog's bark out on the edge of the wood. She slid down, pulled on her boots and was out and beyond the clearing, running out of the wood's edge when she heard them battering on the van door and yelling for her to come out.

Somehow, overnight, her mind had found its answer. She ran until she could no longer hear the men and their dogs. She left them behind with all that had been hers, climbed the hill past the cows and the rooks' trees until the land lay vast all around her, and stood, hands on her knees, breath rasping, tears wet on her cheeks, letting it all go. She needed none of it. It was all hers, wherever she was. She was free.

She walked all day and let the rise and fall of the land guide her into steep-sided valleys, along hedge-darkened holloways, into streams and back up onto the tops.

As the day lengthened, she climbed a gate onto a narrow lane and at a junction spinning out in three directions from a small grassy triangle, she sat beneath the wooden fingerpost and pulled out her phone.

*

Luc's bike wound itself closer, its engine dipping in and out of Starling's earshot as it rounded curves in narrow lanes and dropped behind muffling hedges, until at last its roar grew saw-toothed and clear and brought her to her feet as he curled round the last bend towards her, one knee almost on the tarmac. He righted the bike in front of her, engine still turning over, and gestured at the spare helmet on the pillion.

She climbed on behind him and he accelerated away without waiting for her to put her feet on the bars. She steadied herself, found the bars and put her hands on his waist as he cut tight into the bends of the lane, faster than she'd expected, as if he couldn't wait to be away.

He took the back roads, the noise of the engine bouncing off the hedges. The bike raised sparrows that flew ahead of them down the lanes and swept round the curves as if Luc and the birds were racing to reach the next opening and be free. But with a flick of a wing the birds would vanish through a gap in the branches and Luc would roar on, catching flies in the updraft.

Starling slowly released her hold on him until only the tips of her fingers touched his ribs. They rounded a bend, she leaned, and as they came upright along a long straight she let go and stretched her arms wide as wings, her fingers flickering in the wind, like feathers lifting her away to freedom.

Luc turned his head to see and in that moment, less than a moment, in the flick of an eye, something fast and low, a fox or a cat or a shadow, something too fast to see, too fast to shout a warning, fled from hedge to hedge under Luc's front wheel and spun them both into flight, spinning free in the air together, as they lifted for a moment, and they fell.

And then, nothing.

Chapter Eighteen

Searing pain ripping her arm, her shoulder, her ribs... A claw tearing open her skull... Grit, hot tarmac, the creak and scratch of metal letting go... She can't hear Luc... Luc...

*

A man's voice. 'It's all right. You're all right. Can you tell us your name?' A woman's voice somewhere near: 'Hello, hello, hello? We need more help...'

*

So many voices in the darkness.

*

Mar, lifting her into the cab. 'We're off, Starling!'
  'Can I say goodbye to Luc?'
  'We'll see him later. Where shall we go?'

*

Luc swinging on the gate, welcoming them back.

'Star! Star! There's a river!'

*

A man, close to her ear. 'How is the pain, Starling?'
A melting back into fog.

*

'Does she have family?'

*

'Starling. Don't say anything. I'm here.' Kit. A warm hand on hers.

*

Bleeps and alarms. Rattling trolleys. 'Tea or coffee?' somewhere
beyond. A closing door.

*

Mar, singing along to their road-trip cassette, a laugh in her voice
as she changed up a gear and swooped around a bend.

Beside her, always. Sometimes they left before Starling had time to
say goodbye to Luc. But that was OK because they'd always be back.

*

Em gathering Starling up in her skirts. 'We missed you! Welcome
home!' Luc creeping inside the thick, soft layers to hug her,
squashing her, all elbows and knees tangled together.

*

The pain sharpened, focused, released its grip enough that she could identify it. Upper arm. Shoulder. She tried to sit. Ribs. All on her right side. That groan was hers. Her head. Lie still.

*

She was in a room. High ceiling. Grey walls. Grey floor. Metal-framed bed, sides up, caging her in. Blue blanket. Tube into her left arm. Bright lights. Open door. Nurse outside. Nurse inside.

'How are you feeling?'

She couldn't work out what she was doing here, what had happened. The men at the van? Was that it?

*

She slept and woke, slept and woke, slept and woke to find Kit sitting beside her, eyes closed, pale, like she was praying.

Luc's bag lay on the bed between them.

'Kit?'

Kit opened her eyes with a start. 'Starling.' She pushed her hair out of her eyes. She looked like she hadn't slept for days.

Luc's bag snagged Starling. 'Where's Luc?' her voice creaked. 'Is Luc OK?' Why was Kit here? What had happened?

'He's hurt. He's here too.'

'Where?'

'Wincombe General. How are you feeling?'

'What happened?'

'You don't remember?'

Starling tried to shake her head.

'Don't. You hit your head – you might still be concussed. I'm just glad you're OK. You were lucky. There's nothing too serious, though the nurse said your shoulder's a bit of a mess.'

'Luc? Was he with me?'

Kit nodded. 'I'd better get back to him. Em's coming, but he's on his own at the moment. Look after this for him?' She gestured at Luc's bag. 'They're about to operate.' And she was gone.

*

Starling knew Luc's bag as well as her own. They'd never had secrets. They'd line their best things up in the dust outside Mar's van. Swap? A photo from a magazine. Snail shells and dragonfly wings. Luc's best pebble for her starling feather. She still had his pebble, a tiny white eye, pierced all the way through.

She opened his bag. His wallet, its weave worn and soft. Inside, a small bundle of notes, and a photo of him with Em and his brothers round the fire, years ago, Starling tucked in with them. Her face smudged and grinning beside Em. Who'd taken it? Mar?

Beside the wallet, Luc's knife, a trail of ivy leaves along its handle, the blade folded in.

A battered notebook of songs, with a sketch of Luc on its front page that she'd drawn at his first stage gig and he'd stuck in with tape. He'd looked so happy up there with his guitar.

A card, hand-drawn, the tree of life spreading across it, and on the back, a note: *Love, we're here at last. Come visit. Mum x*, and a little sketched map.

His mug. A lighter. A bundle of cash. All he ever needed.

*

Flea was sitting at the end of the bed.

'Nick sends his love.' She looked away. Was she crying?

'Flea?'

Flea just shook her head, wiped her eyes on the back of her sleeve. 'Sorry. Nothing. How are you doing?'

Starling felt a pit open in the depths of her stomach. 'Have you seen Luc?'

Flea shook her head again. 'No visitors.' She swallowed. 'But I came to see you, anyway.'

*

Kit again, silent as she walked into the room, moving slowly, like the floor was thick treacle.

'Tell me.' Starling didn't want to hear it, but she had to know.

Kit crouched beside her and wrapped her arms around Starling. 'He didn't make it. He's gone.'

They didn't speak again until a nurse came in. 'Just checking your drip. I'll do your blood pressure in a minute.' She rattled out with the trolley. The room was too quiet.

Kit's voice was low and shaky. 'I'm glad you were with him.' She sat with her fists stuffed between her legs, shoulders hunched, looking at the floor.

Starling had to say it. 'It was my fault.'

'He texted me to say you needed help. That's not your fault.'

'He was angry. I said—'

'He told me about the fair. He said he hurt you, he told you something—'

'I needed to hear it. It was just hard, really hard, and I—'

'You know he loved you too much to be angry, don't you?'

'I was going to say sorry.'

'He knew.' They sat in silence. Kit spoke again, as if she had to fill the space between them: 'I just can't believe it. How can he be gone?'

'I don't remember it. Not really. Just fragments.'

'You called the ambulance. I don't know how. You were unconscious when they got there. You were by his side on the road, holding him.' Kit's tears ran onto Starling's neck, and Starling pulled her left arm free and held her.

*

She refused to hear Mar's voice.

*

Did it matter, in the end, that we die alone? Mar would say not.

*

We are the earth's children, with the strength of the air and the water and the soil. We return to earth, all of us. We are but dust and worm-food. Never fear death, Starling. It is life. Em's arms around Starling the night Johnno died, when Mar would not speak or comfort her.

*

Em in the doorway, Kit beside her.

Starling closed her eyes.

Em's voice, worn soft as old felt. 'Starling, my love.' Em's smell, woodsmoke and herbs. Starling's chest a fist. She couldn't do this. She didn't have to. She clenched her jaw.

She had never wanted to make Em sad.

Em's hand on her forehead, brushing her hair aside. 'Let me see your poor head.' A soft kiss, a wisp of Em's breath on her skin. 'We'll get you home and make it better.'

Starling could feel tears coming that she did not want to cry.

'You don't have to say anything, Starling, my love.'

'I'm sorry, Em,' she whispered. 'I'm so sorry.'

Chapter Nineteen

Kit and Em spoke in quiet voices in the front of the car, odd words floating back to Starling. 'Left here, I think.' 'Is she asleep?' For a while they talked about the harvest that Em had left behind, an incantation of courgettes and tomatoes, potatoes and squashes that flowed along with the rhythms of the road beneath their wheels. Then they fell silent.

When she next woke, Em was telling Kit about the day Luc was lost in Glastonbury, and Starling didn't need to hear it because Em had told it so many times before: how even Em was getting worried because he was only three, and every shop in the town they went into had seen him and thought he was with someone else, and how Em and Mar followed a trail of enchanted people who'd met a tiny white-blonde boy trotting along the high street in and out of the shops, singing to himself and casting a spell over shopkeepers, customers, elves and fairies, until at last there he was in Em's favourite herbalists, entirely happy and telling her all about Em's potion to rub on when he fell in the nettles.

'He never changed, did he?' And Kit began to tell Em about how she and Luc had first met, and Starling's mind drifted off.

Starling had missed Luc's funeral, her head not steady enough for her to leave her hospital bed. She'd tried to be there in her mind, but she couldn't imagine Luc lying still and cold inside a box in some anonymous chapel. A scattering of words spoken into the empty air. Em, Kit, Luc's dad the only mourners. Not even his brothers. Em had said it should be simple. They'd say goodbye to Luc with the people who loved him, under the open sky, feet on our mother's earth, back at Bramblehill where he belonged. That's when Davey, Stevie and Gabe would come, she said.

They were taking him home, his ashes beside Starling, impossible.

Starling ebbed and flowed, lulled by the road. She dozed and woke like a small child on a midnight journey, warm in her bed under a summer moon.

She felt insulated from the world that rolled steadily past. A blur of trees and hedges, gates into fields, lamp posts counting her into towns and out again, the swirl of a roundabout, the click of the indicator.

She could not absorb the terrible fact of Luc not being here in the car beside her, not being a mile ahead on his bike, not being anywhere. This box was not Luc. She couldn't think about it, her mind slipping and swerving in a mist. She let go and allowed it all to sweep past, a river in flood, carrying its flotsam and jetsam as they floated on.

The car carried her past places she'd driven through before in her old life: a village of flint walls, the necklace of roundabouts that rattled all the jars in the van, the wide silvery estuary below the road, boats on the mud, all knots in her handkerchief.

Where did that come from? A faint memory that faded with the cries of the water birds as they drove on, west and further west. She slept again.

*

Late in the evening, Em bumped the car over ruts and gravel and nudged it between a battered flat-tyred hatchback and an old pickup. A painted sign with *Bramblehill Forest Community* in awkward, twisting, leafy letters hung from a gate leading into trees. Mar had surely never been here, or she'd have repainted it.

Em leaned over the back of her seat and touched Starling's knee to wake her, though Starling had felt the change in the surface below the car the moment they left the main road, bringing all her senses into alertness. 'We're here, Starling. Welcome to Bramblehill, my love.'

Kit came round to help her from the car, but Starling nudged her away and slowly edged herself out. Every move jagged at her shoulder and ribs, but they were healing and she had to move on her own sometime. When she stood, though, everything spun. She held on to the car door and breathed deeply, making herself look out, away from the pain. The rim of a valley curled around like a cupped hand. It was so thick with trees that she couldn't see the camp below, but she smelled woodsmoke. Somewhere a child was singing.

Em had come here after leaving Mar. She had found her own earth, Luc had said one evening back in the flat. She'd wanted to root herself at last, to bind herself to a small corner of land and give herself back to it. A traveller, she'd told Luc, carries herself away every time she leaves. She gives nothing. Bramblehill would be her place of community between woman and land, a locus for work, worship and weaving the threads that tie us all together, plants, air, animals, water, rock, soil and people.

Maybe. But Luc hadn't wanted to live here. Nor Mar. Hidden away in the cool dark trees, away from the roads and the people they'd always known.

A voice called down in the valley. Someone was laughing. Someone else was sawing wood. Pans clattered. A shout rose up towards them. Someone had heard them.

*

Starling took her time walking down to the camp, stepping carefully on the rooted, uneven path. Halfway down she paused to
rest, holding on to a birch sapling. Its bark was smooth as china,
pale and warm in the evening light. A wren chip-chipped from
the undergrowth and scooted low over the path in front of her.
She hadn't wanted to come, to be trapped by Em, surrounded by
people who loved Em and knew Starling only as Mar's daughter.
But this moment, here on the path, after days captive in the sterile
brightness of the hospital room, this was a cool medicine.

She had let Kit and Em go ahead with the young woman who
came up through the trees to greet them. She was about Starling's
age, skinny and sunburnt, with hand-cropped hair, grubby knees
above battered boots, and a big grin. She'd hugged Em and seemed
delighted to see Kit: 'Hey, Kit! Good to see you!' She even beamed
at Starling: 'Hi!' She turned to Em. 'Is Luc coming?'

Em had said nothing, but put out a hand each to Kit and
Starling. 'Issy,' she said, 'I think Starling might need a hand?' Then
Em had reached into the back of the car and taken Luc's ashes,
carrying them before her as she turned to descend the path.

Starling had refused Issy's help, so the girl bounced on down
the path past Em and Kit, who waited for Starling at the foot of the
hill where the path emerged from the trees into a cleared space. An
open-sided wooden building faced down the valley, a cook shed
with a large table at its centre, shelves of plates and mugs, jugs of
cutlery, and ranks of pans hanging from a beam.

'I was just tidying up,' Issy said. 'Brew?' Kit and Starling nodded
and sat beside each other on logs arranged around a campfire. Em
hadn't told the camp. She'd waited until she was here with them,
holding the news to herself until she was back.

Starling looked up. Em and Issy were talking quietly, holding
hands; tears were running down Issy's face. The light was almost
gone, a faint golden glimmer at the tips of the silver birches all that

was left. Issy stepped across the clearing and seized a rope. A bell rang an urgent summons into the dusk. Em walked away from the fire into the trees, Luc in her hands.

People began to appear from tracks that led to the campfire, finding their places and talking quietly. Five or six people about the same age as Starling and Kit shuffled their boots. A slightly older couple held children on their laps, all four of them dressed in the greys and greens of hand-dyes and seriousness. On a log apart squatted a much older guy with hair in a straying ponytail and a skewy eye. She couldn't take them all in. She was too tired, and the light from the flames flickered on eyes and noses across the fire, making them all one body.

The faces all looked up when Issy carried a big pot of tea into the circle. Behind her came Em, and behind Em a tall, powerful man in a battered straw hat whose face Starling knew almost as well as Em's. Phil looked across the fire. 'Starling,' he said. He didn't smile.

*

Em walked around the fire behind the people of the community, the hoops in her ears flashing in the flame-light. She stopped behind Starling and Kit and placed her hands on their shoulders. The others looked up, expectantly. Issy stopped pouring tea.

Em spoke. 'Some of you know Kit,' she said, in her low voice.

Several voices greeted Kit and waved mugs across the fire at her.

'Welcome back, Kit.' Em patted Kit's shoulder, and Kit lifted her hand and held Em's for a moment. Em spoke again. 'Few of you have met Starling before. I have known Starling since the day she was born. She is a daughter to me. Please make her welcome.'

Faces smiled at Starling across the flames. Voices called quietly, 'Welcome, Starling.'

Em stepped into the fire circle and sat on the log beside Starling. She turned to her and said, loud enough for all to hear, 'I am glad you are with us at this time. Thank you.'

It was a long time since Starling had sat with Em at a fire, felt the heat of flames on her face, and the warmth of the woman who had delivered her at her side.

But across the flames, Phil did not move to take his place in the circle. One by one the faces took notice of his stillness, his standing away from them. He was respected here. That was right, Starling thought. He had lived with the tribe all her life and before. He was a man to be reckoned with, and a just man too. He spoke. 'Starling, I too have known you since the day you were born.'

Beside Starling, Em nodded. 'You are her family, Phil, since that day.'

Phil looked around the circle of faces. 'Kit and Starling bring terrible news. Luc, Em's Luc, died last week in an accident. Starling was with him and has come to us to mend.'

A voice cried out, 'Oh no!' Someone began to cry.

A man's voice said, 'Are we sure?'

Starling nodded. 'Yes. I was there. I was with him. Though I can't remember what happened.' She fell silent.

Phil spoke again: 'Welcome home, Starling. I – we – had wished you would come home to us before, with hope and happiness. But however you have come to us, I am glad to see you. It has been too long.' He nodded, and sat, ever a man of few words, though every word was weighed carefully. Starling felt her throat tighten, and couldn't speak again. She hunched her shoulders and stared at the earth between her boots.

As voices threaded back and forth across the flames, asking questions, exclaiming, repeating Luc's name like a small bell chiming over and over, Starling heard little. A cavern formed in the burning logs, and she felt herself slip into its darkness, gliding through the shimmering heat. A hand on her shoulder, Kit's. 'Starling, are you OK?' She nodded. Em looked at her. 'You need to rest.' She stood and the others fell silent.

'Before we sleep,' she said, 'I thank you all. We are a forest, standing together, each of us bringing our strength and our weakness, strongly rooted in love and care, sustaining each other no matter what comes. Sleep well.'

Starling stood, shaking, the ashes flickering low now, and looked around the circle. She had been around such fires so many times, and always found a place of safety. She spoke. 'Thank you, Em. Thank you, everyone. I've brought you sadness and have nothing else to offer you. I won't stay beyond the night.' She could only bring harm to these people. She had been too long with Mar. She bent and picked up her bag, wincing at the stab of pain in her shoulder, and turned to leave the fire.

Em spoke quickly. 'No, Starling, I won't allow this. You've lost too much already.' She stood before her and looked straight into her eyes. 'And I have been to blame for some of it.' She turned away and looked round at the faces, almost invisible now the fire had sunk so low. 'Starling will stay in my house. Kit, will you stay with us?' She took Starling's hand, holding it firmly so she could not walk away, and led her from the fire.

'Welcome, Starling,' voices said again, one by one around the fire. Then in ones and twos, the people walked into the darkness of the trees.

*

'Come on inside,' Em said, and Starling followed her into the roundhouse. It was dim, lit only by a candle lantern set on a small table by the stove. It shone, golden, at the heart of a circular space rising high up to a twist of beams lifting the roof around a central post. There was a burner, a double bed, a table and chairs, a rocker and a cooking area, but Starling was too tired to take in more.

Em brewed her a mug of camomile and placed a bowl of warm water on the table for her to wash her face. 'I'll be here with you if you wake. Sleep well, Starling.'

Starling slept in a bunk raised above the room and tucked under the thatch, and woke to sunshine through a span of windows that looked out across the valley.

Em had always been able to make any place home. A bunch of flowers, an embroidered cloth thrown over a wooden crate, a mug of tea ready whenever someone knocked on her door were all she needed to turn a shack into a palace.

She was moving around below her, placing a single bowl and spoon on the table, shaking leaves from a jar into a teapot, sweeping the floor out of the open door. She looked up at her and smiled. 'Good morning, Starling. You slept well.'

Had Em been watching her all night? It was possible. But she had no need to watch. Whether it was second sight or deep intuition, she had always known Starling and seen inside her. It was unsettling, a pungent blend of love and intrusion that Starling wasn't sure she wanted to taste again. It was a long time since anyone had enveloped her so completely, and perhaps Em knew it because she placed a tin of cereal and a bottle of milk on the table and left, telling Starling her time was her own, no hurry. She had work to do before the dew burned off the field, and Starling needed to rest.

In the last days Starling's injuries had drained her. She sat in the doorway and watched the community drop down the slope through the trees. They had fields of vegetables and a pair of polytunnels down there, and she could hear their voices lifting from the rows as they started work, hoeing, weeding, harvesting. Em's roundhouse gathered the morning light to its door and Starling sat with her legs in the sun, bare feet absorbing the warmth of the soil.

This earth had been calling her a long time. She pulled the box out of her pocket and opened it. The pigeon's feather she had dropped in when she arrived in Wincombe floated in the warming air across the ground. It landed on a blade of grass, catching the sun. Was it telling her to let go of the town, the airless room above the shop, Flea and Nick laughing in the park, the earthy water-scent of the river and the cool of the woodland edge, the smell of bread in the kitchen, Dinah, even? Starling stretched out and placed it back in the pot.

Her thoughts were everywhere, like a flock of goldfinches in and out of the bush. She tried to let them go, setting her birds free for a while, and rested her gaze on a bed of herbs, concentrating her thoughts to help them find stillness. Bees buzzed from flower to flower, from lavender to rosemary, thyme to oregano. Marigolds glowed orange among them, chives threw balls of purple above narrow stems. And here were Em's remedies: feverfew, camomile, hyssop and lemon balm, tweaking at Starling's memory. She used to help Em gather herbs and prepare them. In the van, she and Mar had grown a few too, in pots that sat on the dashboard when they were journeying. When they paused a while they set the pots around the steps to catch the sun and rain, but none shone with health the way these did, their roots deep in the soil and soaking up the day's light from dawn until dusk. In the wood last winter, Starling's herbs had sat sodden and sad until she cleared the pots and stacked them empty by the log pile.

When she was small, Starling and Mar had parked up in the yard of a smallholding out in the folding hills of south Wales. The smallholder kept Starling in her kitchen garden while Mar was out in the fields digging carrots and potatoes. Starling was eight, and wanted to show her worth with Mar, but the woman said she would not see a child out in the field, glad though she was that Mar was there to work with her.

The woman let Starling help with the herb garden, though, and they knelt side by side, weeding neatly around the marjoram, rosemary, fennel, parsley, thyme, herbs she'd make into wedding bouquets, and would dry and sell in the winter in the villages around. Rosemary was for remembrance, she said, oregano for joy. Violets were for loyalty. She grew rue, too. Rue stank. Rue for regret. And there were clumps of chives that held tiny snails in their tangy, juicy blades. Starling could pick those out without bending the leaves. That was her special job.

After an afternoon of weeding together, the woman had knelt back and stretched, dropping her long fork on the soil beside her. 'Time to stop, I think. Come along, Starling. Let's have tea.'

It was the first kitchen inside a house that Starling remembered clearly. A stone floor, an immovable, vast table beneath rafters that swung with bunches of drying plants, and on that table plates of fresh bread cut into thick slabs and smothered in butter; chunks of cheese; bowls of strawberries and raspberries; a plate of cool cucumbers and carrots; tomatoes from the greenhouse; a jug of squash; and – miraculous to Starling – bowls heaped with crisps and chocolate fingers. It looked like the pictures in library books, but it was real. There was even a cake waiting on the side, with actual icing. 'Is it someone's birthday?' she had asked, and the woman had laughed and shaken her head.

'Just food from the garden for a lot of hungry children, and treats because I love you all. Wash your hands, Starling. I can hear the others.' And her three red-headed children had bounced into the kitchen, back from school and all talking at once and pushing for the sink, ignoring Starling in their fight for first dibs at the tap.

'Tuck in,' the woman said, and soon they were all sat round, silenced by the thickness of the bread, tomato juice and chocolate oozing down their chins. Starling had a fistful of crisps when the door opened and Mar walked in. Her eyes went small and tight, and Starling shrank down into the bench hoping she hadn't seen her, but she knew what would happen next. She dropped the crisps on the plate in front of her and slipped down off the bench.

Mar spoke: 'Starling. Outside, now.' As she ran out, she heard Mar's voice rise. 'We do not accept charity. I feed Starling well, on good, healthy food. Her tea is waiting for her at home.'

Mar was right. *Why would that woman give you food? She is trying to prove herself better than us, because she was born with money in her pockets. She fears us, fears our freedom, fears it will tempt her children away. Well, fuck her.* They left the next morning, abandoning the field half harvested. It was the first of many such leavings.

Kit and Em's voices coming up the path called Starling back. She picked a small chunk out of the roundhouse's clay wall beside her and sniffed it. Earth, heat, dry grass. Em's home. She dropped it into her box beside the feather, closed the lid and tucked it in her pocket.

Chapter Twenty

Mid-morning, the sun high and the thatch rustling with heat and life, Em and Starling were alone in the roundhouse. Em placed the kettle back on the burner with a clang. Starling pulled herself up from the doorway, her limbs feeling stronger and looser already. She crossed the room and took the teapot from Em. It seemed so familiar. She looked around her, feeling the strength of the roof beams, the solidity of the earthen walls, the love in every carved wooden seat and shelf. Em had made a home that felt as if it had grown from the earth beneath it.

'This is beautiful,' Starling said.

'Phil and I made it, with friends from all around. This kind of roof takes a village to raise it. We have three more now.'

They sat at the table, looking out across the treetops, roofs rising between the branches, and making a half-circle around the rim of the valley. Three more roundhouses, a ridge with a dragon on its apex, the poles of a teepee, and glimpses of other structures hidden in the leaves.

Em said, 'There's a green woodpecker in that oak. You see where the top branch was blasted a couple of years ago?'

Starling looked, and saw a bleached white branch rising above the canopy. Em continued, 'He watches me in the mornings, and I watch him. I think we're almost friends, although he likes to hide if he thinks I see him.'

They sipped their tea. Luc should have been here. Starling could feel his warmth beside her, sitting between her and Em. It was like a physical pain. Though her wounds were healing, she felt ripped and scattered over the earth like a hawk's prey. Yet Em seemed serene, as if Luc's death was no more to her than a burnt batch of loaves.

Em reached behind her for a wooden box, and placed it on the table. 'Usually today I would be taking my herbs into the village to post, but I feel a need to stay here for now, close to home. Later we'll prepare for Luc's ceremony, but now I want to set aside time in quietness, and I'd like to spend it with you. I need to make new labels for my herbs. Will you help me?'

She opened the box and took out a stack of square labels, each with the name of a wild herb written across its centre, the weight and use of the herb beneath it. 'I'd like to add pictures of the plants they come from, so people know the plant, feel its essence as they use it. But I'm no artist, as you know.' She laughed. 'You, on the other hand...'

'Do you hand-make every single label?'

'Lord, no. Rob scans them in, and Caryl in the shop prints them out for me in return for a bottle of whatever I've been making. Elderberry cordial at the moment. It's been a good year.'

She set out the labels side by side on the table. Flax, houseleek, calendula, lady's mantle, elder, nettle, evening primrose, feverfew, loosestrife, lime... 'Do you remember them all, Starling?'

'Of course. If you've still got your herbal, though, I'd like to see it.'

Em got up and ran her finger along the bookshelf below the bunks. 'Aha.' She pulled down a thick volume, bristling with scraps of paper, leaves and grasses. 'I don't often use it now, but it's still my best place to go if I'm puzzled.'

Starling took it from her and let it fall open on the table. Clown's woundwort, dancing up the page, its serrated leaves held wide below its tower of small pink hoods. 'I'll make new labels from scratch, with pictures and lettering. Have you got paper?' she asked. 'I've brought my sketchbook, but—'

'No, don't use that. I know how precious it is. I have paper somewhere.' Em rooted around in the boxes beneath the bench around the room's perimeter. 'Here,' she said. 'If you draw while I get my books up to date, that would be perfect. I can ask Rob to scan the new labels later, ready for the next batch.'

So they sat side by side in the light streaming in through the window, sipping their tea, pouring more, drawing, sucking on their pencils, making notes, and saying little. The door was open, and from time to time someone would stick a head in and ask, 'More leeks, Em?', or 'Thinking of sowing some lettuces, if you reckon, Em?', and Em would agree with them and then laugh with Starling at the mere idea that she knew about growing crops for market.

Phil stepped in and laid a hand on Em's shoulder for a moment. Em looked up and held his hand. 'Thank you,' she said, and Phil looked at Starling and nodded, then turned and went back out into the sunlight. Starling wondered if it was always like this. It had never been this quiet on the road, not for long, at least. As if she knew what Starling was thinking, Em laughed. 'We try, Starling, we try, and we're learning to love each other better, but we're human and not everyone loves everyone here. You'll see. But it helps that we have a purpose. We must support ourselves here, or lose the land. So every member of the community has a role, and it only works if we pull together. This end of the year we all have to work in the gardens to get the harvest in. I know you'll help when you're strong enough. And your skills will be welcome.' She reached for Starling's hand and held it briefly. 'We need to get drying and bottling ready for winter, and to deal with the gluts. Awful word. It's the earth's bounty and we're lucky to be blessed. But it does sometimes feel as if the courgettes are taking over, and the tomatoes are ripening so fast in this weather it's hard to keep up.' She looked out of the window and smiled, as if the best thing she could imagine was sitting here with Starling, talking about leeks and courgettes and seed packets.

It was too much. 'Em.' Starling kept drawing, as if it would make it easier to say what she had to. 'Em, I have to tell you about Luc. I haven't told anyone else because he was yours, and it felt all wrong to tell anyone but you.'

'No, Starling, he was not mine. He was the stars' and the earth's and his own gentle self's. But you can tell me how it happened if you need to let it go. I can help to carry it with you.'

'All I wanted to say was that he came to help me. He always did, and I'd stopped knowing it. And he welcomed me, he and Kit both did, and I hurt him. I was so angry.'

Em took another sheet from her box and started counting down the rows of figures. 'Why were you angry, Starling?'

'Because Mar... Mar had left me, and she'd told me that you and Luc and all the others had left us. I knew that no one' – she paused – 'no one cared like she did. But she left me, and I don't know where she's gone, or why, or what I did.' Starling pressed so hard with her pencil, drawing the stem of a flax rising up the paper, that the lead snapped. Em passed her a sharpener and looked out of the window.

'Mar carried so much anger with her, Starling. She always had it, and for so long it carried us, drove us, kept us going when the rocks came through the windows of our rigs and the police tried to drag you children away from us. We needed it then – we needed Mar's rightness, her refusal to change no matter what came our way.'

Starling sharpened her pencil and began to draw the petals, five in a circle around a tiny cluster of stamens. Flax for bronchitis. Flax for inflamed bowels and cystitis. Flax for burns. Flax for soothing. She remembered it all.

Em continued. 'Mar always found leavings hard, you know. For all she talked about the strength of walking away, she could never do it without pain. I doubt she had the power to tell you she was leaving. But I know she would only have left you because she had no other way to go on. She had come to know her life was broken, I believe. I, too, felt this.' Em turned and looked at Starling. 'We drove around the roads of this country and every mile, every place we stopped at for a day or a week, took us further away from our beloved earth, polluting her with our engines, always taking from her and giving her nothing in return. For all our sweet words, we were denying our love for her in our lives. I came here.' Em opened her arms wide as if to embrace the valley below them. 'Mar continued her journey, but in pain. She cannot put down roots until she allows herself to accept all that has passed. She is on a journey that is a kind of penance, perhaps, and I hope a kind of pilgrimage. I hope she will return to us when she has found her way.'

Could Em understand Mar better than she understood herself? Starling would only know when she could ask Mar, if that day ever came. When it came, she told herself. Em, though, Em was right here.

'Why did you leave us, Em?' she asked. 'That last time, the last time I saw you?'

Em drew in a slow, deep breath. 'I have thought about that day so often,' she said. 'Could I have stayed? I felt I betrayed you, and Mar, and' – she ran her hands through her hair – 'and your father. Wait there.' She got up and went to the cabinet beside her bed, opened the top drawer and took out an envelope. 'This is for you,' she said. 'It is a letter from your father. I hoped you would come. Read it when you're ready, and we'll talk again.' And she gathered her papers into a pile, placed them back in the box, and walked to the door. 'I have to help in the garden now.'

Starling set the envelope on the table, propped up against her mug. Then she pushed it away. She kept drawing.

Nettle: diuretic, good for high blood pressure. Male flowers like catkins, female in little bunches. Soup. Risotto. Disgusting tea. She used to dig up the roots for Em, witchy-hairy and bent like an old woman's legs, decocted for diarrhoea and dysentery. Starling carefully pencilled in the four-sided stem, age-old source of string and threads. She'd spent hours making nettle strings to bind Em's herbs and to tie Mar's winter greens in their bunches to dry for winter. Threads everywhere.

She blocked out the letters across the centre of the label and coloured them. Green for health.

Nettles were strong plants. She would always be Mar's daughter.

Would Mar always be her mother? Mar had let go of her own mother, after all. And Starling's father.

Her pencil skittered across the table, a bird on ice, a gale in a tree, her mind in fragments.

No, she would concentrate. She reached out and picked up the pencil again. The picture in the herbal blurred. She blinked. The colours were all wrong. She'd lie down, lie down and she'd be OK. But her heart was beating so fast, drumming faster and faster, and her breath couldn't keep up. She tried to stand. And fell. The floor gathered her up like a dark cloud, washing over her, sucking her in, taking her breath so she could not, need not, had no choice but to let it in.

She remembered nothing, after.

Fragments, like rain from an empty sky. They made no sense. The bed, dust, smoke, Em beside her.

*

She woke in the bed high under the eaves of Em's roundhouse. Opened her eyes, saw a tiny chink of light above her through the thatch. A mouse hole. Watched the light fall towards her, dust motes dancing. Closed her eyes.

Later, she woke again, someone's hand on her forehead. Slept again.

Kit's voice: 'Starling, drink this.' Cold water.

Rain on the roof, fading in and out as she drifted in and out with it.

As the earth turned, the chink of light crossed her blanket, dropped over the edge of the bed. Starling followed it down into the room below. A table, a mug, the door cracked open. Bright day beyond, footsteps passing.

The door opened and let in a breath of warm air, the buzz of flies. Em stepped into the broad brush of sunlight on the floor and looked up. She smiled at Starling. 'How are you feeling?'

Starling tried to find her voice. 'Thirsty,' she whispered.

Em crossed the room and filled a glass with a liquid from a flask and another with water. She climbed the ladder with them and passed the first to Starling. 'Can you manage it?' she asked.

Starling tried to sit up but sank back.

'Here.' Em balanced the glass on the edge of the bunk and pulled her up. 'First this, and now water. You need to drink. You had a fever.'

Starling drank Em's bitter concoction, then the water cool in her mouth like a river, renewing her with every swallow. She gave the glass back to Em. 'How long?' she asked again.

'A couple of days. You needed it. The infection was a sign it was time to let go. You can release now – you're safe here.'

It was true. These walls, this earth, they welcomed her. 'Thank you, Em.'

Em closed her eyes for a moment, leaned and rested her forehead on Starling's, kissed her gently. 'Sleep. You need rest. But you'll be well now.'

'Will you be here?' Starling asked.

'I'll be near.' Em climbed down the ladder and walked to the door. She turned back to Starling. 'We're preparing Luc's ceremony. As soon as you're well enough – that's all we're waiting for.'

*

Kit brought her soup in a wooden bowl. 'Chicken,' she said, and looked carefully at Starling. 'How do you feel?'

They sat together at Em's table, looking out across the treetops. 'Better,' Starling said. And it was true. Her mind felt clearer, as if her lens on the world had been washed in clean water for the first time in a long while. She moved in her seat, experimentally, testing her bones. The pain was less. 'Em's magic.' She smiled, and Kit smiled back at her.

'I don't know how she does it,' Kit said, 'but I feel better when I come here. Even now, when nothing should help, when every time I see Em I'm reminded of Luc...'

'When is his ceremony?'

'Tomorrow. You'll be OK by then?'

Starling nodded. 'Who's coming? Are your friends from Wincombe going to be here?'

Kit shook her head. 'I wish they could be, but it's so far. And I think Em wants to bring Luc back to the earth more than anything else, to the earth where she is home.' She looked out of the window, silent. Poor Kit.

Starling picked up her spoon and Kit stood. 'I'd better get back to the field. There's so much to do.' Starling watched her make her way down the slope, and drank the soup. She took her time, chewed on the barley floating on the surface, tasted the oil and the herbs, crushed soft leeks against the back of her teeth, dredged the morsels of chicken from the bottom of the bowl, put the bowl aside and slept again.

When she woke, she heard the rasp of a saw: long steady cuts, rhythmic, back and forth. A two-hander, a tree of many rings beneath its blade.

A cockerel crowed and a child shouted. Someone dropped a pan on the ground. A woodpecker – was it Em's? – drummed. Nearby, voices murmured, the sound of people talking as they worked, a man and a woman, to and fro, no urgency. Spoon on pan, knife on board, a scraping as they stirred.

Other voices, passing.

'...almost out of leeks.'

'I thought they'd never end. So much leek soup.'

Footsteps outside the door. A whole world of lives moving past her, people growing, laughing, cooking, fighting and dying, whether she was here or not. She could leave and there would be no absence here, no space that felt empty. But perhaps there was a place for her.

*

Late that evening, the slow rumble of a car dropped down to the roundhouse from the track above them. Starling looked up and Em stood and pulled her shawl tight around her, frozen for a moment in the lamp's glow. Em closed her eyes and Starling saw her stretch out the fingers of her hands, as if she'd been clenching them too long; then she walked to the door. She turned to Starling. 'It's the boys,' she said. 'Don't come. Not yet.'

Starling waited by the stove, listening to the low voices outside, deeper than she remembered, twining strong threads around Em's soft tones. Eventually they fell into silence.

She carried tea out to them, four figures sitting by the fading embers of the fires, Em in the arms of Davey and Stevie, Gabe crouched before her. Em's cheeks were wet with tears in the last flickering light.

'Starling,' Gabe said, the first to see her. He stood and came straight to her, taller than her now. He embraced her and at last she cried.

*

A single flute sang, softly at first. It twisted in through the doorway, grew louder, then faded, blending its notes with the wind in the leaves. Slow feet followed it, walking in a rhythm old as time.

A child's voice: 'Where are we going?'

'Down to the gardens.'

Voices and feet faded, the trees gathering them in.

Starling walked with Kit, the brothers just behind them. Ahead of them, Em's back was steady as she carried Luc's ashes in her arms down through the trees to the fields below. In her hair shone a circlet of flowers, rosemary for remembrance, sweet peas for farewells, thyme for courage, sage for immortality, and oak leaves for strength, bound with honeysuckle, the binding of love. Starling and Kit wore them too, and the brothers, the scents mingling as they walked down the hill through the trees and out into the sun.

The birds of the wood and fields sang above the melody of the flute, but everyone else fell silent. Nobody spoke as they gathered around the small, carefully dug hole in the dark soil. It was too small for a whole life, for the energy and brightness that had been Luc, but the earth would hold him in her arms, welcoming him into the young apple trees that grew beside his grave.

The community formed a ring around the grave, steadying themselves on the uneven grass, placing their bare feet carefully to allow the earth to feel their presence, and to feel her love in return.

Em voice was steady as she led them in the old words that she had long carried for the tribe, reassuring those who had never heard them before that here were ancient truths and powerful energies that flowed through every person in the circle, and through the air and earth, rivers and seas, and all life in them. Though they mourned Luc's passing, he was on his life's journey, and he was still with them even as he moved into a new realm.

They held hands as Em placed the box holding Luc's ashes into the grave. She laid a sprig of rosemary on the box and knelt for a moment, her head bowed. When she stood, each member of the community laid a small object on the box – a tiny crystal, a jay's feather, a circlet of grasses – each giving something they treasured. When it was Starling's turn she set Luc's small white pebble she had carried all these years beside the other offerings. She had nothing more to give. Em would know its meaning. Starling stood, and took her place again in the circle.

Em asked them to remember their love for Luc and the happiness he brought them. She raised her eyes to the sky and called for peace throughout the world so that the spirit might be heard. She looked around the circle from her position in the east, and called on the powers of the air to bring bright memories of Luc and the songs and joy that filled him. She had placed Starling in the south, and she called on the spirits of fire to bring forth Luc's eternal courage, feeling the sun's heat on her face give her the strength to lift her voice. Kit stood in the west, where the spirits of water lay, and in a shaking voice, she called on them to remember his steadfastness and love. Phil took the north and raised his deep voice to call on the powers of the earth – who gave Luc his strength and wisdom, and to whom he was returning today – to hold him safe.

They sang, struggling at first to come together, but one by one picking up the melody, the tune Luc hummed to himself as he worked in the garage and in the fields, lilting and simple, rising above his grave as Davey took his shovel and thew over him the earth they loved.

After, they embraced each other, tears and laughter mingling as they remembered Luc as he was in life, and allowed their sorrow at his sudden leaving to flow freely. Em moved among them, kissing and holding them in turn, all equal, all deserving of her love. Gabe put an arm round Stevie's shoulders. Davey kicked at the ground. Starling stood beside them. They'd always had to share Em. Phil watched from the side as if he alone knew Em's pain and was ready to catch her.

When the woodpecker called, its single note cutting through the trees down to the field, Em looked up. 'Thank you,' she said. She walked slowly to Luc's grave and bowed her head, and then looked around her community, meeting each person's gaze. 'Let us eat and drink and celebrate our love for Luc, and our joy in his life. Come.'

As Starling followed her up the slope to the feast they had prepared, Em's words were like a drug flooding through her, filling her with the love of the women who had reared her, the joy and fear and anger she'd been hiding from, and the courage of all the people she'd known. They were one world, one people, one love. Phil's flute carried them up through the trees into the light. She had forgotten this.

Chapter Twenty-One

The boys had left again late in the evening of Luc's ceremony, walking back up the hill to their car in the darkness. Next morning, it was hard to remember they'd ever been there.

The envelope lay on the table where Starling had left it before the fever swept her away. She read her name in Em's loose writing. She turned it over, looked out of the window, breathed deep and tore it open.

Inside, a sheet of paper, and another envelope, Em's writing on the paper. Starling put it aside. She looked at the envelope, read her name again, in writing she did not recognise, angled, regular, looping, telling her nothing. She opened it.

Black ink, from a real pen. Thick woven paper. She ran her finger along its grain, felt the tree inside it, and made herself read.

Dear Starling,

I've written this letter so many times, and still don't know what to say. Please read it, even if you feel like flinging it away.

I saw you once and didn't know it was you. You were high in a tree, an oak with a horizontal branch that you stood on, barefoot, barely holding on to the trunk, perfectly balanced as you directed your troops on the ground below. I think you might have been six or seven. You were smaller than all the others, but full of assurance and power. I didn't know who you were but I remember that sight, the tiny, formidable commander of all she surveyed.

I should have guessed.

But I didn't, because I was naive and I had no idea. I think it is the only time I ever saw you, and the next day when I woke, you were gone.

Em tells me now that whenever I used to come to visit – and of course I always let Em know I was coming – Mar would take you away until I was gone. Ironically, she'd take you to Norwich most often, painting signs across the city. That's where I lived after I left the tribe. Whenever I go back I see Mar's work wherever I go.

You may know this now. Perhaps Em has told you a little of that summer. Or even Mar has. But I joined the tribe the day I left school. I wanted freedom and space, and dreamed of sunshine and friendship, and I believed in the collective and the strength of the masses against the repression of authority. As I said, I was naive, but I was right. I found all of that. And I fell in love with Mar.

She was a leader in a tribe that had no leaders. People looked up to her because she was informed and articulate, but above all because she had an incredible energy. It fizzed all round her. She was magnetic. No one could resist, least of all me.

I wrote to my parents telling them I wouldn't be coming home, that I was going to turn down my place at university. But Mar found the letter and tore it up. She told me I had to go, that my future lay in learning and in ripping the capitalist world down from the inside. She said I had no place in the tribe. She told me she would not see me if I stayed.

So I left. I was only eighteen, the same age as you as I write this, but I am sure you are far wiser than I was.

I suspected nothing. I visited Em and the tribe every summer, travelled, worked the festivals for years until my research took over my time.

Mar was right – my future did lie in learning.

But she was so wrong too. She hid her pregnancy from me. She made sure I left before it showed. She swore Em to secrecy, and Em kept her promise.

So I had no idea that I had a daughter. I wish I could turn back time.

I found out because Em told me, the summer Mar made her leave. They argued, Mar and Em, about telling you about me, and me about you. Em can tell you why things changed and she decided it was time.

I come every year to visit Em and hope this might be the year that you are there when I arrive. I want to meet you and to offer you my friendship. I would like to be your father, if you would like that, but I understand that this is much to ask.

I am so sorry that I have not been with you all these years.

Your friend, and father,

Tom Bridges

P.S. Em tells me you have a little pot that you carry with you everywhere, the one with three birds on its lid. I carved it one summer with the tribe and gave it to Em, not knowing what it might mean nor that she would give it to you. I am glad you keep it safe.

At the foot of the letter, he had drawn the three birds that flew around the lid of Starling's pot. Below them were his address and numbers. Tom Bridges. She knew that name. The man she'd heard talking to Mar, that day in the library in Wincombe. She'd heard her father's voice and hadn't known.

The camp outside was midday quiet, the heat pressing down on the trees. Even the silver birches were still. The community must have been seeking shade if they could find it. In the dim of Em's roundhouse, Starling still felt the heat, the thickness of the air, a storm brewing in the pewter sky. Had everyone known, except her? Even Luc, all these years?

All of them, everyone Starling ever trusted, had lied.

Except maybe her father. Dad. That felt wrong. Tom, then. She felt in her pocket for the three little birds flying round the rim of her pot. That much was true.

She turned her head and read the first words of Em's letter, lying sideways on the table, half in sun.

Dearest Starling,

I love you, know this above all.

I love Mar too, and I could not see another way. I was wrong, I think now, but everything I did, I did from love.

Tom is your father. Mar knows it, and you and he look so alike there is no mistaking it.

Starling reached out a finger and dragged Em's letter closer. She read on.

Like you, he has to move, to read and draw and make. That's what brought him and Mar together. That summer they painted the van for the first time. Those birds that fly across the sky of its roof? He drew them, looking up at the vast sky above the Levels, the summer he and Mar made you. You were made with deep love.

He will be coming here in September and I hope you may meet at last.

I could tell you much more, but I hope we will talk, and you can ask me what you need to.

I am sorry to have kept your father from you for so long.

In love, peace and hope,

Em

P.S. I am writing this, although I hope we are together again when you read it, because I feel that you will want to take time before we speak.

The strange thing was that Starling's mind was clear. She understood. Hidden truths had lain beneath their lives ever since she was born, like rocks on a river bed, invisible and out of reach beneath the water, but always shaping the flow.

Mar had always loved her, and Em loved Mar as a sister, and they had stood beside each other, protected each other, sworn to be loyal no matter what.

But something had changed it. Why did Em decide Starling needed to know the truth?

Starling could feel her heart beating like a tambourine in her chest. She stepped out into the sun.

*

The air in the polytunnel was thick with the bitter scent of fresh-picked tomatoes. Em was at the far end, moving between rows of plants that reached above her head. As Starling came closer she could see that she was slicing off side shoots and training the new growth up the wires, tresses of yellow flowers jiggling and tangling in her hair. Em heard her coming and smiled. 'Just look at the crop. It's taken me years to learn that I must be cruel to be kind with tomatoes – I used to let every shoot grow and wonder why we had so few fruits.' She cut another shoot and dropped it to the ground at her feet.

'Shall I pick up the cuttings?' Starling asked.

'Please. There's a barrow at the end door.' Em looked carefully at her.

'I read the letters.' Starling knew Em could tell. 'I don't know if I want to see...'

Em nodded but said nothing.

'What's he like?'

Em paused before answering. 'I think you need to make up your own mind about Tom. When – if – you meet him, you will understand the kind of man he is.'

'But—'

'All I will say is that he is a good man, kind and honest. He's not perfect, because none of us is, but he's always reminded me of you, full of life and curiosity and open to love. He has been hurt, though never by you, of course. He's never turned that hurt to anger and that's a wonderful and difficult thing for any of us, as you know.'

'Is he coming here next month?'

Em turned back to the plants. 'He is. I heard from him not long ago. He too has a home here whenever he needs it, and he's always welcome.' She dropped another shoot on the floor.

Starling picked up the shoots by Em's feet, gathering them into a bundle, and carried them to the far end of the tunnel. The barrow was already piled high. She tried lifting it, but set it down fast. Her shoulder wasn't ready for that yet. She dropped the cuttings onto the heap, and stepped out of the tunnel.

In the hay field, two figures moved through the long grass swinging scythes. Starling leaned on the fence and watched them reach the far end and turn back towards her. They waved and she saw that it was Dan and Leila. Last night they'd sat by her at the fire, curious to hear how Starling knew Em and Phil. Dan had grown up on the land. 'My grandad used to work a farm ten miles over, up and down on the tractor, dawn till dusk and beyond. I could see the headlights from my bed at night, this time of year, and I'd climb out my window to join him.' Leila was town-bred, had hated school and all its rules. 'I'd stay at home and read instead – school didn't like that, even though I learned way more that way. But at least I met Dan. They sent us on a programme for kids who never turned up, and that's why we're here. We came to learn about growing and never left.'

Later, Starling helped Issy with the cooking – Issy loved company and chatted without stopping – and as the days went by it became a regular task for her. She drew labels for Em, and when she was free, she wandered the camp, settling down with her sketchbook to draw the community while they worked.

Everyone shared tasks, but some had particular skills. Phil tended the animals. He had a flock of hens in a coop beside the polytunnels, a goat, two pigs and their piglets, and four cows with their calves in a field by the edge of the wood. She found him there enjoying the shade with the animals, scratching their ears and whispering to them before the evening milking: 'Good girl, good girl.' He reached over the fence to pick up his stool and saw Starling watching. 'Do you want to try?' he asked.

Starling shook her head. 'I'll watch. Maybe tomorrow, if you'll show me?'

He nodded, and placed the stool on the ground. 'I reckon you'll be good with them, Starling. Bel has a gentle touch, but she's often busy in the wood workshop.' He laid his head against the cow's side and began to milk, rhythmic and steady, filling his metal bucket slowly and surely as he moved from cow to cow. The largest cow gave him only a few squirts of milk, and ambled off when he patted her side. 'I let them feed their calves first,' he told Starling, 'and if there's enough for us, we are lucky. Soon I'll move the calves to their own field, with this old girl for comfort, but for now they're best with their mothers.'

Bel was up the hill. She had taught herself to work green wood, making spoons and bowls for local markets, each stamped with a curled bramble stem. She was learning to bodge from a man in the village, turning wood to make chair legs and bowls, and they'd set up their pole lathes side by side next to a pile of ash logs they'd cut only hours before. Keith was quite deaf so Starling could hear his voice well before she saw them. 'A good bodger, young Bel, has everything in mind from the moment they step out of their door of a morning.' He laughed. 'You do have a door, don't you?'

Bel chuckled. 'Of course. So how did you pick the best trees?'

'Well, it takes a while to get your eye in, mind, but see this one?' He laid his hand on the trunk of an ash. 'Good and straight, it is. And the right size, too. See how I cleave it like this?' And he swung his axe, clean strokes that echoed out across the valley. The tree creaked and fell to earth, shocking in its sudden end.

Bel knelt beside it. 'I promise to use you well, tree.'

'Right,' said Keith. 'So now we make a billet that we'll shape with our knife on the horse.' He hefted a log onto the sawhorse and began to carve it into a cigar shape. 'And we're ready to make the first leg.'

Bel spotted Starling. 'I'm going to make myself a milking stool,' she called out.

'Phil says you're a natural.'

'I love the cows, they're such good and generous girls.' She took the billet from Keith and set it on her lathe. 'Like this?' He lifted it and replaced it, nodding his approval.

Bel shared a ramshackle house with Lizzie at the far end of the ridge. They'd made it from an old shed that they'd extended with another, adding doors and windows from skips, tarps overlapping on the roof, and strings of hagstones and feathers hanging from the eaves. Bel was hardly ever there, always busy in the woodshop, with the animals, or hanging out with the others. Lizzie retreated to the quiet of their house whenever she could. She told Starling she was in search of something beyond the day-to-day life of the community. Living here was the start of her journey, learning to love and respect the earth and the food she gave them, but Lizzie sought a deeper communion with the land and her spirits. 'I am seeking a way to belong to her sacred gentleness, to learn to live as one with her generous love.' She uncrossed and stretched her legs. 'I am only just beginning my initiation,' she said with a serious expression. Then she smiled. 'I feel the love you bring, Starling, and it's strong. Thank you!'

Late in the evening, as the storm began to break over the far hills, rumbling towards them, Starling helped Rob, Kit, Lizzie and Haz, whom she'd only seen across the fire until then, to lay the tomatoes out on racks ready to carry out into the sun to dry the next day. Tomorrow, they'd sow autumn lettuces, dig potatoes and pick berries. 'I can gather berries,' Starling offered.

Rob dragged another bucket of tomatoes over. 'I need to fix the water filter.' He was the practical one who fixed everything: panels and pumps, cars and ploughshares.

'Do you need help?' Starling asked.

'Maybe. I hope it doesn't need a new part.'

Dan carried a pot of soup over. 'Come and get it. Food for the workers!'

The storm broke as they were finishing their meal, and everyone ran for shelter. Back in the roundhouse, Em, Kit and Starling watched the lightning slice into the trees as the rain clattered on the thatch and the ground outside. They carried mugs of tea to the table by the window and sat together.

'I wonder where the woodpecker hides?' Starling mused.

'It's a wise bird,' Em replied. 'It's been here longer than I have and must have seen many storms.'

They fell silent, within the energy of the storm that surrounded them. Eventually, the noise of the rain began to fade. Kit spoke. 'I'm going to go back to Wincombe tomorrow.'

Starling was startled. 'Oh?'

'I need to open the shop.' Kit turned to Starling. 'Do you want to come with me?'

Em said, 'Starling is not yet fully healed.' She turned to Starling, 'You're well enough to make the journey, I'm sure, Starling my love, but I know that you've been through much pain and I would love to be beside you as you heal. I hope you'll stay with us. More than that, Bramblehill is your home. You have a place here forever.'

Starling couldn't think about forever. All she could do was watch the community and wait until she knew what she should do.

Kit hugged Starling. 'No need to decide now,' she said, quietly. 'I just wanted to say, you're welcome to share the flat with me as long as you like. And to help me run the shop. But get better first. Spend time with Em. Take time to think. It's your life.'

*

The next morning, Kit left, walking out of the camp to catch the first of a string of buses home.

'I'll ring you,' Starling promised, as they said goodbye. Kit had pressed Luc's phone into her hands the night before. 'Use this, send me pictures,' she'd said. Starling hadn't expected to mind her going. It felt odd that Kit would be back at the shop, propping the sign up outside, baking flapjacks without her. Starling had given her the secret recipe. 'It's dead easy,' she reassured her. 'And I left berries in the freezer.' But Kit wouldn't be able to forage or bake bread, and Starling knew now how much work it took just to run the shop, even without preparing all the foods they'd been piling up on the counters. It couldn't be helped, though: her shoulder was still too sore to be much use to Kit. So she waved goodbye and went to help Issy make breakfast. She had work to do here, too.

Over the days that came, Starling found her way deeper into the community, treading its tracks and fencelines, working side by side with its people on light tasks, listening to their stories if they shared them, watching the way they moved and worked.

As she healed, she began to spend time in the fields and gardens, learning the feel and smell of the earth in her hands, and how it varied. Even as she walked from the gate to a field's centre she could sense how its soil became looser or heavier, richer or sandier. Haz showed her the line where clay turned to loam, halfway across the main field. 'Amazing, isn't it?' he said. 'Before I came here I'd never even looked at the earth beneath my feet. I didn't even know there was more than one kind – it was all mud to me. But look, the beans here grow way better than the ones over there, and down by the stream it's so fertile. It's wild to imagine this all being a sea, once – but when you know, you know!'

Haz had come to Bramblehill with Issy. 'My mum can't believe it! My nani came all the way to London from a village in Bangladesh, and here's me, working like a peasant again. She is not impressed.' Haz and Issy had grown up in inner-city Peckham, but when they lost their jobs they took to the road in her uncle's old van and followed the festivals, dancing every night, living off whatever they could earn as crew. Issy stomped across the field and joined them. 'God, yeah,' she said, 'when winter came, it was something else.' They'd parked up in industrial estates where a battered white van wouldn't look out of place. 'Man, that was tough,' Haz said. 'That first winter was so cold, and we were skint.' They learned to dive the bins behind supermarkets, and other van-dwellers shared blankets, but it wasn't a way to live. So they drove west, picking up jobs as they went, until one day they met Bel outside a craft shop where she'd been dropping off spoons. 'And that was it!' Issy grinned. 'We're the least likely hippies you'd ever meet, but how brilliant is this? Outdoors all day, snug as a bug at night, and no one can throw us off. I can't believe our luck.'

Everyone had a story. Some, like Haz and Issy, loved to tell it; others kept their counsel. Joff, the guy with the ponytail, worked silently in the fields from dawn to dusk, taking on the toughest jobs, lifting potatoes from the storm-sodden soil, lugging logs up the hill. He lived in a bender halfway down the slope, apart from the others, joining them only for meals and meetings.

The meetings were a surprise. The tribe had never had meetings on the road but left problems to sort themselves out with a quiet word or a flurry of fists in the woods. At Bramblehill, the community gathered every week to talk through the work ahead and to hear grievances as a group. Em led them, calling on each person around the fire to speak in turn. Rob was concerned that they were behind in gathering fuel for the winter, and Haz and Dan said they'd help. Joff nodded his head to show he'd be with them. Phil asked if Em was ready to make cheese, and who was going to help this year. At this, the serious couple with children, Kev and Nix, stood up. They kept themselves apart much of the time, and Starling had barely met them. Their children stood beside them, arms folded, jaws jutting. They could no longer accept the community's continued abuse of animals, Nix announced. It was bad enough that their meals were prepared in the same space as the meat was but their children were traumatised by the sight of Phil stealing the calves' milk and keeping them captive. And as for the hens, forced to lay every day...

Bel jumped in: 'But Phil loves the cows, and they love him – anyone can see that.'

Em looked at Phil, and he lifted his hat and scratched his head. 'I do love the cows,' he said. 'I ask myself every day if I am doing my best by them.'

'What would you have us do with them?' demanded Dan. 'They're not wild animals, are they? You can't just release them!' Voices were raised all round the fire, shouting Nix down.

Em spoke, not needing to stand or shout to make herself heard. 'I doubt that's what Nix means, Dan. Tell us, Nix, would you propose that we simply care for the animals, and take nothing from them?'

Nix's face was taut. 'We should never have brought them here. We have done evil by them. Every animal on Mother Earth has the right to live free of torture and abuse.'

'Are you calling Phil a torturer?' Haz was on his feet.

Em's voice was still soft, but everyone heard her. 'Let us take a minute of silence to reground ourselves and remember the loving kindness in which we try to live.' She stood and held her hands out to Bel and to Phil on either side of her. Around the fire, people pulled themselves to their feet and reached for their neighbours' hands. Starling wished Kit was there, and even more she missed Luc. He'd have known what she was thinking, would have squeezed her hand to say yes, what a pair of tossers, and kept his face solemn as the community stood in silence.

Later, Em told her that they had long agreed as a community that they would rear a small number of animals for their milk and eggs, and for their meat too, though that only rarely. In the hungry months, they relied on their animals to help them stay healthy and strong. 'It hasn't been easy,' she said, 'as you can see from tonight, but we have drawn on the wisdom of our ancestors. They would have loved and respected their animals as we do, and understood the circle of life we all belong to.' Nix and Kev were deep thinkers, she said. She hoped they would come to hear their wild inner voices too, and to respect the others', but if not... well, they would have to move on.

Starling lay in bed that night listening to the mice in the thatch above her head, scratching and scampering. Tawny owls screeched and hooted to each other across the valley. A pale line through the grass of the cows' field led to an earthy bank in the wood. The badgers would be out looking for worms and bugs.

In the morning, she worked in the field, sowing seeds for winter crops. Would she be there to harvest them? All her life she'd kept moving from one patch of earth to another. She'd carried plant pots of soil with her in the van, doing her best to raise herbs and salads, marigolds and tomatoes, as if sowing herself alongside her seeds.

Kit texted: *Hey Starling yup I got back fine thanks – shop is mad – miss you!*

Starling took a photo of the skinny ridge of earth she'd laid across the field. *Winter lettuces in the ground already!* she texted back.

*

She began to know the birds of Bramblehill. The martins swooping low over the hay field before it was cut. The chiffchaffs shouting in the hedge leading from the cow field to the wood, and the blue tits and wrens that dotted around them everywhere. She learned the sounds of the warm wet wind as it blew from the west up through the trees, and the cool dryness when it whistled from the north over Em's roof. The acrid smell of the hen coop when she gathered the eggs. Where the best blackberries grew, down by the stream. The shape of the land, rearing up from the wide river valley far below, much starker than Wincombe's tangle of ups and downs, copses, streams and patchwork fields.

She watched the community and learned the land as she always did when she landed somewhere new, treading lightly, ready to leave. This time, though, she could stay. Why did she resist?

Somehow it all felt so familiar. Em and Phil in charge, the ragtag tribe of people who almost fitted together, the lives they brought with them, even the way they spoke. She understood Bramblehill; it would be easy to step into its rhythms, to see the seasons dance their circle around Em. It felt like returning to childhood, and maybe that was it.

She felt herself fitting in, moulding herself back to this lifelong shape that Mar and Em and Phil and all the tribe had made for her. As she always had, she took up little space, a small body on a high shelf, a voice that knew the words and silences that completed their melody. She pulled out the parts of herself they expected to see, and it was a familiar camouflage. But it was too snug a fit, a coat grown small that pinned her arms to her sides and stopped her breathing.

But leaving – that wasn't easy either. Maybe she was more like Mar than she liked to believe. Or perhaps it was more that she'd never had to leave. All her leavings had been done for her. She pulled on her boots and headed down to the fields. Today she was going to pick berries for jam.

On her way down, her phone buzzed. It was Kit. *OMG. Look at this.* A photo of a field of kale, a small barn blurry in the background. It was a smallholding just outside Wincombe, Kit said. *I went to see them last night, she texted. They'd like to grow for the shop!*

Starling wondered if there might be a room above the barn, maybe.

She put the phone in her pocket and kept moving along the hedge by the stream, filling her box with blackberries, piling them high like shining black jewels. When she carried it back up to the cook shed, Issy was there, stirring some kind of stew.

'I'm thinking of going on a journey,' Starling told her.

'Oh? Where to?'

Starling hadn't known she'd say it until the words came out of her mouth. 'Don't tell anyone else. I'm not sure. I think I'll know when I get there.'

Chapter Twenty-Two

It was late August already, and the days were slowly getting shorter, warning the community that autumn was on its way. A week of short, sudden storms soaked them as they gathered the crops as fast as they could, the warmth fooling all of them into thinking it could be this easy always. But autumn meant winter, and they had to get ready.

Starling's dad would be coming soon, but she pushed all thoughts of him into a box and closed the lid.

As she did every morning, she woke early and lay with her eyes shut, listening to the wind in the trees outside. She'd missed that sound so much in Wincombe. All night the rain had slapped and clattered on the roof above her, but now it had passed. Everything – trees, thatch, cook shed – dripped. The robin in the holly sang, first to announce the morning. Starling turned over and looked down from her bed. The room below was dim, pre-dawn. The windows faced south, and as the sun rose through mist its light leaned away from Starling, tipping the tops of the trees below with its first glow while she lay in pale greyness. Em stirred and appeared, wrapped only in a shawl, standing in the doorway, surveying her domain. She turned and looked straight at Starling, as if she'd known all along that she was awake too and watching the coming of the day. She smiled, and walked out into the pale light.

When her dad came, it would be like this. Em would gently bring them together and drift back into the light, leaving them in her

roundhouse like characters on a stage. Starling could picture herself
sitting at the table waiting for him to come, his entrance – but then
a curtain fell across the scene. Em hadn't given her the words, and
while she was on Em's stage, Starling had none of her own. She had
to walk off that stage and into her own life, whatever shape it took.

She began to map out her journey in her mind. She would walk,
that much was sure. She needed the rhythm, the earth beneath her
feet, the measuring of time and place in footsteps. She would walk
into the dawn, and by evening she would follow her own shadow,
the sun sinking behind her back. She imagined the changing land
beneath her boots, the earth and rocks of the Old Ways shifting in
ancient time as she moved across their rippling, rising and falling,
as she stepped into their slow time, synchronising with the land's
heartbeat as her own heart slowed too and found its own path.

She might pass camps she'd lived in with Mar and rivers she'd
swum in with Luc, but she would allow her feet and the shape of
the land to lead her.

First, though, she had to finish Em's labels, and she had to
tell Em.

*

She was looking for a reference for milk thistle, to remind herself
of how the leaves sat on the stem, when Issy burst in, leading Em.
Em was holding her hand up high, blood pouring down her arm.
'Starling, my love, can you fetch my box?' she said, as Issy bustled
her to a chair.

'I'll make a cup of tea.' Issy rushed outside with the kettle.

'How did you do it?' Starling asked Em, who was looking
determinedly at her hand.

'It was that silly gate, the one out to the river that Mr Griffin
insists on smothering in barbed wire. I was looking to see if I could

see the curlew and sliced my hand. So stupid. You know where my box is?'

Starling placed it in front of Em on the table. Em's emergency box always sat close and ready. Its lid was deep crimson, her name at its centre, its painted sides bound tight by the entwined flowers and leaves of the herbs she used. It was so familiar that Starling barely noticed it any more. But here were Mar's brush strokes, every petal, thorn and leaf laid out in perfect balance and harmony. She had run her fingers along those flowers often as a child.

'Will you clean the wound for me, Starling?' Em asked.

She didn't need to tell her what to do. Starling washed her hands and opened the box, and there was a small green bottle of tincture of calendula waiting ready.

'Hold still,' Starling said, and poured the yellow liquid into the wound.

Em flinched, but took a deep breath and kept still. She looked with Starling at the wound. 'Oh dear. It's deep.'

'What do you think?'

'I think you're going to have to stitch it.'

Em had stitched Starling many a time, but Starling had never thought she'd be the one to stitch Em. 'Are you sure?'

Issy was hovering by the burner. 'Do you know how?'

'In theory I do.'

'You'll be fine, Starling. I trust you. Everything you need is in the box and I'm here if you need me.' Em smiled ruefully.

Em's box was packed in layers. Starling took out small packets of dried herbs, a bottle of iodine, carefully wrapped cotton bandages, lint, a small packet labelled *Poultice – broken bone*, and another labelled *Poultice – infected wound*. She unwrapped a small waxed cloth, found a scalpel wrapped in greased paper. Another held a small glass pipette. She wrapped them again and laid them aside. At the bottom of the box lay two tobacco tins. On one, in Em's writing, it said *Hemlock. Not to be taken lightly.* She had drawn a small skull and crossbones beside her words. Starling took out the other tin and opened it. On a bed of cotton lay a row of curling needles and a roll of catgut.

Starling set out a bandage, scissors and the catgut on the table and stood. 'Issy, can you put some of that boiled water in a bowl?'

She laid out a clean towel on the table and placed Em's hand on it.

'This is going to hurt.'

Em shook her head. 'I know you'll be gentle.'

'OK, here we go.'

She pushed the metal needle straight in beside the wound, pressing hard and then harder, as Em's skin resisted. She hoped she was doing it right. How far was far enough? The needle entered Em's flesh, and Starling took a breath and pressed more so it crossed the cut, took hold and began to hold the wound together. As she stitched, she asked Em to tell Issy how she came to be on the road all those years ago. She was glad to be distracted as Em told the story of how she had spent a summer on Dartmoor with her mother's sister when she was very young. Her aunt's garden was planted entirely with the herbs she used to prepare medicines. She had a peace about her, Em said, that she had never met before. Once she let it in, felt the power of such a connection to the earth, she knew it was her destiny. So the day after her sixteenth birthday she hitched down and turned up at her aunt's cottage.

'Did you ever go home?' Issy asked.

'Oh yes. I went to see my mum every time I was near, once I was on the road. But I never lived in a town again. My home was my aunt's cottage, till she died. She was a lot older than my mum.'

Starling chipped in, 'I met her once.'

'You did, didn't you? She was very old by then, but she took you into her garden to show you where the fairies lived.'

'I thought she was my granny.'

'Well, in a way she was. We all need many mothers, you know.'

Starling pulled the last stitch taut, knotted it, and reached for the scissors.

'But why did you leave?' Issy asked. 'I mean, you had a home, your aunt, the herbs, and it sounds beautiful there.'

'Well, you know, I was young. And I loved my aunt, and in a way that made it easier. I wasn't running away from her – I was off to find my own way. I knew I could always come back. And I met Mar, and we just clicked.'

Issy came and sat beside Starling. 'So Mar is your mum, yes?'

Starling nodded and took a cloth to clean Em's hand and arm of blood. 'Tell me again how you and Mar went on the road, Em.'

So Em told Starling and Issy how she'd gone to Bristol to see some friends, and they'd persuaded her to go to Stonehenge for the solstice. 'I wasn't really part of the scene then, but some of my friends were, and that's how I met Mar. She'd been in a squat making art, and that summer she joined the tribe on the road. She was amazing – so sure of herself, so grown up. She really knew who she was.'

Starling unrolled a length of bandage. 'Hold still.' She paused. She'd never asked this before. 'Did you ever meet Mar's family?'

Em shook her head. 'I never knew the whole story, but she told me once that the only people in her childhood that she felt any connection to were her dad's parents. They were fun and let Mar dance and make art, and they didn't really care about school and all that.'

'What about her mum and dad?'

Em was silent a moment. 'Issy,' she said, 'I think I'd like some raspberries. Do you think you could pick us a bowl?'

When Issy had gone, Em began. 'This isn't my story, so I hesitate to tell it, but it is yours. Mar has always stood up for what's right – she's never been afraid to speak out. You know that, and she was like it even when she was very young. The eighties, when we were teenagers, were difficult, full of conflict. I was tucked away in my aunt's house, and didn't see most of it, but Mar was in the thick of it. She grew up in Sheffield – did you know that?'

Starling shook her head. 'I knew she was from the north somewhere. But she wouldn't talk about it. She was from a city?'

'A lot of us were. They were grim places back then for many of us. So much poverty. There were kids barefoot in the streets because they had no shoes, you know. She told me that.'

Starling couldn't imagine Mar in a city, treading paved streets, walking between high walls under smoky skies.

'It wasn't all bad.' Em smiled. 'Mar got to know some really good people. She was still at school, but every weekend she'd get out and march and write flyers and try to help. I think it was exciting, and it was important. And then the miners' strikes happened. You know about them?'

Starling nodded. Thatcher destroying the working class and the unions. Breaking up communities. Sending in her bastard police to beat up decent people trying to stand up for their rights. They'd all heard the stories in the tribe, growing up. They were like origin stories, binding them together with all the oppressed who'd ever been outlawed.

'Mar was right there,' Em continued. 'When the miners went on strike, she went out and protested with them. She helped run soup kitchens. She was on the front line. But the thing was, Mar's dad was police.'

'Shit.' Starling couldn't believe that. 'No way.'

'Yorkshire Constabulary.'

'She never told me that.'

'It was too painful, I think. She was ashamed. They clashed, of course. On opposite sides, and neither would listen to the other.'

'He was the enemy.'

'And he was her dad. And that was the thing in the end. Mar was on a protest with her mates, supporting the miners, and he knew where she'd be. He'd found out somehow. He could have asked to work a different patch that day. But he made sure he was there and he waded into the protestors with his baton alongside the other police, laying into innocent protestors like Mar and her friends, dragging them off the street. Arresting them.'

'He didn't?'

'He did. He arrested Mar. It was like he had to show her who was in charge. And he couldn't handle his own daughter shaming him by being out there on the barricades with the miners and their families. It was like she'd betrayed him.'

'But—'

'People can get things very wrong, Starling. I've no doubt he's regretted it ever since. He lost Mar that day. When she was released, she went straight home and packed her bag. She stayed with mates for a bit. She finished school but gave up her plans for university and all that, and by the time she was eighteen she was on the road. She shared a bus with a bunch of anarchists, and that's when I met her.'

'Oh my god. Poor Mar.' Starling had never felt sorry for Mar.

Em put her unbandaged hand on Starling's. 'I'm sure she's OK. And she knows where we are if ever she needs us. That's what home means, you know, Starling. You don't have to stay here for Bramblehill to be home. It's your place of safety and love, where you'll always be welcome.'

'I have to go, you know?'

'I know.'

'I have to make my own journey this time. I feel as if all my life I've been carried along by others – Mar, you, the tribe. I need some time, and I need to let my feet take me there. I will meet my dad, but not yet, not here, not this time. I have to spend time with myself first.'

'You're wiser than you know, Starling.'

Starling snorted. She checked the knot on Em's bandage. 'Keep it clean and dry. You don't want to risk an infection.'

'Thank you, Doctor Starling.' Em smiled at her.

Starling stood. 'I'm going to check the tomatoes. I'll leave tomorrow, if the weather's fine.' She embraced Em. 'Thank you, Em.'

Chapter Twenty-Three

The day Starling left, the sky had cleared in the early hours of the night and the morning air was chilled for the first time in months. The sun was still below the trees, but already everyone sat warming their hands round mugs of tea, looking forward to the day ahead. The Discoverys and Worcesters in the orchard were ripe, and today was Apple Day, when the community would work side by side, filling the bins with sweet-scented fruit to last a whole winter.

Rob stood. 'Right, I'm going to set up the storage racks. Bel?'

Bel swigged the last of her brew. 'Starling, I've got to go,' she said. 'You're not leaving right now, are you?'

Starling was tempted to stay, to be part of Apple Day, to help line up the apples in the winter store above the sandboxes of beets, carrots and turnips, to stay another week and push salad seedlings into the warm soil of the tunnels where they'd grow in the pale cold days of winter, carrying the community through to the first leaves of spring. She had a part to play here, and she felt guilty leaving when they had so much to do. But it was time to go.

'I've got to get moving,' she said. 'The days are getting shorter, and I've got to make the most of the light.' She hoped she could leave it at that, but Bel jumped over the ashes of last night's fire and swept her into a sudden hug.

'I'm going to miss you!' She stepped back, holding Starling's hands. 'We all are.'

Bel's hands were warm and Starling could feel the calluses from her woodworking ridged across her palms. Starling's own hands were rough from the digging and field work. She looked around the circle. They were the kind of people who'd annoy you the way they left their dirty bowl out every night, or told the same stupid joke every time they saw you trip on a root, but whose hands fitted yours because you dug the same soil, scythed a field in rhythm, and lugged crates of potatoes up the hill, staggering and swearing at the weight, and knowing this was the food that would keep you warm in the dark cold days ahead. Why was she leaving?

She'd told Issy the night before that she needed to go now because she had things to do, things she'd left undone when Em whisked her away from Wincombe. She didn't tell Issy that she wasn't sure what they were, but it was true. She felt transplanted and unfinished here. And it was true, too, that she had to go now because it was late August, and the weather would turn soon.

She'd lain in bed last night, listening to the owls calling from the towering oak above the cook shed. She recognised them now, the female's screeching *kew-eet* in asymmetric duet with her partner's floating *whoo*, call and response as if they needed to reassure each other they were still there, night after night. She'd never seen them, but she'd found their pellets under the tree, neat packages of tiny shrew bones, beetle wings and bird beaks. Such powerful birds, they could surely fly anywhere, but they stayed here year after year, nudging their brood out to the neighbouring woods as they grew up, calling across the darkness until, one day, one of the couple would fall silent.

If Starling called, Em and Issy, Bel and Haz and the others would respond, and she could always return.

But she couldn't stay. She had enough of Mar in her that she needed to go now, before she was planted in this soil. It wasn't her soil. She knew they'd miss her – she could stitch a wound and gather wild herbs, and soon, when her shoulder was fully healed, she'd be able to lug a crate alongside the others – but they didn't need her. And over the last few weeks she'd begun to understand Luc, and his need to find his own place, his own language, in a way she hadn't when he was right there with her.

It was too early for all this. Too much thinking never did anyone any good.

'I'm going to miss you all too,' she said. 'You haven't got rid of me, though. I'll be back. Don't let Em have any more accidents.'

Em stood quietly beside Phil, holding her bandaged hand against her chest. 'Let us all stand a moment in peace,' she said, smiling at Starling and at the community in its ramshackle circle, 'and let us send Starling back into the world with love and joy.'

They stood side by side, dusty boots and bare feet on the earth around the fire pit as the woodland woke about them. A breeze blew through the treetops and Starling bent to pick up her bag. It was time to go.

*

She walked along the lane out of Bramblehill as the morning sun rose behind her. A hairline crack ran along its surface, coloured by a fine thread of green grass, reclaiming the earth from the road. She followed it, her boots crunching on loose gravel as she left Em and the community behind.

She walked. It was always the best way to see and know the world. She had no map but places that mattered needed no map. She would trust the hills and woods and fields and rivers. She would find her way.

In the sky, a buzzard circled high, its call puncturing the cool air before it slipped the wind and vanished over the horizon. She walked on, shaking out the months of going nowhere. Woods dropped away below her on one side. On the other, a field rose steep behind a hedge of holly, hawthorn and dog rose, the red berries and haws already glowing amongst the late summer's dusty-green leaves. Beyond the hedge the corn was flattened by rain, the farmer caught out by the storms.

The road was empty of traffic, running narrow between its thick and thorny hedges and set into high banks. But it was alive – robins, tits and goldfinches chattering and scooting from hedge to hedge, voles rustling in the bank, a weasel rippling across the tarmac ahead of her. She wondered what the world would be like if everyone lived their lives within walking distance of home, knowing only the land they could reach in a day, but knowing it as well as they knew their sofa and fridge and their car's dashboard. Would they love it more if they felt it under their feet rather than watching it through a windscreen? She'd always thought of herself as a daughter of the land, but she'd spent her life looking out through a wound-down van window, elbow on the sill, wind in her hair, rolling past as if all of it and none of it belonged to her.

Miles behind her, Bramblehill tugged an invisible thread. She let it unravel, loose and fine.

The sun rose slowly behind her, finches scattering from the ruby haws and late-summer seeds ahead. A side lane turned up the hill and she stopped and listened. A plastic feed sack flapped in the hedge; a tractor was grinding up and down a field. Sheep baa-ed somewhere – she couldn't tell where. A lichened signpost pointed up the hill, half the letters missing, to a place she'd never heard of. She was walking on a lacework of lanes suspended between invisible villages, made centuries ago by long-forgotten people treading a path from farm to farm, brother to sister, friend to friend. Enemy to enemy too, of course. Scared servant running from brutal master. Connections, threads and ties made stronger with every passing, that never broke however far you ran.

She'd once seen a film of a brain, a tracery of tiny filaments crossing, linking, firing across gaps from neuron to neuron to find paths and make new connections and tiny threads of knowing, like letters sent and read, carried in a pocket and read again, making those ties stronger with every reading, every step. She could choose the threads she wove, now.

She climbed the hill, passing a badger's run that opened like a doorway up through the hedge's thorns into a field. As she pushed through the gap, her sweater snagged and left a twist of wool twined with strands of fur. She climbed the field, through long grass, molehills and bleached thistle tops, following the badger's track.

At the top she turned and looked back. Below her the road was invisible, hidden by the curve of the hill. Now she was on the tops where the oldest tracks lay, keeping out of the worst winter mud and following the land's natural mapping. She could see right across the valley to the hill that rose on the other side and the hills behind it, field after field, and no sign of anyone. Was this what Mar had always dreamed of? A world empty of people?

Starling walked along the field edge and climbed the gate, and there lay a small church, its walls golden in the morning sun. As she made her way towards it, a mess of rooks lifted and scattered into the sky above the spire.

She trod slowly towards a row of cottages, a pub and a small shop. Nothing moved. It was too early for most people. She looked in the window of the shop at a display of footballs and pencil cases, and beyond them to shelves of plastic-wrapped bread and tins of beans, last week's magazines and a fridge of chilled drinks. She wondered who bought the princess's tiaras and faded calendars, who would push open the door at nine o'clock, if a bell rang to call the shopkeeper out from her kitchen. It was a whole world, unknown. But to the people who lived here, it was everything.

She left the sleeping village behind and as she walked, the land woke up around her. Milkmen clattered past on their way back to their depots. Builders left their engines running outside early bakeries. She bought a cream bun and munched it as she walked. Gaggles of kids waited in lay-bys for the roof of the school bus to appear over the hedgetops, the hiss of its brakes as it stopped to gather them in. Walkers crossed the road ahead of her, nodded greetings, whistled their dogs to heel, vanished into the fields.

She walked all day, following little lanes along the ridges when she could, and cutting away when an ancient route had become a major road, finding parallel tracks and hopping through hedges, keeping high, dropping only to cross rivers and streams, and watching the shadows move around until in the late afternoon the sun dipped down ahead of her.

As dark fell she headed down a farm track looking for buildings, watching out for a chink of light in a window that would warn her away. A fox ran past her, so close she could smell it, but nothing else moved. The silhouette of a something square and solid formed as she rounded the bend and she slowed, her boots loud on the broken track.

It was an open-fronted timber barn, almost empty, the smell of last year's hay lingering on the old brick floor. They were late with their harvest here, holding on for more dry days, perhaps. They wouldn't be coming out to the barn, at any rate, not tonight. She sat on a half-slumped bale and waited for the dark to be complete, watching the starlings settle on the phone wire that ran down the track. They'd be flying home to Africa soon, though maybe home was on the breeze within their swirling murmuration – or on the joists of a seaside pier, or along the metal limbs of a factory, or under the roof of this barn.

A flurry of bats threw silent semi-quavers and triplets above her head. She pulled out a cold potato from her bag, her water bottle, dried tomatoes, an apple, a slice of cheese. Issy had packed her supplies for days ahead. She slept curled on the hay, and when she woke in the morning the sun was raising a soft mist from the fields.

From then on, she kept to the farm tracks, field paths and woods whenever she could as she headed east and the ridge roads grew busier. She looped her way from church spire to church spire, the sun acting as her compass, and if her cross-country route took longer, she didn't mind.

She took water from cattle troughs and streams, gathered chestnuts and cobnuts from hilltop copses and picked unharvested apples from valley orchards. With her supplies from Bramblehill she ate like a queen. When the last dog walkers had gone home, she slung her tarp from low branches and lit a small fire to make a brew and keep the dark's chill away. She made camp behind walls, in old hollow quarries, in the depths of woodland, beside rivers far from any houses. No one saw her unless she wanted them to.

Her thoughts spread out, taking time to find her, and for most of the day she simply moved along, seeing the colour of the soil change, hearing the sound of the wind in the hedges turn to the sifting of wind on bare open downland, and on she went, into the land of trees and rippling earthy hills. Her mind became a soft net and all she had to do was keep moving.

She wondered if there was a thread in the land that tied her to Mar, pulling them closer as they wandered. When her instincts guided her to her nightly sleeping place, she might be only a mile from Mar, each of them curled in the hollow of a tree, unaware of the other, but held in the same palm of the land. When the moon rose, she watched it as it watched her and Mar.

She thought about her dad, and how Mar had tried her best to cut their ties. She wondered if he still looked like her. She wondered if she wanted to pull that thread. She tweaked it, carefully, and let it rest again.

The sun shone day after day, ripening the berries, drying the tracks. Miles behind Starling, the farmer would be glad she'd waited for the weather to change. Her barn would be full now. Bramblehill's drying racks would be a rainbow of tomatoes and courgettes, plums and carrots, beans and pears. Issy and Em would be bottling and making jams. Who was making the cheese? She couldn't remember.

Luc had spent almost a year at Bramblehill. Kit had shown her where, when he got back from Spain, he'd carved his name on Em's centre pole alongside his brothers'. He'd sown and gathered the harvest, stayed a winter, singing in the firelight as he'd done all his life. He'd helped raise the roof on Phil's house.

'Why did he leave?' Starling had asked Kit.

'I think he wanted something more.' They had been sitting on the bench outside Em's house one evening, looking into the sunset, the dusk chorus rising around them. 'Bramblehill, it's wonderful. I mean, just look at it. It's beautiful, a place to feed your soul, to feel connected to the earth, and it's complete. That's the thing. It's a whole world on its own, isn't it? I love it here too, but I get why Luc left. He wanted to be out in the messy, complicated, dirty world where everyone else lives. This isn't how he said it' – she laughed – 'but I think he began to see Bramblehill as a bit self-indulgent. I mean, what difference does it make in the world, it being here?'

Starling had been shocked. 'Really? Self-indulgent?' She held out her battered hands, nails cracked and filthy with so much time in the soil, and Kit turned her own hands over, exposing the broken blisters across her palms.

'I'm not saying it's easy here,' she'd replied. 'But it's inward-looking, isn't it? It's kind of like a retreat from the world, and I do get that and why it's important for some people. But Luc, when he came to Wincombe, he was just so happy. He got the job in the garage and every day he'd sit in the pub in the evening with me and my mates, and they'd all gripe a bit about their days, and he'd just be smiling because he completely loved the fact that he'd spent the day fixing other people's stuff, people he didn't know or even always like, and then he got to hang out with us, and I think it was the first time that he thought his life was meaningful to other people, I mean, people outside his community. It's quite closed, you know, the tribe.' She looked at Starling.

It was true. Anyone could get a rig and go on the road, but there was a code, and if you didn't get it, you'd be out on the edge, always wondering what it took to be on the inside. Starling had been in the heart of the tribe since she was born, but Kit – Starling hadn't wanted to welcome her in.

Kit carried on: 'Luc made me see my life differently, you know? He made me realise I wasn't just filling in time, working in the shop. I actually wanted to be there. It's only because of Luc that I saw how important it is, selling good food that nourishes people and the land.'

That conversation seemed an age ago. Starling wondered how Kit was doing in Wincombe, back to running the shop on her own, without Luc to hug her and pass her a brew at the end of a day. Without her to bake and forage. She wondered about the small-holding people. She set that thought aside, and kept walking.

As the days passed, Starling took more time to lean on gateways looking out over the rising and falling land, watching kestrels hover and drop, meadow browns and commas cluster on the brambles, the late air change from blue to pearl as the sun set, and next morning back to starling's egg. She settled on fallen logs and sketched the swoop of a hillside, the waltz of honeysuckle and columbine through a hedge, the distant clutch of roofs in a nest of trees. Every time she drew, she saw more.

Sometimes, from a ridge or hilltop path, she saw trucks running on a wide road below, engines roaring, cars overtaking them sleek and fast, half hidden by hedges, glinting through the gaps like secrets. They seemed out of place, out of touch.

She left the fields to explore small villages and towns, peering into shop windows, experimenting with walking past their houses as if she had the right to be there. She bought fresh rolls, queueing with the early workmen and the young mums chattering on their way back from school. One evening she bought herself a pint of bitter and a packet of crisps and sat outside a pub that was so old it looked as if it had grown out of the land, its roof and walls clad in rust-red tiles the colour of the earth she'd walked over all day. From her bench she watched couples and groups of friends drive, cycle and walk to be here together for a few hours. When the sun set, she returned her empty glass to the bar and walked back to the riverside thicket where she'd set her tarp.

She greeted everyone she passed and, mostly, they called out 'Morning' or 'Lovely day' in return. If they didn't, it was their loss.

In one village, just after breakfast, three old women sat in a row in front of the Fox and Hounds. They sat on velvet-seated chairs they'd heaved out of the saloon bar, holding cups of tea in their laps, and they waved to Starling as she approached.

They offered her tea, and she brought out a chair and sat beside them for a while. They'd taken over the pub, they said, when the last landlord gave up. It belonged to the village now, and in the day they were in charge while the others worked. It was still a farming village, they said. They used to work the fields themselves, long ago – they gestured up the hill and she could see small figures on the far valley side, moving slowly across the curve of the land. Organic, so it took more labour than the big farms with one giant tractor, they told her. But far too many greens for their liking, whole fields of cabbages and kale. They preferred a nice steak and chips.

So many villages had no pub left, no school, no shop. The buildings were still there, now houses with cars parked outside to take their owners to the nearest town for a drink with friends, or to school, or just to buy a tin of beans. They felt like toy villages, those ones, pretending to be real places where people lived their lives, when really they lived them miles away and only came back to sleep. Sometimes she saw a farmer beetling across a field on his quad bike, checking on gates, moving sheep, clearing a ditch, but dog walkers apart, once she left the villages behind she saw almost no one.

She didn't mind. It was enough to share a couple of words with a woman in a shop, or a walker admiring the sunset. She could feel herself getting closer, tugged by threads as strong and invisible as spider silk, but still she wasn't sure where she was heading.

After one day of walking in hot sun, she followed the palest deer trail through a high field to a coppice of chestnuts, long uncut, with silvered trunks muscling up to a canopy of shivering leaves. The shade was wonderful, and Starling sat to drink from her bottle, looking down over a tiny field enclosed by ranks of dark trees. It was a golden jewel of long grasses and late flowers that buzzed with insects, and a whole county's worth of birds. Rooks circled over the wood, goldfinches clung to teasel burrs, and martins sliced the air, jazz soloists making impossible patterns only they could hear.

She pulled out her sketchbook, and drew the fizz of seeds and wings and shimmering light, and the gate on the far side, tied shut with orange baler twine that startled out of the shadows behind it.

She drew her own feet, pink and crumpled from another day in hot boots.

She turned the pages back. There were Luc's feet, as if he was still here. She gazed out over the field and sent her thoughts up with the martins to Luc. She wished he was here with her, lying in the grass. They'd have had no need to talk.

'Where shall I go?' she asked him. But he would never have told her. He'd have opened his eyes and smiled, and said, 'I don't know, Star. Where do you want to go?' She couldn't believe he was gone. All the years they'd been apart, he was the one she'd talked to when Mar withdrew into silence. When she lay in her bed in the van after a day of journeying, she'd tell him where she'd been, the places she'd passed through, the sounds outside as she lay sleepless again in the dark of the night.

Over the years she'd talked to him every night, even though she had no idea where he was. It didn't matter. He'd always been by her side and always would be. On her last birthday, she'd sat outside in the dark, cradling a brew, and told him how all day Mar had kept the silence she had begun weeks before. How she, Starling, had done all her chores and then sat in the cab of the van and listened to her and Luc's journey tape, turned down so low she could only just hear it. And because she'd told him everything over all these years of journeying alone with Mar, she'd thought that when she got to Wincombe he'd know it all. He'd know how she'd learned to fix the alternator on the van because she'd worked it out from watching him. He'd know she cut her hand down to the bone when she was sawing up logs too fast, trying to grab them off the side of the road, and how she'd wished he was there to hug her better, because Mar strapped up the wound and went out for a walk. She'd told him when Mar burned her book, and she hadn't needed to tell him how that made her feel, even though he'd never wanted to read a book in his life.

So when she'd got to Wincombe, and he'd heard nothing of what she'd told him, had no idea what it had been like, and she couldn't tell him because of Kit, she'd felt betrayed. And she couldn't tell him that, even though he'd been right in front of her.

Not once had she ever asked him how he was, what he was up to, how he felt about what had happened in his life.

And now he really was gone.

So she told him how she was following threads across the land, holding them so gently, listening to them sing in the breeze.

She was glad he was still there, humming a quiet song beside her, reminding her that she would always be home somewhere inside herself, laying out her threads to all those she loved even as she laid herself down to sleep in a darkening coppice under a moonlit sky.

*

The next morning, she rang Kit.

'Starling! Where are you?'

'Um, I'm up on a hill with the buzzards, heading east – otherwise, not sure. Look, I can't talk long because I'm almost out of charge and there's no plugs out here. I just wanted to see how you are.'

Kit was good, she said, taking it day by day. The shop was busy and she barely had time to stop and think. She sounded tired. 'Are you heading this way?' she asked, and Starling could feel the tug of the shop, the purpose she'd felt gathering berries and leaves, chopping and peeling and baking, and seeing people walk out with a pot of soup she'd made, dithering over a spinach pasty or a nettle pie, or biting into a berry flapjack she'd baked only an hour before. But she still didn't know.

'I'll come and see you. Definitely. But I've got to go now – battery's about to go.'

Kit's voice stayed with her as she packed up her tarp and rolled up her sleeping bag. 'I miss you, Starling,' she'd said. 'And I still can't bake a decent loaf – come and help me.'

Starling let the conversation fade as she walked, until it was part of the contours she followed, curving around the rounded hills and steep drops that carried her on easily, high above the river valleys and woods below.

Her path dropped down between high hedges, cut into a holloway by centuries of drovers and villagers, traders and pilgrims. In the small village at its foot, she bought a pack of blank postcards and two stamps – old-style communication Mar-and-Em-style, no need for a phone or a plug, and no difficult conversations with questions she didn't yet know the answers to.

She bought a takeaway coffee and a cheese roll from the bakery and sat on a bench in the sun. A pair of old men walked past in cord trousers and neat jumpers, talking loudly as if they owned the place. Three young women with toddlers chatted outside the post office, chasing after their children, sweeping them into their arms and depositing them back on the pavement, all the while talking and laughing, before one looked at her phone and they all rushed off in different directions.

A weathered man with a stick stumped past her. 'Morning,' he said, nodding at her boots. 'Going far?'

'Maybe,' she said, 'I'm seeing where my feet take me.'

'Best way,' he replied. 'Watch out for the mud if you're heading that way. Round the wood is better.'

Starling thanked him and pulled out her postcards. She'd been thinking about the battered paint of Kit's shopfront and while she sipped her coffee, she sketched out the letters CORNUCOPIA in barley and corn, entwined with cornflowers and poppies, bramble berries and rosehips. If she'd had paints with her she'd have used gold for the letters, but she could see how glorious it would look, if Kit didn't mind the change. Maybe she liked her old name. Cornucopia, though – it felt like a mouthful of all the riches the sun, rain and soil could conjure: honeycomb ice cream, barley broth, a fresh-picked tomato, and a winter's leaf of cress. Surely she'd love it. Starling slipped the card into the top of her bag inside her sketchbook. No need to post it.

The second postcard sat on her knee, blank. She had no idea what to say, though she'd been trying out phrases for days, letting them loose to see if any sang true. But what did you say to a dad you had never met? She looked at the card, white and empty. Come on. She could do this. She didn't need words.

She put her hand in her pocket and ran her finger over her little round pot and its carved circle of birds, flying together all these years. She didn't have to look at it – it was as familiar as her own hand. In the middle of the card, she drew three starlings flying in a jubilant circle. Around them, she drew more birds, every kind, a murmuration of all the birds, filling the sky, drawing lines and patterns that would never fade or rest. She turned it over and wrote Tom's address. But she still had no idea what to write beside it. Just *Starling*, to let him know she was here? *Hi Dad…, Hi Tom, it's Starling…* But what then? She slid the card into her sketchbook and stood up. She needed to walk.

She followed the old man's directions around the wood. There were springs everywhere, he'd said, and some tracks never dried unless the whole of the summer was gripped in drought. She sang as she walked, old tunes with new words, and new tunes with old ones, letting the words loose, and moving on.

She climbed an escarpment and when she reached the top she found herself looking over a wide river valley that crooked its elbow around a rising hillside on the far side. She knew immediately where she was.

Down the slope ahead of her was a pulsing main road. If she crossed the new bridge that took the road over the river, she'd be in a village on the far side where every house was exactly two years old. There were no children or shops or pubs, only empty streets and lost fields beyond the last garden fence. She and Mar had driven through it almost a year before.

Starling was less than a day's walk from the van. She could be there by nightfall. She could check if Mar had returned and left her a sign, a secret note on the board, or under the sun visor. Or maybe, just maybe, Mar would be there, standing by the burner, stirring the pot, and Starling would see her through the open door, and then it could all be just as it was before.

If she walked back to the van tonight, the fat hen at the head of the track would be rampant. She could pick a handful to take with her to the van, a peace-offering, a sharing. The track would be dry and the bramble leaves along its edge would be purpling. Would Mar have picked the berries, made jam, squashed a handful on her tongue and let the juices flow sweet in her mouth?

In her mind, Starling crossed the clearing, reached up for the door handle and pulled it open. She knew the van would smell of mildew again; a trail of snail slime would run across the floor to the food cupboard. The door of the stove would be ajar, just as Starling had left it. Mar's bed would be empty, the blankets tidy. She wouldn't have been back.

When Em and Starling had sat working together at the round-house table, Em had said, 'Mar says she doesn't need people, but she always did. We all do, to know who we are. And she loves you deeply, and always has, no matter what it cost her.' Starling had stopped drawing and looked a question at Em. 'Poor Mar,' Em had carried on. 'She needed more space around her than any of us could give her, even you. Her peace was only to be found in solitude in the woods and fields. I hope – I am sure – she has found it. And I'm sure she will come to find you when she is ready.' Em had taken Starling's hand. 'I am so glad you came to us, Starling. Thank you.'

Mar had always called Em sentimental, sometimes to her face, and maybe she was right. Trees had no sentiment, after all, nor the buzzards that flew over them, nor the worms beneath.

Starling turned away from the roaring main road and the bridge over the river, away from the paths that led to the van. She walked south until she found the place where the river was narrow enough for small cattle bridges and fallen willow trees to join its banks.

Chapter Twenty-Four

Dinah's wasn't open yet, the chairs upended on the tables inside, the ketchup bottles lined up on the counter. But a van of builders was waiting on the other side of the road, and a line of fluorescent light ran round the rim of the door into the back room. Starling knocked on the window. 'Dinah?' she called.

The back room door opened and Dinah peered out, fag in mouth, ready to slam the door shut again. She saw Starling, though, and grinned.

'Long time no see,' she said, as she bolted the shop door behind them. 'I heard about Luc, though. Bloody shame. He was one of life's good ones.'

She let Starling through to the back. 'You come to work? Tabitha's back in London. You knew that?'

'Nah, I didn't. I'm only just back in town. I wondered if you'd have a cuppa going. I've been walking since half five.'

'Bleeding hell. You haven't changed. You look like you've been living in a hedge.' She slung tea bags into a pot. 'Need breakfast? I haven't had mine yet.'

Dinah didn't seem to mind that Starling wasn't coming back to work in the café. 'Don't blame you,' she said. 'It's bloody hard work.' She set a plate of eggs and bacon and beans and fried bread in front of Starling, and another by her own chair. 'So where've you been?'

Starling told her how Em had swept her away to the community. She reassured her that they did have toilets, and beds. She told her how she'd decided to walk back, because it made sense at the time.

'Does it still? Long way, isn't it?'

'I think it does. Yeah. And it's not so far if you just let your feet do the walking.'

Dinah pulled herself to her feet. 'Can't sit around all day gossiping. Let yourself out.'

Starling heard her opening the café door and letting the first workmen in, telling them to wait their turn – she'd be ready when she was ready. There was the hiss of the urn, the clank of mugs and plates, the sizzle of fat, men's voices, the radio. Starling carried her plate into the café to finish her breakfast. 'You don't mind, do you?' she asked Dinah. 'I'll move if you need a table.'

She recognised some of the men and they greeted her across the room, raising mugs, nodding, and carrying on with their conversations.

She took a seat by the window, and when she'd finished eating she ordered another mug of tea. 'I'll pay,' she said.

When she saw Flea's red hair bobbing past, she knocked on the window and beckoned her in.

'Oh my God!' Flea exclaimed. 'I'm so glad to see you! You just vanished – I didn't know if you'd come back.'

'Get you a brew?"

Flea looked at her phone. 'I don't have time. I'm opening up today, got to be there early. But later? Nick's got a gig – fancy it?'

'Ooh. I might? I'm not sure yet. I'll text you?'

The café began to empty as the builders and decorators started work. Dinah was busy in the back room. Starling stuck her head round the door and said goodbye, and Dinah just raised a hand, like she'd never left.

*

Starling walked into town along the river path, past the yards and the industrial units, past the back gardens, to the bridge where she and Luc had swum in the heat of the summer. The water flowed on, slow after so little rain, and dusty from pollen and wind off the fields, but it kept moving, linking the hills and the smallholding and the town and the little cottages with washing on their lines, and the hills beyond, and the wide estuary where the road surged past, and the sea and the sky, and the rain that would eventually rise from the water and the land and fall again on the hills.

She paused before she stepped into the alley from the river into the town. But she refused to be afraid, and walked on through into the main street, Kit's shop ahead of her. She'd be in the kitchen baking and stirring and tasting the soup, and Starling could so easily ring the bell and join her.

Not yet.

She walked on up the high street and up the path between the graves to St Stephen's. She thought of Bel, how she would appreciate the weight and grain of the oak door, and wished for a moment that she was back in Bramblehill where people loved and understood such things. But she pushed the door open and stood, her eyes adjusting slowly to the gloom.

A small candle burned at the altar, and Starling walked to her usual pew, letting the church settle around her. She sat a while, and then she pulled her bag towards her, and slipped out the two cards. She turned over Tom's card and drew a simple map, then added an arrow pointing to the shop with the words, *I'll be here. Starling.*

A priest appeared and nodded at Starling. She wondered if he minded her being there, not praying or singing, but he vanished through a door at the back, and the silence settled again.

Starling looked at the picture she'd drawn of Kit's shopfront. It looked unfinished, somehow. She drew in the door below the letters, and the window piled high with pies and breads and vegetables of every kind. Her hand kept drawing, and a pair of Green Women emerged smiling on either side of the shop's name – Kit and Starling with hair of loaves and flowers, looking down on the wonders they would make.

Starling didn't know the words she was supposed to say in this church, and didn't believe in them anyway, but she closed her eyes and in silence she said, 'I'm sorry.' And then she said, 'Thank you.'

She posted the card to Tom on her way to the shop. The sun was shining on the pavement, and her bag was full of fresh berries and leaves.

Acknowledgements

First and foremost, my love and thanks to Ian, Tom and Isobel and to my friends who kept listening through the long years it took me to write (and talk endlessly about) *Starling*.

Especial thanks to my mum, Janet Mace, for a lifetime of words and books and unfailing love. You are nothing like Mar.

Thank you to Sue Wicks: if you hadn't told me to send out my first story, I'd still be writing in secret.

Thank you to Dr Stephen Carver for giving me the boost I needed to write this story.

And thank you to Laura Shanahan, my editor at Fairlight, for seeing what *Starling* could be and giving me the chance and the freedom to write it.

I am ever grateful to my early readers: Will Sutton, for sitting up with my first draft in the wild midnight hours, and Isobel Butler, whose sunburn and enthusiasm told me I was onto something.

And thank you to everyone who shared their knowledge and experience, in particular to Andy Hope for your generous reading of that early draft. Daniel Thompson-Mills, of Steward Community Woodland, thank you for introducing me to your wonderful forest home. Thank you to Emma Cunis (Dartmoor's Daughter) and many other wise people who shared their deep understanding of plants, and to Nic Wood, who gave me an insight into the delights of living solo in the wilds. And many, many years ago, a young woman welcomed me to her beautiful bender when I was lost in a midwinter forest in south Wales as darkness fell. I'm sorry I don't know your name. Thank you all. Any errors left in this book are all mine.

About the Author

Sarah Jane Butler grew up on the edge of Southborough Common in Kent. She studied languages at university and spent time living in France and Spain. Her short stories (some published under the name SJ Butler) have appeared in literary journals and anthologies and she has twice won the 26 Project Writer's Award. *Starling* is her debut novel. As well as writing fiction, she is a copywriter and communications consultant. She lives in Sussex with her husband, and has two children.

RICHARD SMYTH

The Woodcock

In 1920s England, the coastal town of Gravely is finally enjoying a fragile peace after the Great War. Jon Lowell, a naturalist who writes articles on the flora and fauna of the shoreline, and his wife Harriet lead a simple life, basking in their love for each other and enjoying the company of Jon's visiting old school friend David. But when an American whaler arrives in town with his beautiful red-haired daughters, boasting of his plans to build a pier and pleasure grounds a half-mile out to sea, unexpected tensions and temptations arise.

As secrets multiply, Harriet, Jon and David must each ask themselves, what price is to be paid for pleasure?

'*The bleakness of the coast, the mist, the shifting nature of the sands all speak of contingency, brutality, deception*'
—*TLS*

'*Smyth's evocation of place and nature ... is imbued with a compelling sense of closely observed realism*'
—*Literary Review*

JOANNA CAMPBELL

The Fish

There is a fish on the sand; I see it clearly. But it is not on its side, lying still. It is partly upright. It moves. I can see its gills, off the ground and wide open. It looks as though it's standing up.

A few decades into the twenty-first century, in their permanently flooded garden in Cornwall, Cathy and her wife Ephie give up on their vegetable patch and plant a rice paddy instead. Thousands of miles away, expat Margaret is struggling to adjust to life in Kuala Lumpur, now a coastal city. In New Zealand, two teenagers marvel at the extreme storms hitting their island.

But they are not the only ones adapting to the changing climate. The starfish on Cathy's kitchen window are just the start. As more and more sea creatures leave the oceans and invade the land, the new normal becomes increasingly hard to accept.

'An impressive debut: beautifully written, immersive, prophetic, terrifying and wonderful. I could not put it down!'
—Melanie Golding, author of *The Replacement*

'Brilliant, clever, and important; READ IT!'
—Karla Neblett, author of *King of Rabbits*

PHOEBE WALKER

Temper

There's a gap where my sense of place should be. It's quite a useful one sometimes. It allows me to sit on the cusp of an opinion.

Following a move to the Netherlands, a young woman dissects the developments of her new life: awkward exchanges with the people she meets, days spent alone freelancing in her apartment, her confrontation with boredom and unease. In her newfound isolation, she develops an unusual friendship with Colette, a woman she neither likes nor can keep away from. As her feelings of dislocation grow, larger anxieties about her purpose – or lack of it – begin to encroach. And underneath it all, a burgeoning frustration bubbles.

Intimate, incisive and brilliantly observed, *Temper* explores loneliness, self-worth and disconnection with head-nodding accuracy.

'*Stark and brilliant; a must-read for anyone who has ever felt like an outsider*'
—Jessica Andrews, author of *Saltwater* and *Milk Teeth*

'*Subtle, incisive, and rich*'
—Naomi Booth, author of *Exit Management* and *Animals at Night*